"An entertaining and insightful look at black life in postwar Southern California."
—*Booklist*

FEAR ITSELF

"Twisty, taut, and tantalizing."
—*TIME*

"Paris and Fearless are vital characters who make a dynamic team."
—*New York Times Book Review*

"There's no escaping the pull of the story."
—*Los Angeles Times*

"Mosley's consistently taut, poetic tones remind you why the best mystery fiction qualifies as art."
—*Entertainment Weekly*

"Another winner."
—*St. Louis Post-Dispatch*

"As always, a brisk pace and Mosley's wry prose mix . . . a clever tale."
—*People*

more . . .

FEARLESS JONES

"Mosley is back to basics . . . [This] is the dense, dark, urban noir that made him a household word."
—*St. Louis Post-Dispatch*

"Drenched in the bleak conventions of the hard-boiled thriller . . . a beautiful piece of work."
—*New York Daily News*

"Another triumph. The book sizzles with all the heat of classic noir fiction where sex and violence collide."
—*San Antonio Express-News*

"Fearless Jones is complete, strong, and satisfying. The writing is vivid and powerful, with an almost musical flow. Mr. Mosley's style of interweaving mystery, morality, and amusement makes him one of this country's best writers. He continues to be mystery's master."
—*Cincinnati Enquirer*

"The charm of the characters and the author's seemingly offhand but brilliant powers of description make the tight plotting all the more fun."
—*Entertainment Weekly*

ALSO BY WALTER MOSLEY

THE EASY RAWLINS NOVELS

Devil in a Blue Dress
A Red Death
White Butterfly
Black Betty
A Little Yellow Dog
Gone Fishin'
Bad Boy Brawly Brown
Six Easy Pieces
Little Scarlet
Cinnamon Kiss

NONFICTION

Workin' on the Chain Gang
What Next: An African
    American Initiative
    Toward World Peace
Life out of Context

OTHER NOVELS

RL's Dream
Always Outnumbered,
    Always Outgunned
Blue Light
Walkin' the Dog
Fearless Jones
Futureland
Fear Itself
The Man in My Basement
47
The Wave
Fortunate Son

WALTER MOSLEY

FEAR
OF THE
DARK

GRAND CENTRAL
PUBLISHING

NEW YORK   BOSTON

Copyright © 2006 by Walter Mosley
Excerpt from *Blonde Faith* copyright © 2007 by Walter Mosley
All rights reserved. Except as permitted under the U.S. Copyright Act of 1976, no part of this publication may be reproduced, distributed, or transmitted in any form or by any means, or stored in a database or retrieval system, without the prior written permission of the publisher.

Grand Central Publishing is a division of Hachette Book Group USA, Inc.

The Grand Central Publishing name and logo is a trademark of Hachette Book Group USA, Inc.

Cover design by George Cornell
Cover photo of 8 ball by Getty Images

Grand Central Publishing
Hachette Book Group USA
237 Park Avenue
New York, NY 10017
Visit our Web site at www.HachetteBookGroupUSA.com

Printed in the United States of America

Originally published in hardcover by Little, Brown and Company
First Paperback Printing: September 2007

10 9 8 7 6 5 4 3 2 1

*To Ken Brecher, Michelle Satter, and
all my friends at the Sundance Screenwriters Lab*

FEAR
OF THE
DARK

I WAS EXPECTING ONE KIND of trouble when another came knocking at my door.

A year or so after I opened my Florence Avenue Used Book Shop, I installed four mirrors; one in the upper-right-hand corner of the door frame, one just outside the lower-left-hand side of the window, and the third, and second-largest, mirror was placed inside the window. So by daylight or lamplight at night, all I had to do was pull back the bottom hem of the inside drape to see who was knocking.

I installed my little spying device because if a man wanted to kill you and you asked "Who is it?" on the other side of a thin plank of wood, all he would have to do is open fire and that would be it. You might as well just throw the door open and say "Here I am. Come shoot me."

Someone might wonder why the owner of a used-book store would even think about armed assassins coming after him at any time, for any reason. After all, this is

America we're talking about. And not only America but Los Angeles in the midfifties—1956 to be exact.

We aren't talking about the Wild West or a period of social and political unrest. That was the most serene period of a democratic and peaceful nation. Most Americans at that time only worried about the cost of gas going above twenty-nine cents a gallon.

But most Americans weren't black and they sure didn't live in South Central L.A. And even if they were my color and they did live in my neighborhood, their lives would have been different.

Through no fault of my own I often found myself in the company of desperate and dangerous men—and women. I associated with murderers, kidnappers, extortionists, and fools of all colors, ages, and temperaments. By nature I am a peaceful man, some might say cowardly. I don't care what they say. It does not shame me to admit that I would rather run than fight. Sometimes, even with my mirrors, I didn't go anywhere near the door if the knock was too loud or too stealthy.

And during business hours, from 10:00 a.m. to 3:45 p.m. Monday through Saturday, I sat at my desk at the top of the staircase so that if someone dangerous walked in I would be able to get away before they even knew I was there; the fourth, and largest, mirror was on the ceiling at the head of the stairs for just that purpose.

Don't get me wrong; most of my customers were readers, primarily women and children, and unlikely to be looking for trouble. Whole days could go by and no one came to my bookstore (which was also my home), so I could spend long days reading books, uninterrupted and blissful.

But even though I was alone most days and the people who sought me out were, 999 times out of 1,000, looking for a book, there was that one time now and again when someone came to my door bearing malice and a gun.

I often think that this was true because of my decade-long friendship with Fearless Jones. Fearless was tall and thin, jet of color, and stronger of thew and character than any other man I had ever met. He wasn't afraid of death or love, threat or imprisonment. Fearless Jones wasn't even afraid of poverty, which made him a rare man indeed. No one could intimidate him and so he went wherever he wanted and associated with anyone he cared to.

Those anyones often came to me when they were looking for my friend and expressed themselves in ways that Fearless would not have stood for — if he were there.

Sometimes Fearless came to me when he was in a jam and needed the clear eye of logic to see his way out. And, because he'd saved my life more than once, I most often agreed to help, with the caveat that my aid wouldn't throw me into trouble.

The problem was, Fearless didn't ever feel like he was in trouble.

"Don't worry," he'd tell me. "It ain't all that bad."

And then someone was shooting at us, and Fearless did some impossible maneuver, and the gunman was disarmed, and Fearless was there smiling, saying, "You see? I told you it was all right."

So when I heard that knock on my door at 3:51 in the afternoon, I moved the hem of the drape expecting one thing, but instead I saw Ulysses S. Grant IV staring up into the mirror and waving.

"Open up, Paris. It's me."

I was a fool. I knew it even then. So what if Useless saw me in my mirror? I didn't have to open the door. I could have walked upstairs, opened up a copy of *Don Quixote* that I'd just acquired, and read to my heart's content.

"Come on, Cousin," Useless said. "I know you there."

I should have walked away, but Useless worried me. The kind of trouble he brought was like an infection. He never had a simple yes-or-no kind of problem; it was always "You're already in a mess. Now how do you plan to get out?"

I opened the door and stood to bar his entrance.

"What do you want?" I asked him.

"Let me by, Cousin," he said with a grin. "I need some ice water."

"I'm not askin' you again, Useless."

We were the same height, which is to say short, and he was fairly light colored, where I am considered dark (that is unless you see me standing next to Fearless Jones). Ulysses S. Grant IV, whom everyone but his mother and Fearless called Useless, was a petty thief, a liar, a malingerer, and just plain bad luck. His mother and mine were half-sisters, and I'd been dragged off by the ear because of him as far back as I could remember. As young as nine years old I was avoiding Useless.

The last time we'd seen each other was at my previous bookstore. He'd come over asking for a glass of ice water and use of the toilet. After he'd gone I didn't think much of it. But that night, while I was sleeping, I began to worry. Why had he been there? Who drops by somebody's place in L.A. for a glass of water?

It was three o'clock in the morning, but I pulled myself out of bed and went into my bathroom. I searched the medicine cabinet and behind the commode and in between the bath towels stacked on a shelf. Nothing.

I made coffee in my hot-plate kitchen and then went back to lift the heavy porcelain lid off the tank of the toilet. Down in the tank was a waterproof rubber sack filled with gold chains of various lengths and designs. Solid gold. The whole thing must have weighed two pounds.

That was 4:00 a.m.

Fearless was at my place in less than half an hour and he took the swag to hide it elsewhere.

I was in bed again by five.

At 6:47 the police were at my door with a warrant.

They went right to the toilet. Somehow they managed to shatter the lid.

It was late morning before they stopped turning over my bookstore. Those cops flipped through more books in that one day than most librarians do in a year.

After all that they arrested me. Milo Sweet, the bail bondsman, got me a good lawyer who told the cops that they had nothing on me and that any accusations made against me had to be proven or at least strongly indicated.

A week later an ugly guy named José Favor came by my house.

"Where the gold, mothahfuckah?" he said to me right off. One of his nostrils was wider than its brother, and the knuckles of his fists were misshapen, probably from beating on smaller men like me.

"You will have to speak to my agent," I told the man, who had already grabbed me by the collar of my shirt.

"Say what?"

"Fearless Jones," I said, and he let me go.

"What about him?" the ugly black man with the round eyes asked.

"He told me that anyone wanna know anything about gold they should come and see him."

José didn't say any more. I never heard about the gold again. Fearless came by the next week and took me to Tijuana, where we drank tequila and met some very nice young ladies who taught us Spanish and made us breakfast four mornings in a row.

I hadn't seen Useless since then and I hadn't missed him for a second.

"I'm IN TROUBLE, PARIS," Ulysses said, looking pathetic.

"So?"

"I need help."

"I sell books, not help."

"It's about that time with the gold chains, right?" he asked me.

I didn't even answer.

"That wasn't my fault, Paris. The cops got a hold'a me and like to beat me half to death. I told 'em that I hid 'em in yo' sto'. I told 'em you didn't know nuthin' about it."

I could have asked him why did they arrest me, then? But that would have opened a conversation, and I didn't want to have anything to do with Useless Grant.

"I need a place to hide out," he said.

"Not here."

"We blood, Paris."

"That might be, but I ain't bleedin' for you."

I thought Useless was going to break down and cry. But then he looked at my face and saw that I wouldn't let him in if he was having a heart attack. He wasn't getting across my threshold even if he fell down dead.

"Well, do me one favor, okay?" he said.

I just stared at him.

"Tell Three Hearts that there's a man named Hector wrote my name on a black slip'a paper. Tell her that I tried to make it work with Angel, but I guess I was mudfoot just like she said."

I didn't say a thing. Nothing. Useless was less than that to me. I heard his words and I would repeat them if I ever saw his mother again, but he wasn't going to make it into my house.

No sir, not in a thousand years.

2

I CLOSED THE DOOR on Useless and took a deep breath. I had to send him away, had to. Useless was the kind of trouble that could get a man killed. He had no sense except for the sense of survival. That meant he would deal with thugs or criminals just as if they were upstanding citizens; he'd invite those men into your house and then leave out the back door when trouble started.

The next day he'd call and ask how you were just as if he hadn't seen his partners come after you with a butcher's knife. He'd come to visit you in the hospital and hit you up for a loan even after you explained to him that you couldn't pay the doctor's bill.

Useless was trouble from the git-go.

But still I felt guilty.

I loved my auntie Three Hearts. She was the finest individual that you could imagine. She never passed judgment on people without cause and she was loyal. I once had a fever of 105 degrees, and she sat there sponging me down for days while my mother was laid up sick with the same flu. She stayed with us another week, cooking and looking after us while her son, Useless, broke every toy I owned.

Three Hearts's only blind spot was her son. Useless could do nothing wrong in her mind. If he got in trouble it was always somebody else's fault. If he lied it was for a higher purpose. Her son was a perfect man, and woe be unto those who thought otherwise. She lived in Lafayette, Louisiana, which was a good thing because that meant I wouldn't have to face her wrath at my turning her boy away in time of need.

Maybe I would have offered Useless a glass of water but, as I said before, I was already expecting trouble when he came knocking.

THREE WEEKS EARLIER I had been having dinner at a diner in downtown L.A. It was an Italian-American place at one of the crossroads between the races. There were all kinds of patrons eating there: whites, blacks, Asians, and even one Mexican family.

I liked integrated places. I guess that's because my time in the Deep South had been defined by segregation. They wouldn't let me into the library in my hometown. I wasn't even allowed to urinate where a white man had gone.

I had ordered eggplant parmigiana and was sitting there reading *Ulysses* by James Joyce. The book was no longer banned in the United States, but there was still a stigma attached to it, and I wanted to see what that was all about.

Between Joyce's playfulness, the eggplant and Italian bread, and the satisfaction of being able to sit where I was sitting, I was pretty happy.

Also, at the booth across from me there was this skinny young white woman. She had natural, if dirty, blond hair and blue eyes that looked like pale quartz. She used her tongue a lot while eating and I was quite enchanted by her wandering gaze.

The meal and Stephen Dedalus went along just fine, and I was completely satisfied. But then a disturbance occurred.

The plump waitress, who wore a tight red uniform, had delivered a check to the blonde's table, but then she came back with the cook. The cook was dressed all in whites. He had a sailor's cap, a stained white T-shirt, bleached white trousers, and an apron that was once buff colored but now had faded to a kind of off-white.

"No, no, miss," the burly, all-white cook was saying. "This is the dinner menu. The meat loaf is two ninety-nine, not one fifty."

"It says right here that meat loaf is a dollar fifty cent," the young woman said, pointing.

"It says lunch from noon to four right here," the cook, who had a kindly face, insisted.

"You shouldn't have the lunches on the same menu with the dinners," the girl said. "I wouldn't have even eaten here if I thought I had to pay all that."

"I'm sorry," the big man said.

The woman took out a small red purse and reached in.

"Oh, no," she said.

"What now?" the waitress, who was almost as large as the cook, said.

"I must have left my wallet at home."

"I do not trust you," the cook said, and I wondered what his native language might have been.

"I'll just go home and bring it right back," the woman went on as if she had not heard his words.

"No," said the man. "You will be staying here and Diane will be calling the police."

The woman attempted to rise, but the man with the kindly face held up a warning hand.

Diane turned to go toward the counter.

People all over the diner were craning their necks to see what was happening.

"Rita?" I said. I was standing next to the cook with a restraining hand on the waitress's elbow.

The dirty blonde looked up at me, trying not to seem confused.

"Hey, Rita. It's me . . . Paris. Don't tell me you lost your wallet again. I told you you got to remember to put it in your purse before you leave the house."

"You know her?" the cook asked.

Instead of answering, I handed him a twenty-dollar bill, the first twenty I'd had a hold of in a few weeks. That's the reason I had come to the diner, because I was flush and didn't have to eat pinto beans and rice for once.

"Rita Pigeon," I said, lying easily. "We work at the Lido Theater. I take tickets in the afternoon, and she's the nighttime usherette."

"Bullshit," Diane, the obese waitress, said.

"Watch you language," the cook said. "Don't speak like that around customers."

"What customers?" Diane spat.

"Come on over and sit with me, Rita," I said to the blonde. "And could you bring us some coffee with milk?" I asked the waitress.

Diane was going to tell me where I could go, but one gesture from the cook and she was on her way.

"I don't know what kind funny stuff this is," the cook said to me, waving the Jackson note. "But I will take your money."

I remember thinking that there was a great deal more truth to what he said than he meant.

The blonde moved to my booth, and the rest of the patrons returned to eating.

"Jessa," she said, introducing herself. She held out her hand and I shook it. "Thanks."

"It was a good scam," I said. "Three out of four places would have just thrown you out and said not to come back. But you should at least have the two bucks so that the one hardnose won't send you to jail."

Jessa was wearing an orange sundress that had little white buttons all the way down the front. The collar had a little dirt on it. Her red purse was scuffed.

"If I had two dollars I would have gotten a burger someplace," she said, smiling at me. "My boyfriend took off with our money, two weeks behind on the rent."

She didn't have to ask where she was going to sleep that night. I might be a coward, but that doesn't prevent me from being a fool. Watching that girl masticate her meat loaf had wiped any caution from my mind.

I had seen Jessa every third day after paying for her meal. I even went into my sacrosanct bank account and came out with money for her weekly rate on a room down on Grand.

That woman knew how to talk to a man.

But eight days before Useless came knocking, I had gotten information from a guy who worked at the front desk of Jessa's downtown rooming house.

"Mr. Minton," Gregory Wallace, the night manager, said, speaking to me as if we were equals. He was a white guy from Idaho. He'd never understood racism. There are many white people like that, even in the South.

"Yeah?"

"You know your friend Jessa had another boyfriend before you," the skinny young man said.

"Uh-huh."

"This big mean guy called Tiny."

Greg had my attention then.

"What about Tiny?" I asked.

"He's been comin' around on days that you're not here. And last night he asked me what the name was of the guy paying her rent."

Gregory had a pale, crooked face, with permanently bloodshot eyes, but he looked to me like a savior right then.

"Thanks, man."

I hadn't gone back to the rooming house for a week. That meant it was time for the rent to be paid and so Jessa would be looking for me. My phone had been off the hook for three days. I'd taken sixty-five dollars from my savings account to give to Jessa if she came by, but I intended to tell her that she needed to leave me alone.

So, Three Hearts notwithstanding, I had to turn Useless away. Because if he was there when Jessa was, I would most certainly come to grief. Useless was like monosodium glutamate for problems; he brought out the evil essence and magnified it.

I HAD JUST FINISHED rehearsing my speech to Jessa for the thirteenth time when her gentle knock came on my door.

I pulled the drape back to be sure she was alone, took a deep breath, and then opened up.

She was wearing a tan dress that hugged her slim figure and somehow wrapped around her calves.

"Hi," she said, letting her head loll to the side.

"Hey."

"Can I come in?"

No died on my lips as I backed away from the door. She swayed twice and crossed the threshold. She pushed the door closed, and I shivered.

Jessa Brown reached out as if she was about hold my hand, but instead she unzipped my pants and reached down into my shorts with quick and deft fingers.

"That's what I need," she said, looking into my eyes. "You know a girl can't give up a treasure like that."

I took half a breath and held it.

I am what the genteel folks call well-endowed. Some women like that. It gives them a de facto sense of power, I believe.

I'm small and weak and scared of my own shadow, and so my sexual prowess is one of the only things I have to be proud of in a masculine way. So when a woman looks me in the eye like that and tells me she needs me, I can't say no.

"Let's go upstairs," I said.

"No."

"Huh?"

"Let's do it right here on the floor, with your pants down around your ankles and me riding that monster."

THERE WE WERE, lying on the wood floor, naked where it counted. Jessa's feathery touch was keeping me excited, and her kisses on my shoulder and cheek delivered me from fear.

I would be thirty years old later that year, but in my heart I was still a kid. When a woman laid her hands on me, there was nothing I could do. That's why I hadn't as of yet entertained the idea of marriage. My auntie Three Hearts had always told me, "A man shouldn't say I do until he can say I don't."

I was a long way from *no* in the presence of a woman like Jessa.

She was a good seven years younger than me, not pretty but fetching. White women were another taboo that I liked breaking now and again. But there were other qualities about that girl.

The first thing was that she didn't feel compelled to talk and didn't mind listening. She liked masculine company and so never complained about toilet seats, dirty dishes, or the errant eructation. And when she did talk, she knew how to speak to a man.

"How come you haven't been by to see me, lover?" she said with her head on my chest and her left thigh over both of mine.

"Tiny."

"Him? Why you worried about him?"

"Because he's big and the jealous type."

"Big? He's not even half of you."

"Maybe not in the bed. But I'm not talkin' about love, J. I'm talkin' about gettin' my ass kicked—hard."

Jessa sat up to look down on me. "I'm not gonna tell Tiny about you. I don't tell him nuthin'. He just came back because he thought I'd take him in. But you know I'm easin' him out. By next week he'll be gone and forgotten."

"I don't know if we should be seeing each other," I said. I might have been more convincing if my voice hadn't gone up an octave.

"Come on, lover," she said, looking deep into my eyes. "You want this."

I did. I really did. Even though I knew better, I saw no use in that knowledge. The only reason I learned things was to be in a situation like I was there: lying on the floor in the entranceway of my bookstore, all tangled up with a girl that made my blood boil.

She kissed me.

"I can't let you go, Paris," she whispered.

Jessa Brown was from a whole slate of southern states. Her mother had moved around quite a lot. Her family was from the Midwest somewhere, but she never saw them because they called her and her mama trash. She could barely read, but she sang beautifully and had come to Los Angeles with a man named Theodore who had promised to get her an audition.

I didn't know that much about her, but it was enough to know that she was trouble.

But there I was on that floor, floating in a dream and not even thinking about waking up.

That's when the front door slammed open, breaking the lock and splintering part of the frame.

Jessa was on her feet in no more than a second. I was on my back, moving backward on all fours, under the shadow of one of the largest white men I had ever seen.

"Tiny!" Jessa shouted, and I remembered, quite clearly, why I stayed away from women like her.

"Kill you, bastard!" came from Tiny's lips. He had a movie star's voice, loud and strong.

It was his threatening tone that got me to my feet.

It was my youth and sexual prominence that saved my life.

Tiny was mad but not blind. He did a double take when he saw my diminishing erection. That one moment of hesitation was enough for Jessa. She grabbed a hardwood bookend from one of my shelves and threw herself at the behemoth. I didn't wait to see how it went.

With my pants in one hand and my drawers in the other, I made it up the staircase in triple time. At the top of the stairs I kept a large oak bookcase that only had towels and sheets on it. This light load was by design. I tipped the bookcase over so that it blocked entrée to the second floor. Then I scooted out the window and onto the tar paper roof.

I plan for calamity. The roof I was on covered the back

porch of my house. There were three beams along it that could bear the weight of a man. I knew the route of those beams and went quickly along the center timber and into the apple tree in the yard.

A great bellow came from the house as I stepped onto the top pole of the wire fence that separated my backyard from the alley behind Florence. The volume of that shout made me lose my footing. My bare foot got tangled up in the top mesh, and I fell to the asphalt below.

The fence was only six feet high, but I landed on my right shoulder blade and it hurt like hell. For a moment I lay there feeling as though I could never get up. But then I saw my maple desk chair crashing through the window I had just gone through.

I dropped my underpants and jumped into my jeans as I ran.

I came out on Central in a matter of moments. I couldn't hear Tiny, but that didn't mean he wasn't after me.

There I was in the twilight, wearing only my jeans with no shoes or socks. The pain from the fall was returning. Somewhere on the run I had cut my right foot, so I was limping now and trailing blood behind me on the white sidewalk.

I looked like a hobo. And not only that, I looked like trouble and so I had to figure what establishment I could duck into that wouldn't eject me into Tiny's murderous embrace.

"Paris!" a voice called. I nearly fainted.

"Paris, what's wrong?"

The voice was coming from the street, not the alley. There was a yellowy green Studebaker, maybe ten years

old, right there in the left lane. Sir Bradley was sitting behind the wheel.

I heard a shout. It might have been anybody, but I
couldn't take that chance.

"They tryin' to get me, Sir," I cried.

"Jump on in, boy. Let's move."

I opened his car door and hopped into the backseat.
Before the door was closed, Sir hit the gas and we were
off across the intersection. I heard a loud thump, turned,
and saw Tiny running only a foot or so behind us. Cars
were honking in the intersection, and Sir swerved to
avoid a collision. Tiny swung his fist and struck the trunk
of the Studebaker again.

"Oh, shit!" Sir screamed.

The tires squealed loudly, and we were off down Central, leaving Tiny to swing his fists in the crossroads.

"Wow," my savior said. "That suckah's big. What he
after you for, Paris?"

"His girlfriend forgot to tell him about me."

"White girl?"

"Yeah."

The woman sitting next to him gave a disapproving
grunt.

"Hm. That's what you get runnin' 'round with them
white women," she said.

"Paris, meet Sasha," Sir said.

"Pleased to meet ya," I said while glancing out the
back window and putting pressure on the cut on my foot.
Now that I was safe from immediate harm, I began to
worry about what Tiny would do to my store.

Turning my attention to the front seat, I saw that the
woman with Sir was a deep chocolate color, with big eyes

and high cheekbones. She was a beauty by any standard—except for the sour twist of her lips.

Sasha was born to be a queen and Sir was just a pawn. He was medium brown, middlebrow, and five eight in street shoes. His forehead was low, but he had a long skull from front to back. His eyes were crafty and his smile ever present. He was a union man from the first day he got a job at the Long Beach docks and he voted Democrat without even a glance at the candidate's name.

Mrs. Bradley, Sir's mother, had christened him so that no white person could insult him by refusing to call him Mister. He might have been a peasant by breeding, but there was a natural genuflection in just the mention of his name.

Maybe that's why the sour-faced beauty had hooked up with him: because saying his name did her honor.

"That boy was out for blood," Sir said.

"Uh-huh," I agreed.

Crossing the cut foot over my knee, I began teasing out the splinter of glass.

"You wanna call the cops?" Sir asked.

"A white cop?" Sasha said. "And tell him what? That he been sleepin' with a white man's girl and the white man wanna kick him? The police probably hold him down."

She was more than half right.

"Naw. I don't wanna go to no cops," I said. "Take me over to Slauson."

"Where?" Sir asked.

"Milo Sweet's new office. Fearless is there playin' bodyguard for a little while."

"Fearless Jones?" Sasha asked.

I recognized the longing in her voice. Fearless was coveted by women all over South L.A. and beyond. They liked his power to begin with and then his heart once they got to know him.

"Hear that, Paris?" Sir said. "I'll let you off on the corner. Either that or I'll be sleepin' alone tonight."

4 SIR LENT ME A BEAT-UP yellow
sweater so that I wasn't bare chested walking
down Slauson. When he and Sasha let me out
on the darkening corner, I was almost shaking. I was feeling the exhilaration of survival and mortal fear at my
close call. I was proud of myself for my letter-perfect escape, knowing all the while that I was a fool to be in a situation that could bring me so close to pain.

MILO SWEET'S BAIL BOND office was upstairs
from the haberdashers Kleinsman and Lowe. They spe-
cialized in old-world hats that they exported throughout
Europe and the Orient. At one time they had used the
third floor for the managing office, but when they decided
to move the nerve center of their operation downtown,
they let the space to Milo Sweet and his jack-of-all-trades
assistant, Loretta Kuroko.

I climbed the outside staircase to the third floor and
knocked.

After a few moments Loretta opened the door and smiled for me.

That day she was wearing a green ensemble. The jacket was silk and so was her skirt. The black blouse might have been cotton, and the hand-carved jade rose that hung from her neck was exquisite.

Loretta was ten years my senior but looked younger than me. She was beautiful and smarter than her boss. But Loretta revered Milo Sweet, and I do believe that she was the only person in the world he would have laid down his life for.

She had long dark hair rolled up into a bun at the back of her head and eyes that looked at you from some other epoch, when there were no cars or jitterbugs, no white people at all, and when men, once they made up their mind to fight, would not give up until they had bled their last drop.

"Hello, Paris," she said.

I felt something then. It was the feeling I'd had as a child when I returned home after a long day away. My mother would be there waiting for me, and I felt a joy that I had not expected to feel. Loretta's greeting was a delight. And I think that she saw my reaction.

She smiled and nodded by moving her head in an elegant semicircle.

"Are you here to see Milo?" she asked.

"No."

Her lips pursed. "Fearless?"

"Have I ever told you how happy I am to see you whenever I come to this office?" I asked.

"Come on in, Paris," she said.

I followed her up the three steps to the circular room that she and Milo shared.

When Milo told Loretta that they were moving offices again, the thirteenth time in nine years, she informed him that she would only go if he let her find the place and design and furnish it. What came of it was a thing of beauty.

The room wasn't actually round. It had eight walls of equal size. Every other wall had a large window with a roll-up bamboo shade. The floor was the most wonderful part. It was a perfect circle, twenty feet in diameter, raised half a foot above the original floor and made from cherrywood. Fearless had constructed it. He had also built the oak file cabinets that sat against the windowless walls and on the floor outside the circle.

Loretta's desk was a simple plank of ebony wood on white ash legs. She had no drawers or doodads to obstruct the elegant lines.

On the other side of the circle, Milo had his hideous drab green desk made from sheet metal. His chairs didn't match, and he was perpetually swaddled in a thin blanket of cigar smoke. When you looked at the room you got the feeling that it represented a planet, one side of which was in permanent midnight and the other washed in eternal noon.

No one would have expected this particular meeting of East and West in a third-floor office in black Los Angeles. It might be that no one, outside of Milo's clients and friends, ever knew it was there. People from the style section at magazines went to see how John Wayne and Clark Gable lived. They wanted to see foreign queens' palaces when they should have been looking at that bail bondsman's office on Slauson.

•   •   •

WHEN I TOOK A STEP and faltered, Loretta noticed my bare feet. A moment after that she saw that I was bleeding on her cherry floor.

"What happened?" she asked.

"It's kinda hard to explain," I said. "But it's not all that bad."

"Come sit down."

Milo had a favorite guest chair. It was a spindly light brown creature that most resembled a half-starved dog. The legs didn't look as though they could bear the weight of a big cat, but there Fearless sat with his feet on Milo's desk, leaning back on the two quivering hind legs of that chair.

Fearless wore a charcoal shirt and blue jeans. He was drinking a glass of water.

"Paris," he said with a true friend's smile.

"The prodigal son," Milo rumbled. If they ever put him in a choir, he'd have to be placed somewhere behind the bass section.

"Gentlemen," I hailed, allowing Loretta to help me to a red stool that Milo had also refused to give up. Behind him there was an open window with a fan blowing out; another demand of Loretta's.

"What happened to you, Paris?" Milo asked.

Looking at Milo you would have thought he was once tall but somewhere along the way he'd gotten jammed up in a compactor that had made a shorter, broader specimen.

He had the big hands of a heavyweight and the shoulders of a bull. For all that, Milo was not a physical man. Nine times out of ten when I saw him he was sitting, and the only sport he excelled in was darts. He was most often the darkest man in the room, that is unless he was in the room with Fearless.

"Cut myself runnin' barefoot through an alley," I said. I didn't need to say any more.

Loretta came up with a glass of water and a first aid kit. She knelt down in front of me and started ministering to my wound.

"I come to borrow my friend," I said, wincing from a dab of iodine.

"This is prime time right here, Paris," Milo said, shaking his big head at me. "And Fearless is on the clock."

"What you need, Paris?" Fearless asked, as if Milo had not said a word.

I told them the story. It didn't bother me that Loretta was there listening. Milo's assistant never passed judgment on someone for being the victim of his instincts.

"Unless the man come to your house is Albert Rive, Fearless ain't goin' nowhere," Milo said when I finished my tale.

Fearless had grinned now and then while I spoke, and Loretta had let out with an "Oh, no" here and there. But Milo was all business.

There was a thug in Los Angeles named Albert Rive. He was an armed robber who got caught, tried, and sentenced to fifteen years in the California penal system. But before he could be sent away, his lawyer, Philip Reed, a friend of Milo's, got the conviction set aside on a technicality. Rive came to Milo for bail with his mother's mortgage in hand. Then he went somewhere down South and disappeared.

Milo was out fifteen thousand dollars when Rive jumped bail. And though he hated to do it, he had to foreclose on Mrs. Alberta Rive's home. She lived there with her daughter, granddaughter, and four great-grandchildren. Milo was about to put them all out in the street.

Somehow a message came to Milo that he had better lay off Mrs. Rive or Albert would make a surprise stop at his doorstep.

Milo was a thinking man, but he was also almost as brave as my friend Fearless. He had hired Mr. Jones to be his bodyguard until the Rive property was liquidated and hoped that Albert would make a move so he would get caught and Alberta could remain in her home.

Toward this end, Milo had hired the only official black private detective in Watts, a man known as Whisper Natly.

Whisper was a man with no distinguishing characteristics. You never saw him even when he was right there in front of you. He wore a short-brimmed brown hat that was a shade darker than his skin. He had a gray hatband but no feather. His shoes were dark, maybe brown, and his clothes were neither new nor old, natty nor disheveled. He spoke in a low voice, not a whisper, and no one I knew had ever seen where he lived.

Whisper was the kind of man who could get information out of a deaf-mute. He moved quietly, always paid his bills, and never bad-mouthed anyone.

If Albert Rive was anywhere near Watts, Whisper was sure to sniff him out.

"Get your hat, man," Fearless said to Milo. "We gonna take a ride with Paris."

My friend rose from his leaning position effortlessly, like some being more graceful than a human. When he squared his shoulders, I spied Loretta appreciating him.

"I'm the one payin' you, Fearless," Milo reminded him. He stayed in his chair.

"If I was wit' Paris here doin' sumpin' for him," Fearless said, "an' you come to me an' say your house was on fire, I'd tell Paris to get his hat. Now, if you want me to leave you a gun, I'll be happy to do it."

Fearless wasn't the smartest man I ever met. I sometimes wondered if he could do long division. But whatever he said was usually the last word in any argument. That's because Fearless thought with a pure heart.

Milo got up.

"Come on, Loretta," he said. "Get your bag and go on home."

"But what if someone needs bail?" she asked.

"Have the answering service call you at home. I don't wanna leave you here with that killer runnin' free out there."

"Wait a second," she said, jumping up from her knees.

She'd done a good job cleaning and bandaging my foot. She went behind Milo's desk and came out with a beat-up pair of light brown slippers.

"Put these on," she told me, tossing the house shoes to the floor.

I glanced at Milo, but he just shrugged resignedly. He knew better than to argue with Miss Kuroko.

WHEN WE GOT TO THE STREET, I told Loretta that I'd walk her to her car. She was driving a tan Volkswagen Bug. At the door she reached out and touched my upper lip.

"What's this?" she asked.

"Mustache."

"It looks good."

We stood there for a moment longer than was necessary.

"Call me," she said.

I breathed in and forgot about expiration. Loretta gave a little laugh. It was as if I had never heard her laugh. It was wonderful.

5 | WE TOOK MILO'S dark red '52 Cadillac. He drove while Fearless sat shotgun. I reclined in the backseat, thinking about my bookstore and that angry white man.

I wasn't scared, because I was with Fearless and Fearless always inspired calm in me. In his company I had my greatest acuity due to the peaceful security of his aura.

I wasn't scared, but I was worried that maybe Tiny had burned down my store.

I was thinking about Loretta behind me and Jessa up ahead, wondering why it was that I could never make it work with women, why there was only a short time for love before something went wrong.

"What's the matter with you, Paris?" Milo asked, as we turned onto Central.

"What you talkin' 'bout, Miles?"

"You. Why a smart man like you spend half his life in trouble?"

"Me? What about you, needin' Fearless and Whisper

t'covah yo' ass?" I asked in the street banter that was the glue of Negro life in every corner of our nation.

"That's business," Milo said flatly. "That's money in my pocket. Man gotta do business or him an' his starve. But you got people up on your ass an' you don't hardly have a pot to piss in. Here you worried 'bout that bookstore, an' we both know that you be lucky to clear forty dollars in a month's time."

"Maybe so," I allowed. "But you the one been up to his kneecaps in loan sharks every year since you been out on your own."

Fearless let out a low chuckle on that one.

Milo gave his temporary bodyguard a sidelong glance and said, "Again, all you talkin' 'bout is business. Businessman got to cover his debts, got to grow his capital. I own a business that's worth somethin', Paris. People, white people, have offered me big money to sell out to them. Big money. How much somebody gonna give you for that bookstore?"

Milo was ragging me because he was mad that Fearless had made him leave his office. I was arguing back to keep my mind off the troubles that lay ahead. But I tripped up on that last question. I didn't want to sell my bookstore. I would have gotten an extra job in order to keep it running. I loved sitting there with those dusty books. I loved it.

MILO PULLED UP AT THE CURB across the street and down a few houses from my place. Fearless turned sideways in the front seat and gave me his serious look.

"Okay, Paris," he said. "Now tell me what you did to this white boy."

"Nuthin'."

"You sure?"

Fearless was a killer. He didn't have a bad bone in his body, but somewhere along the evolutionary trail he had been endowed with a gift for violence. All through World War II, and in American cities from Houston to S.F. to L.A., he had dealt out terrible punishment. He never shied away from trouble, nor would he turn his back on a friend. But Fearless didn't want to be tricked into hurting someone who didn't deserve it, and so he asked me about Tiny.

"What I told you at Milo's is all there is, man," I said. "I should have sent her away, but you know . . ."

Fearless smiled and opened the car door.

"I'll drive around the block a couple'a times," Milo told us.

"It won't take long," Fearless replied.

THE FRONT DOOR TO MY STORE was closed. That in itself wasn't so strange. It was just that I remembered the splintering wood from the frame and the violence in Tiny's voice. I found it hard to imagine such rage closing a door like that.

Fearless and I took the stairs together, side by side.

With the fingers of his left hand, Fearless tapped the door, and it swung open. This meant that someone had gone to the bother of reattaching the hinges.

Ten feet from the doorway Tiny lay, in the same spot where Jessa and I had rutted like alley cats. He was on his back, his left arm under him and his right flung awkwardly over his stomach. His green eyes were open wide, and there was a small dark cavity in his right temple.

I moved closer to the body, not really realizing what I was seeing. It made no sense. In my fear I had wished this man dead, but wishes couldn't happen. I tried to come up with an explanation as to how the killing might have occurred, but there was no thought that could take hold. I didn't believe that I was seeing what was in front of me. I expected Tiny to sit up any minute and say, "April fool."

"Paris," Fearless said. I had the feeling he'd said it more than once.

"What?"

I turned to see that he had closed the door.

"What the hell is this, man?" he asked. Fearless rarely cursed.

"I swear, Fearless. I don't know. I ran out over the eave of the back porch. He might have falled or somethin'. . . ."

"Fall my ass. This dude been shot."

"I don't know how."

"What about that girl? Maybe he went after her and she shot him."

"She didn't have no purse," I said. "Damn, man, she wasn't even wearin' underpants."

"What about your piece?" he asked.

"I don't have a gun."

"No?"

"Uh-uh."

"Maybe," Fearless said, straining his mental faculties, "maybe *he* had a gun and she took it from him."

"Fearless, what the fuck I'm'a do about this?"

That started him chewing on his bottom lip. He shook his head, staring at the body.

"Call the cops?" he asked.

"Come on, man," I said. "What the hell can I say to the cops? That I was fuckin' his white girlfriend on the floor when he busted in? They hang me for that right there."

"You right," Fearless agreed. "Even if the girl did it, she's probably long gone by now, and if they catch her all she got to do is cry rape and say you shot the guy."

"Maybe we should bring Milo in," I suggested.

"Uh-uh. Unless Milo see dollar signs he won't do nuthin'. Anyway he's not gonna put himself in trouble for us."

Us. That's why I could never turn my back on Fearless Jones. Who else would walk into my house, find a dead body, and stay to share my trouble?

"So what do we do?"

"How come you standin' funny, Paris?" Fearless asked me.

"What the fuck that got to do with anything?"

"Okay. I'll tell you what. You lift his feet and I'll get his shoulders."

I knelt and grabbed Tiny's ankles. When I tried to lift them, a spasm went through my right shoulder that sent me to the floor.

"Now you wanna tell me 'bout how you standin'?" Fearless asked.

"Okay, yeah, I fell an' hurt my side. So what?"

"So if we don't tell the cops and we don't tell Milo, then the only thing we can do is get rid'a yo' friend here. But he too big for me alone. And you don't have the strength to help, not with that hurt back."

I wanted to scream. How could a bookworm like me get into so much trouble over a meat loaf dinner?

Fearless smiled.

"You get too upset, Paris. Don't let it bother you. We just need some help."

I couldn't even talk.

"I'll tell you what," he said. "Let's put our friend here down in your cellar. I'll drive Milo around until he goes to sleep at his hideout and then I'll get somebody we can trust to help."

Under the rightmost bookcase in my store was a blue carpet covering a trapdoor. This door led to a small brick-lined cellar that had come with the building. I don't know what the previous owners did down there. It didn't have a hot-water heater or even an electric outlet. It wasn't big enough for a pool table. I'd always thought that the original owners might have been crooked in some way and they installed the underground room as a hideout in times of trouble.

I had had Fearless run a wire through the wall so that I could have light down there, but other than that I hadn't changed a thing.

Fearless moved the bookcase and I kicked the carpet away. I also pulled up the trapdoor. Fearless dragged the heavy corpse to the hole and dropped him in.

"Hey," he said in a moment of sudden inspiration. "We could just bury him down there."

"Naw, man. Naw."

"Why not?"

"Jessa's not here but she's somewhere. Sooner or later she's likely to talk to somebody and then they will talk to somebody else. One day somebody's gonna talk to a cop, and he's gonna come here with a hard-on and a search warrant. Naw. We got to get rid of Tiny."

"Okay," Fearless said. "Throw that carpet back down there."

I did as he said, but before he could move the shelves
I stopped him.

"Maybe I should go down there with him," I said.

"What for?"

"I don't know. I mean, I don't know who killed this
man. Maybe he gonna come back. Maybe Jessa already
talked to the cops. I can't go with you 'cause Milo'd
get suspicious. But if I'm down there, nobody gonna find
me."

SO I CLIMBED DOWN the short ladder into the ten-
by-ten-foot brick-lined hole. Tiny had fallen on his head
and broken his back in the fall. His torso was bent in a
most unnatural pose. I clicked on the reading lamp I had
down there, and Fearless closed the hatch. I heard him
moving the bookcase and sat myself on the floor in the
corner — as far away from Death as I could manage.

6 BEFORE HE LEFT, Fearless called down through the floorboards, "Paris, you still got that trunk with the padlock on it in the back?"

"Yeah," I said in a deep tone.

"Where's the key?"

"In my tool drawer. Why?"

"I'm'a put the lock on the front do' so nobody come in here."

I heard him walking around for a while after that. He went back and forth a couple of times, and then the house was silent.

The first thing I realized after Fearless was gone was that I didn't have a book to read. At the best of times that would have been bad news. Reading is how I made it through life. While other children were out getting into trouble, I was in the schoolroom or at the back of the church reading *Treasure Island* or *Huckleberry Finn*. Books were my radio and my daily drug. I could live without almost anyone or anything as long as I had a book to read. A long queue became a luxury if *Anna*

Karenina was there to engage me. The doctor's waiting room became my private den if he kept up with his magazine subscriptions.

Sitting there next to a heap of flesh and bone that once made up a man, with no book and no way out, made me jittery, pressed me to the edge of panic.

I tried to go over how I had come to that place. Should I have left Jessa alone? Probably. But she said her boyfriend had left her. Should I never have believed what people told me?

Within five minutes of Fearless's departure a peculiar pinging sound began emanating from the corpse. It had a nautical ring to it. His body juices settling, no doubt, I thought.

I turned off the lamp and closed my eyes, determined to sleep until Fearless returned with his helper. No more than a minute later came another greatly extended bodily note. I turned on the light and wondered if I could push the trapdoor open.

Tiny's head was on the floor and his middle was bent backward so that his feet were next to his head. I decided that it was this uncomfortable position that made him so musical. Maybe if I straightened him out he might calm down.

With great difficulty because of my hurt back, I pulled on the big man's legs until he was lying flat on his stomach with one hand underneath him and one behind his neck. I would have straightened him out more, but he had soiled himself and was beginning to smell pretty bad. For a moment I worried that the odor might overwhelm me. I panicked and climbed the ladder, but when I made a tentative shove against the trapdoor I realized that I'd never be able to push my way out.

I kept a tarp down there that I used sometimes when I had to do work around the house. I used this to cover the body and to contain the odors it was emitting.

Then I turned out the light again. The next sound that came from Tiny was like that of a giant toad being pressed underneath him.

I turned on the light.

I was caught between my fear of the dark and the terror that light brought.

"You gonna be fine, Paris," I told myself. "It's gonna be okay. You didn't kill this boy. You didn't ask him to come over here after you, actin' a fool."

For a while there I blamed Useless for my problems. Just the fact of him dragging his unlucky hide to my doorstep, I reasoned, had brought this misfortune down on my head.

But I couldn't blame Useless. He hadn't even come in my house. Anyway, if my cousin had caused the problem it would have been me stretched out on the floor instead of Tiny.

For some reason that thought made me laugh. The laugh, in turn, made me smile; as long as I had a sense of humor I was on the way to recovery.

That's when Tiny twitched under his canvas blanket.

It wasn't a violent motion, more like a twist and a shudder. But when the man you're sitting with is supposed to be dead, you don't want to see any movement whatsoever.

I leaped to my feet, uttered five or six unintelligible syllables, and ran smack into the wall. I hit the ground and then looked around for a weapon to protect myself from the man I was entombed with, the man whose only words to me had been that he intended to take my life.

My forehead was bleeding. My fists were up in front of my eyes. I was panting like a spent dog. Sweat was coming down my face, and I shivered from cold. I had never been so frightened in all my life, and then Tiny shifted under his rough pall again.

This next motion could only calm me. I mean, things couldn't get any worse. I took a step toward the prostrate figure and nudged him with my toe.

He didn't respond.

"Tiny," I said. "Hey, man, you okay?"

I thanked heaven that he didn't answer.

It was then that I remembered reading that corpses in morgues and mortuaries often exhibited some characteristics of life. They shifted and farted and made all kinds of sounds and motions. Some bodies had been known to sit upright hours after their demise.

Tiny was dead. If the bullet in his brain hadn't killed him, his broken back from that fall would have finished the job. He wasn't going to rise up and kill me in that cellar. All I had to do was sit there and wait for Fearless to return and everything would be just fine.

That last thought was the wrong one to have because it aroused a question. When would Fearless return?

Milo went to bed before ten every night. He had a switchboard answering service that connected to him or Loretta on alternating nights in case an important call came in. Fearless would drop Milo off, pick up his helper, and return to get me out of that hole. If everything went well, I figured, he'd get there no later than 11:30.

It was the *if everything went well* clause of this logic

that got stuck in my craw. What if something went wrong? A car accident or the police stopping Fearless and finding his illegal gun. What if there was a shoot-out with Albert Rive and he got the drop on my friends? It could happen. Anybody could die. And Fearless was the only person in the world other than me who knew about the crawl space under the floor.

Even if my back was in perfect condition, I wouldn't be able to push that heavy bookcase off the trapdoor. If Fearless didn't make it back in time, I would die.

The cold in my chest was like a new ice age creeping down toward my feet. I was a fool and I was going to die because of it. I sat in the corner, turned out the light, and buried my head in my hands.

A moment later I forgot about all my worries.

I heard a footstep above me. I almost called out, but then I thought that it couldn't be Fearless because not enough time had passed. And it couldn't be anyone else who was there by accident because Fearless had padlocked the front door for sure.

Someone had broken in. He was walking around, sending shelves and furniture crashing to the floor. I heard glass shattering and table legs crying across the wood floor. And whereas just a moment ago I was afraid that no one would ever find me in the tomb below my home, now I was scared that whoever it was searching my house would kick the blue carpet, discover the trapdoor, and climb down to kill me.

I felt around Tiny's pants, locating a fairly large pocketknife. This I unfolded and held in both hands. Maybe I could wound the invader before he knew I was armed.

That was the worst night of my entire life. Everything

that happened was a potential threat. No matter what I did, Death was dogging my tail.

AFTER QUITE A WHILE the footsteps and crashing subsided. After ten minutes of silence I turned on the light. The fears then began to pile up like stones in an avalanche. I worried about carnivorous insects burrowing after Tiny and then deciding they'd like to have living flesh too. I wondered how much air there was in the underground room and if I'd have enough to last me until Fearless returned, if he returned.

Then my fears became more complex. I worried that the burglar hadn't left but gone into hiding. Maybe he was lying in wait for me. Maybe he had come to kill me but bumped off Tiny because the big white fool had come on too strong. Now the killer was waiting in shadows for me, and when Fearless got there he'd be ambushed and I'd die of starvation there under the floor.

The fears heaped up so heavily on my mind that I retreated into a mild catatonia where all I could do was sit and stare.

I was sure that my death was imminent and so for one of the very few times in my fretful existence I knew no fear, only hopelessness.

7 | I HAVE NOT BEEN ABLE to spend
more than a few minutes in a completely dark
room since that April Fools' night 1956. I always have a candle and a match somewhere nearby and
one of those pale blue night-lights that parents have for
frightened children plugged in the wall of every room in
my house.

Blackouts in plays and movie theaters never fail to
give me the willies.

After my four or five hours with Tiny and every fear
that my mind could manufacture, I promised myself
that I would never be such a fool again. It didn't matter
that going down into the temporary tomb probably
saved me from whoever had broken in. No. I would
rather have faced Death himself than the fear I experi-
enced. I couldn't turn on the lamp because if someone
was lying in wait he might have seen the light through
the floor. So I huddled in darkness, my mind a cold sea
of dread.

•   •   •

A FOOTSTEP. Another. Then there were the sounds of two men walking boldly across the room.

"Paris," Fearless called out.

"I'm here," I said, but my tone said *help*.

Somebody mumbled something and Fearless said something back. There was a chortle from one of them, but I couldn't tell which one.

I heard the bookcase move and the trapdoor came open, flooding my abyss with electric light from above.

"Damn," a man said and snorted. "It sure do smell bad."

I had reached the ladder and grabbed the rungs, but between the blinding light, my silent terror, and the growing pain in my back, I was unable to climb.

"Come on, Paris," Fearless said. I looked up and saw his dark and smiling face. "One foot after the other."

After four steps, Fearless grabbed me by the forearm and lifted me into the light. I landed on my feet and looked around. Everything that had been upright was on the floor: books, bookcases, tables, and chairs. Everything had been tipped over, opened, and turned out. The only things standing upright were me, Fearless, and the man he had brought with him: Van "Killer" Cleave.

Seeing Cleave there grinning at me was almost enough to send me back down into the crypt.

Van Cleave. He was the living legend of Watts. Only an inch taller than I, he was a giant. Dark-skinned and bright-eyed, he was a killer of vast talent. No man, or group of men, crossed him if they were smart. He was a stone-cold killer, the consummate ladies' man, and the best storyteller anybody knew of.

Back when he first came to L.A. from Georgia, he was stalked by three white gangsters for robbing a department store that was under their protection. The white men were from down South and used to colored people taking their punishment. They came into a crowded bar and called Cleave's name. Everyone expected him to throw up his table and run, but instead he stood up with his long .45-caliber pistol and casually squeezed off shots.

"Them white men was dead 'fore they knew it was comin'," Randolph Minor told me the next day.

"Did Killer go back down South?" I asked him.

"No, sir," Randy, a big man, squeaked. "He went home with Bea Langly. She said that she asked him wasn't he worried that somebody would tell? An' he said, 'They bettah not.'"

And no one did. Killer became a hero overnight. He stood up to three white gangsters and went home with the most beautiful bar girl our city had to offer. After that night he never had to pay for a drink, a haircut, or a meal. Tailors gave him clothes just to say he was their customer. He'd been to prison for another crime. But he survived that too. Van Cleave was as oblivious to danger as was Fearless, but on top of that he was flamboyant and dangerous—just the kind of man our dark manhood needed to maintain our dignity.

I loved hearing stories about Van, but I wasn't happy to have him in my house. Even standing there with Fearless I felt in peril.

"Hey, Paris," Van said easily. "Hear you got a problem."

I gulped and nodded.

"It smell bad," he said with a wink.

"What happened here?" Fearless asked me, looking around at the debris.

"Somebody broke in an' tore up the place," I said. "I heard 'em."

"I thought you said that the only trouble you had with that white boy was the girl," Fearless said.

"It was, man. I swear."

"Go on, Van," Fearless said then. "Pull the truck around in the alley and we'll get everything ready in here."

Cleave nodded and made his way around the debris to the door. After he was out of the house, I started in on my friend.

"What the fuck you bring him to my house for, Fearless?"

"Because you can't hardly lift up your arm and we got to take Tiny way out somewhere."

"But that's Killer Cleave," I argued. "You cain't trust a killer."

"Yes, you can," Fearless averred. "He's the second-most trustworthy man in all Watts. He will nevah talk to a cop. He will nevah turn a brother over. It's true he will kill you if you cross him, but he won't evah talk about this night, not to no one. Not evah."

I knew eighth graders who could think circles around Fearless, but I never met a college grad who owned more truth than he.

FEARLESS HAD BROUGHT a heavy rope. He climbed down into the hole and created a hemp hoist under Tiny's shoulders. Then he came back to the ramshackle room and pulled the 250 pounds of dead weight up with very little effort as far as I could tell.

I remember thinking that if Fearless and Van had a duel of tug-of-war, my friend would win hands down. But

Watts wasn't some ancient Scottish hamlet. They used guns and knives in my neighborhood, and the killers I was rolling with were duelists extraordinaire.

When we had Tiny laid out on the floor, Cleave returned. He and Fearless hefted the dead man, carrying him through the back porch (which was also my hot-plate kitchen) and out the screen door back there.

I noticed a big hole in the tar paper roof. Tiny had fallen through according to my plan, but the fall hadn't hurt him. He'd just busted through the screen door and bounded over the fence.

"How do we get him over the fence?" I asked.

Cleave reached into his back pocket and came out with wire cutters. He snipped a hole big enough to pull Tiny through while Fearless climbed over the top. Van positioned the body and Fearless pulled it through. Then Killer climbed over.

I could neither climb nor crawl with my hurt back.

"I got to go through the house," I said.

"Go down into the cellar and get that canvas sheet," Fearless said.

By the time I made it around to the alley, they had Tiny neatly folded into the back corner of a flatbed Ford truck.

FEARLESS LET ME SIT next to the passenger's window while Van drove the '48 Ford truck he'd borrowed from some friend. I was on the alert for police cars, jerking my head around every time a light flashed.

"What's wrong, Paris?" Van asked after my body went through a fairly pronounced spasm.

"Worried about the cops stoppin' us. It's late. They might grab us just for drivin'."

"That ain't our problem, man," the killer said. "It's their widows and fatherless children got to worry 'bout them."

The certainty of Cleave's tone and the depth of Fearless's silence put me into a different mood altogether. There I was, in a truck with desperate men. *I* was a desperate man. It was hard to believe that a milquetoast coward like myself could be involved in such a clandestine and dangerous operation. But the reasons were as clear as the quarter moon shining through the windshield.

All three of us were living according to black people's law. The minute I came upon that white boy's body I knew that I would be seen as guilty in the eyes of American justice. Not even that—I *was* guilty. There was no jury that would exonerate me. There was no court of appeals that would hear my cries of innocence.

I wasn't a brave man like Fearless or a born criminal like Van Cleave, but we all belonged in that truck together. We had been put there by a long and unremitting history. My guilt was my skin, and where that brought me had nothing to do with choice or justice or the whole library of books I had read.

WE DROVE SOUTH and a little east of San Pedro. Van was driving us through a fallow strawberry field. It was maybe two in the morning, and we were the only souls within miles.

When we got out Van said to me, "Take off your sweater, Paris."

"What?"

"Take off that yellah sweater," he said.

I realized what he was saying. Fearless was still in his

dark colors. Van was wearing all black. Only I had on a bright piece of clothing: Sir's sweater. There I was, afraid that the law might see me, but that sweater was like a lightbulb under that moon.

While I was disrobing, Fearless and Cleave hefted the corpse out of the back of the truck and carried him over the tilled soil into a stand of oaks. There they used two short spades to dig a shallow grave.

Before they put him in, Van went through his pockets and pulled out a slender wallet. He threw the billfold to me, and then they covered Tiny over. There was no money in the wallet, but instead of throwing it down I put it in my pocket.

"See ya later, my friend," Van said by way of prayer.

Fearless saluted.

BACK AT MY FRONT DOOR at four in the morning, Fearless and I climbed out of Van's borrowed truck.

"Thanks, Van," I said, extending a hand.

"One day I'm'a come ask you for a book, now, Paris," he said.

"What kinda books you read?" I asked.

"No kind. That's why I'm'a come to you. When I need a book, you the one gonna tell which one I'm after."

It was the only time in my life that a book request scared me.

8 | FEARLESS SLEPT ON the couch in my front room that night. The next morning he was off to protect Milo, and I worked on fixing up my bookstore, jumping at every sound.

The first day I straightened, swept, and sorted through my stock. The next day I got out my tools and went to work on the structural damage that Tiny had wrought. I'm not all that good with my hands, but I come from poor stock. I never hired a plumber or carpenter because I didn't have that kind of wealth. So the door frame looked mismatched and crooked, but it held the door in place. The tar paper roof looked as if it had a black bandage on it, but when it rained eight months later I had nary a leak in my kitchen.

I even knitted together the wire fencing in my backyard.

Fearless dropped by every night after letting Milo off at his hideout. He'd bring peach schnapps, a liquor we both got a taste for from an older Jewish lady who had died on our watch. We'd toast the old woman when we took our first sip.

After a week had gone by, I began to calm down. Whoever it was that had broken into my house either got what he was after or didn't — either way he didn't return.

I had eight customers in that time, all of them in the last four days.

My first patron was Ashe Knowles. She was what I called a Lady Poindexter. She was the only person I ever met who had read more than I. She had bought and traded back almost every book I had in stock.

Ashe was an inch or so taller than I, and her coloring was what I call a buttery brown: lighter than your average Negro's but not by much. She wore glasses and had absolutely no sense of style. Her clothes were old, and she wore brown leather shoes with black laces and white cotton socks. She braided her hair into pigtails every morning, tying them with primary-colored ribbons on the ends.

I was happy that Ashe was such a poor dresser for two reasons. The first was that she liked me. I was one of the few eligible black men she knew who actually read for enjoyment and who could engage her on most topics that she was familiar with. Because of this she often came by and spent long hours talking about arcane subjects like coats of arms in the Middle Ages or the dynasties of Egypt. Ashe had taught herself the rudiments of Latin and Greek, and she liked to play word games, looking for the ancient roots in English words.

Ashe would give me long hungry looks as we conversed, but all I had to do was glance at those ribbons in her hair and I knew that I wasn't going to make a move.

The second reason I was happy about her appearance was that I suspected that she was beautiful under that dowdy facade.

I didn't want to get romantically involved with Ashe because she was my best customer and I really liked talking with her.

She was a deep thinker. Sometimes she'd say things to me and it wasn't until days later that I figured out what she'd meant.

If I became her lover something was bound to go wrong. Pregnancy. Expectations of marriage. Both. I wasn't ready for a good woman like Ashe, and as long as she dressed the way she did, she couldn't tempt a fool like me.

"Hello, Mr. Minton," Ashe said on that Thursday morning. She was wearing a Scotch plaid skirt that came down to the middle of her calves, a dark green sweater that didn't go with anything that wasn't a uniform, and pink hair ribbons.

"Ashe. How are you today?"

"I read that book about dreams," she said.

"*The Interpretation*?" I asked, referring to Freud's seminal work.

"It was very interesting," she allowed. "He wants it to be a science, but it cain't be, not really."

"Why not?" I asked. "He's a doctor."

"A doctor's not a doctor when he's sittin' in church talkin' to the preacher," she said. "When a doctor is talkin' to a minister, he's just a man."

Even though she was looking as homely as a woman three times her age, Ashe made my heart flutter then.

"But Mr. Freud wasn't in no church," I said. "He was bein' a doctor, curing psychosomatic symptoms."

"But he couldn't prove it. He talks to you and explains dreams, but some of what he says has to be wrong and he doesn't have the tools that could quantify and compare his findings."

"So you don't believe it?" I asked the drab young woman.

"No. I didn't say that. But it seems to me that Dr. Freud has opened up a question about how we understand things. He's discovered something that no chemist or physicist or mathematician can prove or even begin to prove. That's wonderful."

Ashe smiled then and I forgot, for the first time in many days, about Tiny and Jessa and that stand of bitter oaks.

"I hate to rush you off, Ashe," I said, "but I just remembered that I have to make a call."

"Oh," she said. "I thought you might have some time."

"Sorry."

I hurried her out because I knew myself. I'd be in love with her for a day or a week, maybe even a month, but sooner or later we'd crash and burn; she'd walk away from my bookstore and never return with her brilliant insights and goofy smiles.

I HAD OTHER CUSTOMERS. Two neighborhood boys came by for comic books and copies of *National Geographic* magazine (hoping for a glimpse of the naked breasts of so-called primitives). A couple of ladies from up the block who bought romance novels dropped in twice.

One dusky-skinned guy with an island accent of some sort came in looking for a French dictionary.

"You mean French-English?" I asked the guy.

"*Non*," he said. "I wish to look up words in French."

"I don't got that, man," I told him. "You should try Cutter's Books downtown or better yet go to the library."

"I like to own my books," the deadly handsome foreigner said, affecting an aloof air.

He was almost six feet tall, with skin that was not exactly the color of that of most Negroes you meet. He had a thin mustache and bisected eyes that were both a dark and a darker brown.

He was looking around the place as if he were searching through the books, but I could tell that he was looking for something else.

Finally he asked, "Do you have a toilet for your customers?"

"Hang a right before you walk into the porch," I said, pointing the way.

He went in. Made all the appropriate noises and came out again.

"How do you keep that mustache so perfect?" I asked him. "You know I got this bushy thing here. I'd like something styled like yours, but when I start trimmin' at it I keep goin' from side to side tryin' to keep it even until finally my lip is bare."

The foreigner smiled.

"I go to a barber, of course," he said. "Burnham's on Avalon."

"You wanna leave me a number?" I asked then.

"Why?"

"In case I get a French dictionary."

"I'll go to Cutter's," he said. "I need it now."

NEAR THE END OF THAT WEEK, Whisper Natly came by. He was wearing a suit that was equal parts dark blue and dark gray, his signature short-brimmed hat, and rubber-soled black shoes.

"Hey, Paris," he said. The syllables sounded like a triplet explosion that occurred very far from my store.

"Whisper. What's up, my man?"

"You know a guy named Dorfman?"

"Yeah. White dude. Helms bakery driver. Delivers bread on this block. He comes in now and then to buy war magazines. I sell 'em for a nickel apiece."

"Gambler?"

"Yeah, yeah. I think so." I remembered that whenever the burly white man came into my place he always talked about sports and the odds on any and every competition. "He always talked about it."

"He run a game?"

"Not that I know of," I said.

Whisper took me in for a moment. I can't say he flashed his eyes at me because there was no glitter in his gaze. His presence was flat as a pancake, just as his appearance was tamped down and without character.

"Heard you had some problems the other night," he said.

"What you mean?" I asked defensively. I regretted that because it caused Whisper to regard me again.

"Milo said that some white boy wanted to kick your butt."

"Oh. Oh, that. Yeah. Yeah. It wasn't nuthin'. Fearless came on by, but he was gone."

"Okay, then," Whisper said. He turned away and walked out of the store, leaving less of a wake than a shark's fin along the surface of the water.

•   •   •

MY ONLY OTHER CUSTOMER that week was Cleetus Rome, an elderly white man who had lived in my neighborhood when it was mostly fields and inhabited solely by white people.

Not only did Cleetus not read, he was illiterate. He had told me as much.

"My daddy used to tell me why waste time readin' when you could be swingin' a hammer," Cleetus had said when we first met.

Cleetus couldn't read, didn't own a TV set, and wasn't a gregarious guy at all. He didn't know his neighbors when they were white and he certainly didn't know most of them now. But he owned a radio and he listened to the news all day long. Every few days or so he'd come by my store and bring up things he had heard. I understood that he wanted to find out if I knew more about the stories from reading the paper.

I didn't mind. He was old and toothless. He smelled something like dust or maybe even loam and he always bought magazines from me that had swimsuit models on the covers.

That day he asked, "You hear about the body they fount in the strawberry field down near San Pedro?"

"Say what?" I asked as calmly as a man being stung by a bee.

"Big ol' white boy, they say," Cleetus added. "Farmer's dog dug him up from under some trees."

"I haven't read about that," I said.

"On the news today," Cleetus said. "Prob'ly be in the paper tomorrow. I heard 'em say down at the gas station that some big ol' white boy was chasin' a car right out on Central here the other day."

"Really?" I smiled through the nausea.

"Yeah. Ain't you heard about it? I mean, I don't talk to nobody and I heard it."

I felt that I was in a dream and that I had been walking down the street naked. One thing for certain, I didn't need Sigmund Freud to interpret that.

CLEETUS CAME BY exactly a week after the death of Tiny Bobchek—I had learned his last name from his driver's license before I burned it along with the wallet in the incinerator in my backyard. I spent the rest of the day trying not to worry about the police asking about the big white guy chasing me down the street.

Fearless dropped by that evening.

"You think I need to worry about Sir and Sasha?" I asked my friend.

"Sasha Bennet?" Fearless asked.

"I don't know her last name."

"Girl named Sasha Bennet called up to Milo's the other day and asked for me. She said that she was a friend'a yours and that you said maybe we should all get together sometime."

"Yeah," I said. "That's her. They the ones saved me from Tiny."

"Then you better not think about 'em, Paris. Let it ride. Don't talk to nobody about problems you worried about.

Especially don't talk to Van about it. You know he only know one way to solve problems."

"Yeah, yeah. I know. I ain't talkin' to him. I'm talkin' to you."

"Nobody thinkin' that the white dude chased you is the one dead out there, man," Fearless said. "You think it 'cause you know."

"Cleetus said it."

"But he didn't think they was the same guy."

"I'm just scared, Fearless. What if the cops come around here askin' 'bout that boy? What if Jessa go to them?"

Fearless hunched his shoulders.

"We could run," he suggested.

"Run where?"

"I 'on't know. New York. We could check out Harlem. I bet you you could start a great bookstore there."

"Just pull up stakes and go?" I asked.

"Why not? You know we always on the edge, brother. You don't have to do sumpin' wrong for the cops to get ya and the judge to throw you ovah. All you got to do is be walkin' down the street at the wrong minute. Shoot, Paris. You always got to be ready to run."

He was right. My mind was about to get me in trouble. I had to forget Sir and his wayward girlfriend. I had to forget Tiny in his makeshift grave.

I nodded and Fearless poured me a shot of peach schnapps.

"Drink deep and sleep well," he advised.

I walked up to my bedroom, slept nine and a half hours, and woke up free from fear. The cops might brace me, but I was innocent in my own heart.

•   •   •

THE NEXT MORNING I was sitting down to a plate of pinto beans, white rice, and chicken necks that I had simmered in tomato sauce. The whole meal, including the gas it took to cook it, couldn't have cost more than a dime. I had learned from a lifetime of poverty to live on almost nothing.

I nearly missed the soft knock at my front door.

Two days earlier I wouldn't have answered it.

I shouldn't have answered that morning.

IN MY SECRET MIRROR I spied a middle-aged Negro woman of normal height and slender frame. She was wearing a blue-and-white dress that was loose but stately. She also wore a dark brown hat which brought an extra touch of elegance to her presence.

I wanted to slip away, to call Fearless and say that I was ready to hightail it to Harlem. I wanted to run, but I had not been raised to turn away from that knock.

I opened the door and said, "Hi, Aunt Three Hearts. How are you?"

"Fine, Paris, and you?"

"Fine. Good. Great." I took a deep breath. "Come on in."

There was a carpetbag on the porch next to her. I hurried out and picked it up, ushering her inside as I did so.

I carried her bag past the entranceway–reading room, through the aisles of bookshelves, and into my back porch and hot-plate kitchen. That was my social room.

"Paris," she said. "I like your store. You live here too, right?"

"Have a seat, Auntie. What are you doing here? Do you want something to drink? To eat?" Maybe I thought if I overwhelmed her with hospitality I wouldn't have to give her news about her son.

"Water, please," she said.

I got ice water from a pitcher in the refrigerator and a glass from the high shelf. I poured her drink, staring into the clear liquid, hoping to find a cue in there.

"Have you seen Ulysses?" she asked after nodding her thanks for the water.

My voice sank deep into my chest and refused to come out.

ACCORDING TO LEGEND AND MYTH down in southern Louisiana, there were all kinds of witches and warlocks and people of power. Some could speak to the dead, others had the power to reanimate corpses. A few could look into your future in the hope of steering you out of harm's way. There were benign practitioners who made charms and amulets that would assist in matters of the heart or when you were looking for employment, and there were those accomplished in casting curses upon your enemies.

These fallacies governed the lives of many weak-willed and superstitious people who lived out in the country. As a rule I looked down on these people and the so-called witches that took advantage of them. I was a modern man, an educated man who didn't believe in hocus-pocus or magic spells. But I am a firm believer in the adage that there is a grain of truth in anything you hear. I do believe that there are those who have abilities and influences barred to most mortals.

Three Hearts Grant was one of these special individuals. She had what is commonly known in Louisiana as the evil eye. People who crossed Three Hearts were bound to come to grief. There was no question about that.

There was once a white man in Lafayette who accused Useless of stealing molasses from his larder. The boy was only seven, and one could hardly blame him for being attracted to such a treasure. But that white man, Michael Ogleman, chased Useless down with a cane. He struck the boy twice before Three Hearts interposed her body between the cane and her son. Ogleman struck Three Hearts seven times, kicked her once, and then returned home to die of a heart attack three hours later.

Her boyfriend of some years, Nathan Shaw, stole a jar that contained Three Hearts's life savings and moved to Lake Charles with Nellie Sweetwater. The lovers were to spend their first night in the Alouette Inn, a colored establishment on the outskirts of town. There was a fire that night that started under Nathan's room. He and Nellie were the only ones to die.

Three Hearts's power extended beyond humanity.

Once, when she and a twelve-year-old Useless were walking along Gravedigger's Mesa, they were set upon by a wild dog that was as large and vicious as a wolf. The beast growled and slavered and then cornered the pair at the edge of the elevated plateau. Three Hearts was yelling and waving at the monster, hoping to draw its deadly attention toward her. But the dog, like any other cowardly predator, was after the weakest victim. It was stalking the boy. When finally it leaped, Three Hearts jumped to get in the way, as she had with Michael Ogleman. But the defending mom tripped and knocked Useless down. The dog flew above both of them, went over the side, and broke its neck on a live oak.

Three Hearts did not believe she had the power, but everyone else, including me, did. These examples that went through my mind when she asked about her son were only a few of the terrible consequences that befell any man, woman, or beast that crossed her.

"Yes," I said, forcing the air through my larynx. "He came by about a week or so ago."

"Where is he now?" she asked.

"Ain't he home?"

"I went by the last address I had for him, but they said that he moved. I was hoping he might'a told you where he'd moved to or where he'd gone."

"Maybe he left L.A.," I said lamely.

"Ulysses wouldn't do something like that without telling me."

I don't like to think of myself as a superstitious man, but when Three Hearts looked into my eyes with her steady, serious gaze, I was as frightened as I had been bunged up with Tiny Bobchek. Haltingly, I told her about her son's last visit without letting on that I had turned him away. I made it seem as though we'd had drinks and talked about his problems, after which he'd left of his own free will.

"I had trouble of my own right then, Auntie. There was a girl I was messin' wit' and a man after me."

Three Hearts stared at me from under the brim of her hat. I didn't know which eye was the evil one, but I was sure that it was doing its work while I sat there.

"Come on," I said, standing up from my chair. "Let's go find your son. He got to be out there somewhere."

That turned Three Hearts's grim expression into a grateful smile. I could only hope that that smile trumped the evil eye. And for once I was hoping to find Useless and embrace him.

I HAD A TAN STUDEBAKER at that
time. It was old when I got it, but I didn't
care much for style when it came to cars. I
hardly drove anywhere except maybe to the supermarket
now and then and to libraries when they were getting rid
of old books.

I opened the passenger's side for Three Hearts and
placed her carpetbag in the trunk. There was never any
question about my auntie staying with me; she would not
do it. A woman her age needed a room or house appropriate for her. There also was no question that I would have
to find her a place to stay where she would be comfortable.

"Why did you come up here?" I asked as we cruised
down Central. "I mean, did you have some reason to be
worried about Use . . . Ulysses?"

"Ulysses send me a lettah 'bout a month ago. Said that
he had a new girlfriend and a new business and he was
expecting to make a lotta money and buy me a house in
Lake Charles."

"Nuthin' wrong about that," I sang, hoping to keep the mood light and uncursed.

"It's always bad to have love and money on the same page," she said sagely. "The more I thought about it, the more I worried that he was gettin' himself into a mess. And then too it was the name that girl had."

"Angel," I said, remembering Useless's last words.

"What's she like?"

"I really don't know, Auntie. He said somethin' like he wasn't good enough for her. Somethin' about bein' mud-foot, that's what he said."

"Lord."

"That means somethin'?"

"Feet of clay," my churchgoing, devil-eyed aunt said. "I told him all the time that men had feet of clay. It means that that woman, that Angel, made him wanna overcome his base nature and try to be a real man."

"That sounds good, right?"

"Maybe," she said in a voice so soft that it might have been Whisper Natly speaking in the next room.

I KNEW THAT USELESS liked pool; it was the one thing he was good at. So the first place Three Hearts and I went was Rinaldo's, a half-block-long storefront that sported eleven tables.

Rinaldo had copper skin and slicked-back hair that did not seem straightened. He was missing one tooth and stood and walked in a hunched-over posture that he blamed on forty years leaning over pool tables.

Rinaldo was a busy man. He took numbers, delivered messages to some of Watts's most important gangsters, and sold property, both stolen and otherwise. There was usually a line of people waiting to speak to him. There was that day. I waited my turn and when I got to him he looked at me.

"Fearless's friend, right?" he asked.

"Lookin' for Useless Grant," I said as I nodded.

"Man's Barn," Rinaldo said, and I hustled back out to the car where I'd left my auntie.

MAN'S BARN WAS a barnlike building that sat in Man Dorn's backyard. It was once some hangar or shed that the black Kansan had acquired along with his little blue house. He had subdivided the building into eight apartments and spent most of his time moving tenants in and malingerers out.

Los Angeles was a nomadic city in the fifties. Rent was cheap, and jobs were so plentiful that people were willing to pull up stakes and go for the promise of a neighborhood swimming pool or a change of employer.

Man was a short guy with brick brown skin. He wasn't much older than I, but he seemed to be so, with his bald dome and beefy body. His hands were fat with muscle and his neck was a third the length it should have been. He wore overalls and a faded gray T-shirt. Whatever it was his wife loved him for, he didn't display it on the outside.

"Yeah, yeah," Man was saying to Three Hearts and me. "Useless got the back right corner apartment." He was leading us down the driveway to the building everybody called Man's Barn.

"Ulysses," Three Hearts said, correcting him.

"Oh, sorry. It's just that everybody calls him Useless," Man said.

"I don't," she informed him, "and I'm his mother."

"Well," Man said, "he ain't paid his rent in two weeks, so maybe you wanna take his things with you, you bein' his mama an' all."

"How much does he owe?" Three Hearts asked.

"Forty-three dollars and fi'ty cent," Man said.

Three Hearts carried a brown cloth bag for a purse. She reached in with one hand and rummaged around for a minute or so. She came out with a wad of bills and two quarters. Man counted the bills and seemed satisfied.

"Now it's your place," he said. He handed me a brass key.

"Did he live alone?" I asked before Man could walk away.

"He had a girl . . ." The landlord had to smile. ". . . called herself Angel, and I do believe she was that. She went away a few days before the last time I saw him."

"How would you know that?" I asked.

"One day a tall man came and helped her put her suit-case in his car."

"What did Ulysses have to say about that?"

"He wasn't around as far as I could see."

Man Dorn left me wondering what kind of trouble Useless had gotten himself into.

I opened the front door and we entered the slender hall of the made-up apartment building. The ceiling was low and there were only three weak lightbulbs to make the natural darkness into gloom.

The floor was concrete and the walls were unpainted plaster.

The doors were constructed from pine. Not one of them looked new. One actually had a hole punched into it; another the tenant had started to paint green but then run out of paint and finished the job with dull brown primer.

Useless's door was okay except for a few dozen pinholes in the upper half. I supposed Three Hearts's son and the Angel left each other love notes — for a while.

I worked the key in the lock and ushered my aunt in. There was a light switch to the left of the door. When I flicked it, soft white light bathed the room.

Useless's apartment surprised me. Over all the years I'd known him he had been slovenly at best. His sink would be filled with dishes. The floor was his closet.

But this room was neat as a pin. The ceiling was very high, maybe eighteen feet, and there was a window maybe ten feet from the floor. The table had matching chairs. A rainbow-colored throw rug sat at the foot of the small bed, and paintings of flowers hung on three of four walls.

"My God," Three Hearts breathed. "He must have been in love to let her change his home like this here."

She went over to a bureau and opened the drawers one at a time. I didn't know what she was looking for and I didn't care.

I knew that men kept their secrets in the trash. And so I looked under the sink, pulled out a blue rubber bin, and placed a kitchen chair before the shaft of sun coming in from the window.

There were napkins and white cardboard tubs from some Chinese takeaway restaurant. Under that were envelopes addressed to U. S. Grant, most of them bills, all of them unopened.

Under that layer were a number of tiny white and green slips of paper with "$1,000" printed on each one.

Three Hearts settled on a stool next to the bed. She had a journal or diary in her hand and was turning the pages more quickly than she should have been able to read.

The denomination for the wrappers was probably twenties. I counted seventy-two slips while Three Hearts perused the diary.

Seventy-two thousand dollars. Useless was either in Honolulu or dead. This last thought didn't sit well with me. I didn't want Three Hearts to think that I might have saved her boy when he was in dire need.

I didn't feel guilty about whatever had happened to my errant cousin, far from it. There was no way that he could have garnered that much money legally, and we all knew what the price was for stealing from white people.

I knew that the money came from whites because they were the only ones who had that kind of cash. That is except for religious leaders and black gangsters, and even Useless wasn't fool enough to mess with them.

I rummaged around in the garbage until I came up with a typewritten list on a sheet of white paper. There were thirteen entries on the list: banks, insurance companies, large white churches, and financial management firms.

Useless and I were first cousins; we were of the same blood. I wondered how someone so closely related to me could have been such a fool as to leave a trail like that in his trash.

I stuffed my pockets full with the damning evidence.

I called across the room, "What you got there, Auntie?"

She slapped the book shut and said, "Nuthin', baby."

"Not nuthin'. It's a book."

"It's private."

"Angel's diary?" I asked.

"Just because you're smart does not mean you have good sense," my aunt told me. "These is private papers, and I intend to return them to her."

"Will they help us find Ulysses?" I asked.

"No."

"How can you be sure? You haven't read the whole thing."

"Have you found anything in the trash?"

"No, ma'am."

"I didn't think so."

With that, Three Hearts Grant stood up and marched toward the door. I followed her, wondering if her evil eye was powerful enough to protect me from the people that worked for the companies on Useless's list.

11

MAN DORN WAS ON his blue porch, puffing at a short cigar and sitting in the center of a mesh hammock as if it were a chair.

"You movin' in?" he asked me.

"Ms. Grant's the tenant," I told him. "But you can tell me somethin' if you don't mind."

"What's that?" the no-neck landlord offered.

"Who was Angel and Ulysses hangin' out with before he went away?"

"Mad Anthony," Man said with no hesitation.

"That's it?"

"The only one I knew. People come in and outta there all the time, but I didn't know their names. Angel didn't have many girlfriends, and the men who visited Useless wore suits half the time."

"Ulysses," Three Hearts corrected.

"Any white men come to see Ulysses?"

"No," Man said, shaking his head, "never."

"You know where I can find Anthony?" I asked, all other options being closed.

"He stay at a white door in the alley between Ninety-first and Ninety-second, right off Central to the east side."

I walked Three Hearts back to my car with the detritus of seventy-two thousand dollars in my pocket and the address of a brutal thug echoing in my ear.

"Maybe we should call the police," Three Hearts said as we left the curb.

"No," I said. "No police on this."

From the corner of my eye I saw Three Hearts turn to regard me. She watched my profile for a moment and then looked away. She knew that I had gleaned some information that might have put her son in jail. She knew it and decided that she didn't want to know the details.

That was fine by me. I was afraid even to speak the thoughts I was having.

I didn't like anything about the road we were on: Useless with his rotten luck, his mother and her evil eye. And a woman named Angel in that community didn't bode well either. All of that was just superstition, though. I could have gone to a good John Wayne movie and put those thoughts out of my mind. But those money wrappers and that list were no wild fancy. That was blackmail and extortion — maybe worse.

THE ALLEY BETWEEN NINETY-FIRST and Ninety-second was a rut-ridden dirt path with tiny islets of asphalt here and there to remind you that it had once been an honest road, paved and straight. But now that alley was a place to buy and sell those things that were not legal. It was a place where a teenage boy could lose his virginity for ten dollars and where the woman who helped him could forget her sins for half that in white powder held by a cellophane fold.

The alley was a place where criminals congregated and plotted doomed liquor store robberies and pie-in-the-sky counterfeiting schemes.

I parked on Ninety-first because any car left in the alley was asking to be stolen.

Three Hearts and I walked timidly at midday down the dark path to Mad Anthony. I wasn't as afraid as I might have been because I did believe in Three Hearts's power. But even the thought of standing face-to-face with one of Watts's genuine gangsters made me quiver.

I had never actually been in the company of Anthony Jarman. I had seen him in side glances at glitzy Watts night spots and coming out of big fancy cars. Once I had seen him sitting in a booth in a gumbo restaurant on Florence. But I knew enough not to stare at a man like that. I wouldn't have met his gaze any more than I would look a wild animal in the eye.

Fearless knew Anthony, actually referred to him as Tony. But Fearless was almost as much of a legend as Killer Cleave in our neighborhoods. Most people knew that Fearless had been a behind-the-lines assassin in Europe during the big war. No one who crossed him stayed on his feet.

But I had no intention of invoking my friend's name. Saying that I was there under the protection of Fearless Jones would have been like taking out a pistol and placing it on a table. Everyone knows that once the gun comes out, it's bound to go off sooner or later.

I laughed when we got to the door, set in a decrepit

brick wall at the very center of the block. It was as if Man Dorn had told me a joke when he called that portal white.

It might have once been white. But now it was lined with cracked paint. The cracks were filled with black dirt and soot. The little white that was left had dried gray and green lichen on it like delicate tile work. The doorknob was so rusted that you would have cut your palm trying to turn it.

I knocked. It was like banging on a redwood tree with a bag of mushrooms. I picked up a rock and banged again. This caused some reverberation, but no answer came. I tried a few times more, breathing a little easier after each attempt.

"I don't think he's here, Auntie," I said, not able to keep the relief out of my voice.

"How can we find him?" she asked.

"I think we might have to go to Fearless," I said.

That got my worried relative to smile.

"That nice Fearless Jones?" she asked.

My mother and Three Hearts had come once to visit me and Useless in L.A. Three Hearts was very taken with Fearless; most women, no matter their age, were.

"You think he'd agree to help us some?" she asked.

"Yes, ma'am. Fearless is my friend and he likes Ulysses."

This was true. Fearless had a good time with Useless. But, then again, Fearless would have thought that a lion cub was cute or that an eleven-foot crocodile was grandfatherly.

"Well, let's go and see him, then," Three Hearts said.

That was fine by me. It had taken all of my courage just to darken Mad Anthony's door. We turned back and walked toward the civilized world of paved streets and real white doors.

Half the way toward this goal we ran into a roadblock.

He was so wide that you didn't think that he was as tall as he was.

He must have seen us from some secret lookout and decided to come around from behind.

"What the fuck you niggahs doin' beatin' on my do' wit' that rock?" Mad Anthony roared.

"We, we, we, we, we," I said.

"I'm lookin' for my son," Three Hearts told him with nary a stammer. "Ulysses S. Grant the Fourth."

"Useless? That piece'a shit is your son? He need to die. Motherfuckin' bastid need to have my knife diggin' all up in his asshole." And to prove the point, Anthony revealed a ragged blade with his right hand.

Fearless has often told me that between the two of us I was the brave one. "Man like me," he would say, "man not afraid of heaven or hell, is too stupid to be scared. You cain't be brave if you don't know fear."

I understood his pronouncement on that afternoon. Because you know the minute I saw that knife all I wanted to do was run. I knew I could outrun Anthony. Hell, I could have outrun Jesse Owens right then. My thighs felt like they had motors in them. My feet were pistons waiting to go off.

But I didn't run because that would have meant leaving my auntie, and that was something I just could not do.

"Where the fuck is he, bitch?" Anthony bellowed. He grabbed her by that loose dress and actually lifted her up off the ground.

"Oh," Three Hearts shouted, more in surprise than fear, I think.

"S-s-stop," I managed to stutter. "P-put her down, Anthony. She don't know where Useless is. She here askin' you where."

I know it might sound like a pretty light challenge when I write it down here. But I would like to see how you would respond faced as I was by a man who might just as well have been a hungry tiger lunging at you from the depths of an Indian rain forest.

Anthony pushed Three Hearts against the wall of a dilapidated and condemned building. They were a few feet from me.

It was the perfect moment to run. I could have said that I was looking for help. I could have called for the police.

Tiny Bobchek returned to my mind at that moment. I didn't know why. Months later, when I was sitting up wide awake in my bed at 3:00 a.m., it came to me that I felt guilty about not being able to do more for him than just take him out in the middle of nowhere, strip him of his identity, and drop him into a shallow grave. I had to do it, but it seemed that I should have done more.

I wasn't aware of all that in Mad Anthony's alley. All I knew was that Tiny was in my mind and I was running toward a man who could have beaten me with both arms tied behind his back.

I leaped and struck out while the behemoth raged at my auntie.

Mad Anthony released my auntie, grabbed me, and delivered what might have looked like a halfhearted slap.

I actually bounced upon hitting the ground, first on my left side and then on my stomach. I came to a stop on my back, looking up into a blue, blue sky edged by branches from trees on the eastern side of the alley.

I tried to sit up. For a moment I felt that I'd succeeded, but then I realized it was my will that had risen while the body stayed down.

The sky seemed to be spinning and darkening. A car backfired maybe three blocks away, and then there was a cry for help.

I wondered what it was all about while floating away on a sea of painful darkness.

I WAS WALKING DOWN a Louisiana dirt road not far from the hovel that my mother and I called home. It was a spring day, neither hot nor cold, and there was a lark singing somewhere in the trees to my right. I was trying to remember which was the fastest way to get back to our place.

It occurred to me as I walked that there was no deed to the land that our tar-paper-and-brick home stood upon. We never paid rent. I looked down at my feet, which were bare, and felt a creeping trepidation come over me that we might one day be evicted from our squatters' claim. But with a shake of my head I sloughed off the fear as a boxer shakes off sweat in the middle rounds. I laughed at myself for being silly.

That's when I bumped into him.

I looked up and saw a very tall, very thin, very black, and very old man. I knew this man—his name was Brother Bones — but I didn't know where or when I had made his acquaintance.

He was at least seven feet tall, even hunched over his gnarled cane (which seemed to be crawling with insects).

When I made to go around him, he held up a great spidery hand, barring my passage.

"I cain't let you up there, brother," he said in a deep and melodious but still threatening tone. "You will not be going there again."

I screamed at Mr. Bones. I caterwauled and cried. Inside, I felt no pain or passion, it was just that I knew, or believed I knew, that yelling like an infant would get me through.

When Mr. Bones shook his head at me, I considered running around him. But he seemed to grow larger, blocking any passage with his bony limbs.

Then the apparition stamped his foot upon the dirt road, making a sound like a kettledrum. The vibrations of the drumbeat found a resonance in my chest. The feeling of that tremor became fear in me. I tried to hold it down, but once it began it would not end.

Mr. Bones leaned forward and said, "Boo."

As I ran back down the way I'd come, his laughter reverberated all around me. I was ashamed that he had bested me, angry that he was keeping me from my home, and determined to turn back around and face him. But I kept running.

As I ran, the bright day turned quickly to night. Soon I was running in pitch-blackness, not even able to see myself, much less the road, when I looked down. I realized that I couldn't see the road under my feet or my feet on that road, tripped, and went tumbling down into a gully.

I didn't know how long I was there but after a while I looked around without trying to rise. I was deeply frightened and realized somehow that I was now inside the body of Mr. Bones, that he had taken the whole world into his dark being and I was now his prisoner.

To my right I saw two shining jewels in the darkness. This sight touched a hope that I didn't even know resided in my breast. Maybe these priceless gems would be my reward for all the calamities I had had to endure.

I found a book of matches in my pocket. The first few were chalky, already burned. Hatred took my heart then, hatred for the fool who had lit those matches without tearing them out.

Then I found a match that was live. I struck it and was momentarily blinded by the flare. When the temporary blindness faded, I saw that the jewels I imagined were actually the dead eyes of Useless.

"He's just a damn coward," a woman's voice said clearly.

The match burned down to my thumb, but the pain of the burn was in my jaw instead of my hand.

I opened my eyes, hurting from my fall from the fence and my roll in the alley. Somehow they both had blended themselves into my dream.

There was a white plaster ceiling above my head. I could see the rust-colored veins of the pipes that ran above it. I smelled whiskey and wanted some. I heard murmurs that I knew were voices that would come clear in a moment.

I raised my head and saw Three Hearts, Mona Gibbs, and Fearless Jones sitting around a fold-up card table, the only table Fearless owned.

Three Hearts was the one talking. She had been the one who had called me a coward, I knew that. But she smiled when she saw that I was awake. It was more than a smile, like a friendly grin.

"So you back with the livin', huh?" Fearless said. He said the same thing whenever I woke up in his presence.

"I need a cigarette and a shot'a that rotgut you drinkin'," I said.

Mona got them for me.

Mona was a beautiful young woman. She was Negro and she was brown, but the brown mixed with gray everywhere in her appearance. Her skin was touched by it; her eyes sometimes shone with lunar possibilities. Even her hair seemed to be lightened by the midtone color.

Mona loved Fearless, loved him. She worked as a secretary in city hall and always managed to find an apartment near to where Fearless had moved to. She liked to sit next to him and hold his hand. If they were at a party and he was going home, she'd reach for him and if he took her by the hand, she would go along.

For a time this behavior had unsettled my nearly imperturbable friend. That's because he was not only a natural-born killer, he was also a romantic. Fearless needed to be hopelessly in love to give his space to a woman. She didn't have to be pretty or smart or friendly, even. There was some quality he searched for that I never understood. And so when he realized that Mona didn't have what he needed, he told her so. He said that he didn't mind spending time with her but they would never have a life together.

Most women, when Fearless told them that, would move on — after a while. But Mona said she didn't care. She loved Fearless whether he loved her or not. She let him know that she would be there no matter what he did or who he saw. All he had to do was call or ring her bell.

Fearless didn't have a phone, so she always lived nearby.

While Mona was lighting my cigarette, Three Hearts asked, "Are you okay, baby?"

I was still angry that she had called me a coward when I had tried my best to save her, so I didn't respond right off.

"First he struck Paris with his hand," Three Hearts said to Mona and Fearless. "And then he kicked him."

I remembered the kick as a bounce.

"He was lookin' around the ground for somethin' to hit Paris with," Three Hearts was saying, "when I took out my Colt forty-five. You know a woman always got to have somethin' in her purse for protection. He's lucky I was so mad. Made my aim go wide."

I remembered the shot. It was a car on another block— I thought.

"An' he run like a coward," Three Hearts said. "Just a damn coward."

Fearless gave out a deep belly laugh. Gray-hued Mona brought up both of her hands to cover her beautiful smile.

"He a fool not be afraid'a you, Hearts. Damn. Forty-five. This mama right here don't play." He laughed some more.

"How did we get outta the alley and ovah here?" I asked.

Mona was handing me my whiskey.

"I remembered that you and Fearless used to work for Milo Sweet," Three Hearts said. "I dragged you to the side of a house in that damn alley and went to a phone booth and called."

I slugged back the whiskey and Mona poured me another. One of the nice things about her one-sided love for Fearless was that it seemed to spill over on me some. She looked at me with the same friendly eyes that he did.

"I put Milo and Loretta away and then come over to dust you off," Fearless said.

"Damn," I said. "Gotdamn."

"What you wanna do, Paris?" Fearless asked me.

"I don't know, man."

I looked from him to Three Hearts and back again. What I wanted didn't matter. There was no way out.

I drank my whiskey.

Mona refilled my glass. The aches in my body began to recede.

"Let's walk on down to Mona's place," Fearless said. "I need to make a call."

Because Fearless never had a phone, Mona was also his phone booth.

13 | MONA'S APARTMENT WAS no larger than Fearless's studio, but she had a royal blue sofa, nice chairs, and a fine oak table that supported a small TV set in a pink plastic frame.

Some people felt sorry for Mona. They thought that she should find a good man who wanted to be with her. But I wasn't so sure. Fearless didn't love Mona in the way that she wanted, but he'd accompany her to any restaurant or church event she needed an arm for, he kept her car running and her plumbing flowing, and he never got mad when she had a weekend away with some temporary boyfriend. When Mona's cousin Natalie died, Fearless stayed with her for two weeks, making coffee in the morning and tea every night.

I'd look at his relationship with her and think that if I could have a woman who treated me the way Fearless did Mona, I'd be in heaven. Of course that's a selfish attitude, but I don't know. If Mona had a child and died, I'm pretty sure that Fearless would have taken that baby in. That's the kind of selfishness the world could use more of.

FEARLESS SAT DOWN on Mona's upholstered chair, hung his left leg over the arm, and started making phone calls. While he was doing that, Three Hearts, Mona, and I sat around the polished table and drank iced tea that our hostess served.

"Thanks for savin' my butt, Auntie," I said.

"You were so cute out there, baby," she replied. "You should'a seen 'im, Mona. He jump in the air and screamed like a little boy. An' then he hit that awful man in the shoulder."

Mona grinned and touched my shoulder with her gray-brown hand. Her fingernails had silver polish on them.

"You know he did his best," Mona said.

It was the closest I was going to get to being complimented for my manhood, so I took the backhanded accolade in the spirit in which it was meant. Poor people back in those days didn't know how to give false tribute. They said it how they saw it or they didn't say a thing.

"Yeah," Fearless said into the phone. "Yeah. Ovah at Wisterly's be fine. See you in half a hour. See you then." He looked up at us and said, "Let's go."

That meant me and Three Hearts.

Mona gave Fearless a long heartfelt kiss at the door. He looked down into her eyes and she swelled up like a piece of ripening fruit. I remember thinking that there was more love in that tender good-bye than in many life-long marriages I'd witnessed. Three Hearts was so moved by the spectacle that she sighed.

•   •   •

FEARLESS WAS DRIVING Milo's red Caddy. Three
Hearts got in the backseat and we cruised over toward
Florence and Central. There was a big restaurant there
owned by a white family called Wisterly. It was a broken-
down little diner when Cleetus Rome's family first
moved to town, but it had grown and flourished with the
influx of the colored population. That's because black
people needed fancy spots to call our own and most of the
upscale places still managed to freeze us out.

Wisterly's had a big dining room for dinner and special functions, but they also had a diner for the daytime
with seven booths against a window that looked out on
the street.

We got to the restaurant at a quarter past three. When
we'd made it halfway down the aisle of booths I spied big
ugly Anthony ensconced at the corner table. I hadn't
asked Fearless who we were going to see. I suppose that's
because I was still rather stunned from the beating I'd
taken. But I hadn't suspected that we'd be meeting with
Anthony. I'd thought that Fearless was looking for some
other line on Useless.

Anthony had a big white bandage over his left ear.
When he saw me he tried to get to his feet. But by that
time we were at the booth. Fearless struck out with a right
cross that traveled all of seven inches. You could hear the
impact in the next room. Anthony fell hard on his butt and
groaned in spite of himself.

"Good for him," Aunt Three Hearts muttered.

Fearless gestured for her and me to sit on the bench
across from Anthony while he took a seat next to the big
tough. Anthony was rubbing his jaw, trying not to cry —
or at least so it seemed to me.

"Why you mess wit' my friends?" Fearless asked as if he were a father talking to a wayward son.

"Tryin' t'find Useless."

"Ulysses," Three Hearts said.

"Ulysses," Fearless repeated.

"Ulysses," Mad Anthony agreed. And then he said, "That bitch shot me in the ear."

Fearless grabbed Anthony's shirt and shook him back and forth, letting him know to use proper language around a lady.

I could see Anthony's jaw swelling.

"What you lookin' for Hearts's boy for?" Fearless asked, explaining the rules in doing so. Because once my friend identified Useless as the son of someone he knew by name, Anthony understood that he'd have to kill Fearless to cross that line.

"Use . . . Ulysses brought me to a man named, uh, String, Stringly . . . sumpin' like that."

"A white man?" I asked.

When Anthony frowned at me my heart did a flip of fear.

"If you hear a question outta Paris's mouth," Fearless said, "then that's me talkin'."

The frown evaporated and Anthony said, "Yeah. White dude."

"What about him?" I asked as respectfully as I could.

"He paid me to go with him an' rough up this white dude called Drummund. Paul Drummund. I did the shit and then Use . . . Ulysses cut out."

"How long ago?" I asked.

"Two weeks, a little more."

"Where did you meet this friend'a Ulysses'?" I asked then.

"At a house down around Fairfax. I don't think it was his house. At least he wasn't livin' there."

"When did you first meet this white guy?"

"How the hell should I 'member that?" he said belligerently.

"Try hard," Fearless advised.

"I dunno. Three mont's. Sumpin' like that."

Anthony winced then and put a hand against his jaw.

"So you met him a long time before he had you beat on Drummund," I speculated.

"Yeah," Anthony said. "Yeah. String-whatevah had me put a scare into a dude named Katz too. That was aftah I first met 'im. He paid me a hunnert dollars for that."

"Did you say anything to these people when you beat them?" I asked.

"I cain't talk like that in front of a lady," Anthony demurred.

I could have reminded him of the language he had used in front of Three Hearts in the alley earlier that day, but I felt sorry for him.

"What I meant was did Stringly have any message that he wanted you to give them?" I asked.

"Yeah, uh-huh. He told me to say that they went down this road on they own an' they wasn't goin' back. He said to tell 'em that if they paid, the pain would go away."

"What did you do to them?" I asked. I don't know why. It wasn't relevant to what we were looking for, but Anthony fascinated me when he was no longer a threat.

"Broke some fingers an' knocked out a couple'a teeth."

"For a hundred dollars."

"I'd kick yo' skinny ass for nuthin'," he replied, unable to keep the sneer off his lopsided face.

Fearless placed a hand on Anthony's forearm. It was a light touch, but Anthony flinched.

A sharp pain made Anthony bring both hands gingerly to his jaw.

"Anything else you want?" he cried.

"What was Ulysses into with this Stringly dude?" I asked.

"I don't know."

"Come on, man," I said, selecting my words delicately. "Everybody knows that U-man liked to talk. He wouldn't just bring you somewhere and not say somethin' 'bout what he was up to."

"He said that him an' Stringly was tight," Anthony said, straining at the memory. "He said that they had a scam goin' gonna make 'em rich. That's it."

"He didn't say nuthin' 'bout what they was doin'?" I asked.

"Naw. Just that, just that white people was thieves too, it's just that they never got caught 'cause they stole big."

"That doesn't prove a thing," Three Hearts said with deadly conviction.

"That all, Paris?" Fearless asked me.

I nodded.

Fearless put a hand on Anthony's shoulder.

"You bettah get to the hospital, Tony," he said. "That jaw you got there is broke pretty bad."

Mad Anthony stood away from the booth and staggered toward the door.

14 | "WHAT WAS ALL THAT STUFF about U-man and what Ulysses like t'talk?" Three Hearts asked me when the big man was gone.

I knew she would take umbrage at any hint of an accusation toward her son.

"I was just tryin' to get him to remember, Auntie," I said. "You know sometimes you just have to say the first thing come in your head when you talkin' to a rough man like that."

"But why did you say what you said?"

I swear I saw her left eye flashing.

"Hearts," Fearless said in an impossibly reasonable voice. Impossible for me, that is. My heart was fluttering like a sheet in a Santa Ana wind at that moment.

"What?" she said to my friend.

"You know Ulysses," he said. "You know what he do. If you didn't you wouldn't'a got on a bus and gone hundreds of miles ovah a lettah where he said he was doin' good."

"My son is a good man," she said.

"I'm not sayin' he ain't," Fearless said. "But you know that he was doin' somethin' wit' Tony there. An' you can see what Tony is like."

"But Ulysses did not order him to beat up anyone," she said.

"I don't know about any'a that. All I know is that Paris here is tryin' to help you, an' you givin' him grief."

When Three Hearts looked Fearless in the eye, he gazed back with a sanguine expression on his handsome face. It was like the meeting of two heads of warring tribes. Anyone seeing them would have known that something very important hung in the balance.

"He's my only child, Fearless," she said at last. Tears sprouted from her eyes.

Fearless put his big hand across the table and held both of hers therein. Her forehead lowered to the knot of fingers and the tears flowed freely.

"An' Paris an' me wanna help, baby," Fearless said, "but a lotta people gonna be callin' your boy Useless and U-man and all kinds'a things. An' you know Paris here smart as they come. He cain't be answerin' to you every time he have to ask somethin'."

She raised her head to look at her momentary father. She nodded and freed her hands from his loving grip.

"I know," she said.

She turned to me and smiled, her eyes lowered.

"You wanna go stay at Paris's while we look?" Fearless asked.

There was a moment where Three Hearts seemed to be considering Fearless's ill-conceived offer.

"No. I better not," she said after what felt like a very long minute.

I exhaled, hoping that they didn't register the sigh.

"Where you wanna go, then?" Fearless asked.

"Ovah to Nadine's, I guess," she said.

Nadine Grant was Useless's father's sister. She had moved to L.A. with her first husband, but he had died in a warehouse fire and Nadine had married his brother Otem. Otem got pneumonia and passed six months after the wedding. After that Nadine, who was a very handsome woman, got engaged to a man from Tennessee called Morley. Morley had a college education and two houses. The problem was that his real name was Henderson and he'd murdered a man in southern Louisiana in the late twenties. He'd run to Tennessee, changed his name and his way of life. But when he got engaged to Nadine, one of her cousins recognized Henderson and told a relative of the murdered man. Morley/Henderson was extradited to Louisiana, tried, convicted, and hanged.

After that, Nadine swore off men. She lived in a nice house on Sixty-third Street, where she had a front yard that sported dozens of different kinds of flowers. Nadine worked as a librarian in Compton, and so I saw her from time to time when I'd drop by to pick up books she was discarding at the end of the summer and fall seasons.

"HI, FEARLESS," Nadine said after greeting Three Hearts when we appeared at her door.

Nadine never seemed to recognize me when we met away from her library. She'd always give me a quizzical look and then fail to place my face.

"Ms. Grant," Fearless said in greeting.

The women gabbled at the front door for a minute or two, then I cleared my throat.

"Oh," Three Hearts said. "Honey, would you mind if I stayed here with you for a couple'a days? Ulysses has gone missin' and my nephew here has agreed to go look for him."

"Missin'?" the black widow exclaimed. "I hope he ain't in no trouble."

"I don't think it's nuthin' serious," Three Hearts said, rather unconvincingly. "But I wanna stay around until Paris find him."

"Oh sure, darlin'," Nadine said with a big forced grin. "I could use the company."

We left them there standing on the porch: old Evil Eye and Typhoid Mary among the flowers, counting up the dead.

BACK IN THE CAR I informed Fearless of what I knew.

"Seventy-two thousand dollars?" he said. "Ulysses? Where that poor son gonna come up wit' money like that?"

"Blackmail, extortion, intimidation, and threats," I said.

Fearless laughed.

"What's funny?" I asked.

"That cousin'a yours is sumpin' else, man. I mean, I never seen any boy get in as much trouble as him. Damn, he'd be runnin' numbahs in heaven an' sellin' holy water in hell."

"Whole gotdamned family," I said. "There you got Nadine cuttin' down men like wheat and people fallin' dead all ovah Three Hearts. I don't know how I lived through a Christmas dinner back in the old days when they'd come by."

"Yeah," Fearless said with a nod. "But you ain't much bettah, Paris."

"What you mean?" I said. "I ain't cursed."

"No?"

"Naw."

"Paris, I know men who run in the streets every night don't have half the trouble you got. I know people live more peaceable lives in prison."

"Fuck you, man. All I do is run my bookstore. Ain't nuthin' more peaceful than readin' a book."

"That's what that white boy thought when somebody put that bullet in his head."

This was no simple banter. Fearless wouldn't have brought up Tiny Bobchek unless he was thinking that my current problems had something to do with him.

"Uh-uh, Fearless. No," I said. "Tiny was just a, a coincidence."

"Ulysses comes to your door one minute and then just a few hours later there's a dead white man on your flo' and that's just a coincidence? You know I ain't that fast when it comes to figurin', Paris, but this one looks clear as a bell."

"It was Jessa," I said. "Jessa did it."

"Li'l white girl killed that Goliath?"

"He was shot," I said. "Shot in the head. Women carry guns. Look at Three Hearts."

"You said Jessa didn't even have a bag or drawers," Fearless argued. He had a good memory when he wanted to.

"Tiny could have been armed. She could have pulled out his pistol and opened fire."

Fearless threw up a hand and let it fall. "Yeah," he admitted.

"It couldn't have been Useless," I continued. "He ain't a natural killer in the first place. He never carries a gun and he would run from a big fool like Bobchek."

"Yeah, but that just proves my point."

"What are you talkin' about?"

"First you got Ulysses comin' to your door, sayin' how he got to run," Fearless said. "Then the white girl and her boyfriend aftah yo' ass. Now Ulysses is gone an' Three Hearts comes, gettin' you into trouble up to your ears. If that ain't some kinda bad luck, I don't know what is."

It was my turn to laugh. Fearless wasn't making fun of me. He was reading my life like I'd read a dime novel.

"So what we gonna do about Ulysses?" Fearless asked.

"What can we do?" I replied. "You heard Anthony. Useless is either gone or dead. And with seventy-two thousand dollars in his pocket, he's way beyond where we gonna find him."

"The girl could have took the money," Fearless said.

"Then he's runnin' on empty."

"Come on, Paris. You know we cain't turn our backs on Hearts. You know you don't want that evil eye'a hers on yo' ass."

I knew it. I knew it.

15

I KNEW IT TOO WELL.

Fearless dropped me off at my place at about six.

There was a cardboard box on the front porch. The flaps were folded together and there was an envelope taped to its side. I unlocked the door and kicked the box inside. I sat on the first chair near the entrance and flipped the box open.

Books. Books in which there were many dog-eared pages. I opened the sealed envelope. It was from my literary girlfriend, Ashe Knowles.

Dear Mr. Minton,
Lately I've been taking to underlining those places in books where Negroes are denigrated by white authors, and colored ones too. It seems to me that one day our children or their children might want to know how many lies have been propagated against our people over the years and decades and centuries. You will find in these pages references to our

*low intelligence, our aberrant sexuality, our crimi-
nal nature, and our primitive instincts. In some
places these comments are meant as compliments
and in others as scientific fact. For a long time I believed that everyone was aware of this terrible state
of affairs, but just last Tuesday I asked Miss Harri-
son, the librarian at the 53rd Street branch, if she
knew where such outrageous statements would be
catalogued. She told me that she wasn't even aware
of any great preponderance of racist statements in
American literature. I gave her fifteen examples in
the B's of authors' last names and she was amazed.
But when I asked her if she would set up a catalogue of these gaffes in her branch she told me that
that wouldn't be any help for anyone.*

*Mr. Minton, you are a well-read and therefore a
well-educated man. I know that you will see the
value of these notes. My apartment is just one room
and very small, but you have lots of room in your
bookstore. I was wondering if you might keep these
books for me over the next little while until I can
find some institution that might want to store and
catalogue my research.*

*Yours truly,
Ashe Knowles*

There were eighteen hardback books in the box. Each
one had anywhere from five to fifteen dog-eared pages
proving Ashe's claims. She had a relentless, steel-trap
kind of intelligence. And I had to admit there was something to her assertion. There must have been thousands of
times that I had come across statements in books that in-

sulted and lied about Negroes in America and abroad. Hegel had done it and Karl Marx too. But without a definitive list of these misdemeanors, how could we complain? Even the librarian had denied the allegation until Ashe showed her proof.

I decided to put the books down in the onetime crypt of Tiny Bobchek.

I was happy to have received that box of books, first because of the fact that no one had stolen them from off my porch. Nobody stole books. These bound and printed stacks of paper were the most precious things in the world, and yet no one would have picked them up. That box could have sat on my porch for a week and those books would have gone unmolested and unread.

The second thing that made me happy was that Ashe had distracted me for an hour or so from the worries that had settled all through my mind.

I thought about Ashe and her bumbling brilliance. She would have done much better for herself if she had gone to college and committed all of the plays of Shakespeare to memory. That way the white professors, deans, and provosts would have seen her as some kind of anomaly who would have fit well in the lower echelons of the university hierarchy. There she could have waited until such time that a catalogue of racist quotes in American and English literature might have been presented on a grand stage.

But Ashe could only see truth—not strategy. She worked as a teacher's assistant at a private Baptist elementary school down on Eighty-third Street. They paid her twenty-two dollars a week, and she lived somehow, sometimes unable to buy even a pencil.

Again I thought of how I could have loved a woman

like that. But loving her, I knew that I should leave her alone.

I WASN'T HUNGRY and so I went up to bed at eight. My jaw was aching and my right arm felt weak. I had pains up and down my right side and a thick copy of *Titus Groan* on my night table. I wanted to read it, but I was experiencing too many aches to grapple with that hefty tome.

So instead I started thinking.

I knew that I shouldn't have cut off Fearless's question about Tiny Bobchek's death. Tiny's dying like that was just the kind of trouble that Useless would bring down on you. But Useless wasn't a killer and he'd gone. I hadn't even let him through the door, so why would he have come back? And I was sure there wasn't any connection between Useless and Jessa.

When I'd met her, she talked all the time about how she'd never seen a black man up close. She'd play with my hair and place her white hand against my skin to marvel at the contrast.

And Jessa was a brass tacks kind of girl. I paid her rent and made an exotic entry in her life. If she was working with somebody who was counting money in the thousands, she wouldn't have had a moment for me.

No. Jessa had nothing to do with Useless and Useless had nothing to do with the murder of Tiny Bobchek.

But where had Jessa gone?

I closed my eyes, but I could tell by the thrumming at the back of my head that sleep would not be coming any time soon.

I had an inspiration then. So I got dressed, went down

to my car, and drove over to the blue house in front of Man's Barn.

It was almost nine, well beyond the time when decent people dropped in on one another. Man might have turned me away, but I had a plan to get by him.

I rang the bell and stood there in my brown jacket and black trousers. I was sporting alligator shoes and a blue pullover shirt that had a one-button collar.

Man wore a white T-shirt and navy blue pants that had a drawstring at the waist.

"What the hell do you want?" he asked me. "Do you know what time it is? My little girl was asleep before you started pushin' on that bell."

I twisted my face into a wordless apology. "I didn't wanna disturb ya, but I thought you'd appreciate me coming here over the alternative."

"What the fuck are you talkin' about, Negro?" he said. He grabbed the door as if he were about to slam it in my face.

"Fearless Jones," I said.

For a moment time ceased to pass on Man Dorn's face. Then he looked at me, wondering how to avoid the two words he'd just heard.

"What's Mr. Jones got to do wit' me?"

"You know that woman I was here wit' today?" I asked. "The one that paid Useless's rent?"

"Yeah?"

"She took me ovah to Mad Anthony's, and he got kinda riled. . . ."

"That don't have nuthin' to do wit' me," Man claimed.

"Yeah. I know." I was feeling sorry for Man. "But then Three Hearts went to Fearless and Fearless broke Tony's jaw. Then she said that she was here and she thought that you knew more about Angel than you was sayin' and that maybe he could come on by. I told Fearless that we didn't need to go through all'a that. I said that I was sure you'd give Three Hearts what she needed."

"Hold on," he said, retreating into the blue home.

He left the door open. There was a television on in a room next to the one the door opened onto. Through the second doorway I could see two black women sitting on a couch, illuminated by the light of the TV. They were peering out at me. They looked like dark sisters, maybe a year or two apart. I tried to think of what their relationship to Man might have been but failed.

I did know that neither one of them was his wife.

Man returned with an eight-by-six glossy photograph. It was of a stunningly beautiful woman. She had medium brown skin, straight or straightened hair, eyes filled with knowing surprise, and parted lips that could teach you how to kiss a Greek goddess.

"This Angel?" I asked.

"When she told me that she was a actress," Man said, "I asked her if she had a publicity picture. You know, a lotta these girls got bikini pictures for their Hollywood agents. It wasn't that, but she's pretty, though. Nice girl. She just had bad taste in men."

"Anything else?"

"Naw, man. That's it. I told you everything else."

"How about the car the guy drove her off in?"

"I don't even know, brother. I didn't really care."

"Man?" a woman said. She was standing at the inner door.

She was a shortish woman with big kissy lips and startled eyes.

"Go on back in the TV room, Doretha," Man said. "We almost through here."

She backed away fearfully.

"Couple'a my tenants come up to watch TV," he told me. "So Fearless don't have to come by now, right?"

"No, sir, Mr. Dorn."

16

THERE WEREN'T TOO MANY joints where a woman like Angel would belong. Of course there were all kinds of men who would have wanted to go there with her: garage attendants and gangsters on the Negro side; directors, producers, and other high rollers on the white. But black men couldn't get into the places she would have wanted to be, and white men couldn't take her there — at least not for very long.

In 1956 a sophisticated and beautiful black woman had very few choices unless she wanted to be a good girl and wear midcalf skirts and milky rimmed glasses. I didn't expect that Angel was that type of woman. If she was, I wouldn't find her and I wouldn't need to.

The only black club that would fit her bill was Apollo's at the Knickerbocker Hotel off Central down in the forties. Apollo's had jazz and fine food for black and white patrons. That was before the black part of town became off-limits to the casual white devotee.

I pulled up to a liquor store called Kenny's Keg on

Figueroa. I got a pack of Lucky Strikes and a pint of Greeley's whiskey with a short stack of paper cups and a quart bottle of seltzer. I put the booze and water in the trunk, lit a cigarette, and then walked across the street to a glass-encased phone booth. I looked up a number by the yellow electric light and dialed.

"Hello?" a frightened elderly voice inquired.

"Kiko, please."

"What?"

"Kiko."

"Kiko?"

"Yes."

A few hard knocks sounded in my ear and then, "Hello," came a sultry voice.

"Loretta?"

"Paris?" she managed to evince both surprise and joy in her tone.

"You said call you, right?"

"I'm surprised you did," she said.

"Why's that?"

"I don't know. You seem to think about some things until all the color is washed out, I guess. What do you want?"

"I got fifty dollars and a yen to hear some jazz."

"The High Hat?" she suggested.

"I was thinkin' more in the line with Apollo's."

"You know you need a reservation to get in there," she said.

"I do, but Milo don't."

"And you just came up with this idea on a whim?" she asked. She was playing with me, but even when playing, cats use their claws a little.

"No," I admitted. "I got to find out some things there, but I promise you a good dinner and fine companion-ship."

"I'm not a cheap date, Mr. Minton."

"I know how to act."

I PICKED HER UP at her parents' house twenty-five minutes later. They lived just south of Venice Boulevard on the west side of town.

That night Kiko "Loretta" Kuroko was a sight to behold. She wore a tight-fitting green gown that had sequins here and there, with a black velvet-and-silk shawl draped on her shoulders. Her black high heels made her taller than I by two inches, and her makeup was just enough to make any man from six to sixty-six skip a step in his gait.

I opened the door for her as her frightened parents gawped from a window of their small house.

Loretta's whole family had been imprisoned in an American-run concentration camp during World War II. This caused her parents to be afraid of anything outside their small circle and it made Loretta hate all white people.

"Damn," I once said to her. "My people been under a white man's thumb for three hundred years an' I don't hate all of 'em."

"That's because they never lied to you," she said on that weekday afternoon at Milo's office. "But I always believed that I was accepted as a person and a citizen. After what I saw, I don't care what happens to them."

It was lucky for Milo and the black population of Watts in general. Loretta was a force to be reckoned with.

•   •   •

THE BOUNCER AT THE CLUB entrance at the Knickerbocker was a reptilian-looking fellow named Razor. He was taller than Fearless and broader of shoulder than Mad Anthony. But he smiled, showing more teeth than seemed possible.

"Loretta," he said, not even deigning to recognize my presence.

"Mr. Hanley." If Loretta knew you, she knew your last name and often used it as a mark of respect.

Loretta took a step across the threshold and I moved to follow. A big brown hand covered my chest.

"Where you think you goin', boy?" Razor asked, no longer smiling but still showing his teeth.

I wish I'd said something smart or sassy, but I was flabbergasted and intimidated. All I could do was stutter.

"Paris is with me," Loretta said.

"Really?"

"Yes." Her smile really was something.

"You know you could do a lot bettah than a little man like this here," Razor said, giving her an up and down look.

"I can see that you don't know him as well as I do, Mr. Hanley," she replied. "Paris here can't fight to save his life, but you know when women get a man alone, fighting is the last thing on their minds."

The club was crowded, and the bar was right next to the door. A few of the people standing around heard Loretta's lecture and started laughing.

Razor smiled and bowed his head to me.

"Excuse me, Mr. Paris, sir. I didn't know." He waved his hand and we were taken by a young brown girl in a tight pink dress to a table near the stage.

Milo had a running tab at Apollo's, but I started my own. I lit Loretta's cigarette and ordered good champagne. She was hungry and so we had them bring out a basket of battered and fried shrimp with two salads.

The Winston Marks Trio was playing that night. They were one of the most important components in those early days of the new jazz. Winston could be anything from a lonely whale to a hummingbird's wing with his trumpet. He would have probably been world renowned if he hadn't had an eye for every lady he met. One of those ladies was his bass player's wife. Three weeks after that performance, Billy Stiles shot Winston in the brain, ending the trio's career.

I spent most of my time talking to Loretta. At one point I went up to the bartender, Silver Martin. I showed him the picture of Angel and he admitted seeing her before. I handed him a picture of Andrew Jackson and he promised to send over anyone who knew something about her.

THE MUSIC WAS GREAT. Maybe Winston sensed his death that night because he played like I never heard anyone play before. There was one number where I knew instinctively that he was tracing the cracks of a broken heart that could never be mended. Fool that I was, I even shed a tear.

Loretta placed a hand on mine.

"You're a sweet man, Paris Minton."

"And you're twice the woman of anybody else in this place," I said.

She smiled and let her head loll a bit to the side.

"What?" I asked.

"Are we going to do something about all these fine compliments?"

Loretta liked black men. She liked us because we knew how she felt on the inside. She shared our rage and our impotence; she strained with us at the edges.

"Well?" she asked.

I was frozen in place. I didn't know what to say. It was as though I had just been in my house talking loud and bragging about what I'd do with some movie queen, and then she strolled in and said, "Let's get it on, son."

Loretta grinned. She was not the kind of woman who would belittle the man she was with.

"It's okay," she said.

"No."

"No?"

"You don't get it," I said. "You couldn't understand because I'm just gettin' to it right now myself."

"What?"

Loretta's eyes shimmered and her presence was absolutely assured. She felt more at home in my world than I did.

"I love you," I said, and her smile was replaced with astonishment.

"What?" It was a whole different question this time.

"I see you sitting there with Milo. I see you loving him and caring for him and everybody he cares for. You're beautiful and strong and hurt, but you never complain. That man tried to humiliate me, and you shot him right down. And I'm not even thinkin' that you're askin' me to share your bed. Even if you just wonder if we'll have another date, I'm scared to death about it. You know the girls I hang with might forget my name in the mornin'.

And here you are looking into me like I was this glass'a water."

The smile returned to Loretta's mouth after a moment.

"Maybe later, then?" she said.

"Excuse me. Mr. Minton?"

I looked up and saw a short brown man with pockmarks on his skin that made him seem to be made of leather. He had a flat head and snake eyes but wasn't at all threatening or even off-putting.

"Yeah?" I said, angered by the interruption of one of the few purely honest moments I'd had with a woman.

"Silver said you wanted to know about Angel."

"Excuse me," Loretta said, standing. "I have to go to the powder room."

She left, taking the best part of me with her.

"What you got?" I asked the man, whose name I never knew.

"Angel live with a dude named Useless at Man's Barn."

"I got that already," I said, taking a small fold of cash from my pocket.

The man eyed my money and actually licked his lips.

"What you need, then?"

"You seen her in the last week or so?"

"Naw."

"You know where she work at?"

"Naw." He bit his lip, seeing the possibility of a tip fade.

"What about anybody she's tight wit' other than Useless? Maybe some white dude?"

"I seen her with some white men but not with anyone more than a couple'a times. But she used to know this one guy, an' it seemed like they stayed friends."

"Who?"

"Guy name'a Tommy Hoag."

"You wouldn't have a number for 'im?" I asked.

"Don't need it," the leather man said. "Tommy is the only Negro agent for the Schuyler Real Estate office on Hooper."

Andrew Jackson leaped happily from my hand, and just as happily the nameless leather man jogged away from my table.

I saw Loretta approach from across the room. The men all gave her glances. The women looked to make sure that she kept on going.

17

LORETTA KISSED ME when we stopped in front of her parents' home. It was a long, juicy kiss. I was working with her, but she was definitely the captain of that boat. She licked my throat and nipped my ears, caressed the side of my neck in a way no mother had ever done a child's. Two of her fingers found their way into a small opening between the buttons of my shirt. When she pressed against my nipple, I jumped a little.

"I'm not finished yet," she whispered, just in case my flinching meant that I was ready to walk her to the door.

There was no hurry to Loretta's passion, but my heart was thumping like a lonely puppy's heart does when his master returns after leaving him tied up for hours.

When we finally separated, I felt as if I had spent a lifetime with her.

"I understood what you were saying," Loretta whispered. "I do love Milo, but we aren't like that. And you know, Paris, I need a man to make me whole."

I had nothing to say but I opened my mouth anyway. Loretta put two fingers to my lips and said, "Let's go."

Before we got to her front porch, the door flew open. Loretta's parents were huddled there — a two-headed warden. Loretta kissed me again and then was enveloped in the frightened arms of their love.

I went to my trunk and brought out the whiskey and soda. I sat there smoldering cigarettes and imbibing alcohol until the fervor abated and the swelling went down.

I didn't make it home until after four.

SOMETIME IN THE EARLY AFTERNOON I headed out looking for Tommy Hoag. Schuyler Real Estate was a small office wedged in between a hardware store and a barber's shop on Hooper. The office was red of color and less than six feet in width. There were three desks along the crimson aisle. The first was at the window on the right, the second was just behind that on the left, and the third was against the back wall, removed from the other two by at least seven feet.

For years Schuyler's had had three white agents sitting in that crooked line. The head man was always the one at the back of the room. You had to get past the first two barriers to reach him. These first two agents dealt with colored people wanting apartments and storefronts, churches, and small garages. The last agent always dealt with white businesspeople coming down to open big businesses like supermarkets and lumberyards.

Knowing the system, I was surprised to see the one colored face manning the hindmost desk.

It was one fifteen and I was dressed in my blue suit.

Where I had been feeling cursed and oppressed for the past few days, I now was blessed with thoughts of Loretta and her amazing understanding of my heart. I kept moving forward because that was all I could do. But she was at the back of my mind, kissing my neck and making sounds of whoopee.

"Yes, sir?" the half-bald white man in the green jacket and black trousers asked. He had risen either to greet or to expel me.

"Mr. Hoag, please," I said.

"Do you have an appointment?" the middle-aged roadblock asked, an apology already etched around his eyes.

"It has to do with this photograph," I said, handing Angel over into his bone-colored grasp.

"I don't understand?" he said, looking at the picture and registering something.

"He will," I assured the salesman.

The first man, whose nameplate read ROGER, moved to negotiate between the desks, making his way toward the back of the aisle. The man behind him sat tall and thin, swathed in brown. He smiled and nodded.

"Nice day," he said.

One of the things I love about America is that if you are a potential customer almost everyone is nice to you. They might hate your guts and wish you dead, but face-to-face they smile and nod and talk about the weather in a neighborly cadence.

Roger had made his pitch to Tommy and was returning without the photo. He nodded at me and smiled as he approached and then said, "He has a few minutes before his next meeting. He'll see you now."

I careered around Roger's desk and the next and then

set my pace for the well-dressed man at the back of the room.

He stood up to a good five eleven and put out a hand that had a double fold of fine white cotton and cuff links at the wrist. Tommy Hoag was light skinned and auburn eyed at a time when freedom for black people depended on how closely we could approximate being white. His Caucasian-like features had served him well. His expression told you that he knew it and that he knew that you knew it too.

"Mr. Hoag?" I asked.

"Pleased to meet you, Mister . . . ?"

"Minton," I said. "Paris Minton."

"Have a seat, Mr. Minton."

I sat, looking around.

On the wall behind his desk hung a framed parchment claiming that Thomas Benton Hoag had earned a bachelor of arts degree from Howard University.

The chair was walnut and the desk was walnut veneer. The black carpet would wear down in six months and the walls might as well have been paper. But Schuyler's was an institution in Watts.

"Damn," I said.

"Do I know you, Mr. Minton?"

"No. You might know my cousin, though. Ulysses S. Grant the Fourth."

His eyes registered yes.

"No," he said, shaking his head to prove it.

"Useless, that's what most of us call him, is Angel there's boyfriend." I pointed at the photo on his desk.

"She's a pretty girl," he said noncommittally.

"She's more than that, I hear."

"What can I do for you, Mr. Minton?"

"Can you explain the theory of evolution?" I asked.

"Say what?" he asked. I could almost hear the *Negro* at the end of the sentence.

"You got a college degree, brother. You know that's more rare for a black man than someone actually born in L.A."

Tommy smiled. He liked a quick wit.

"I could explain, but that would take too long," he said. "You'd have to do some background reading, the original texts, you know."

"I done read *The Origin of Species* and *The Descent of Man*," I said. "I understand the position, but what I always wonder about is what I call the horizon point of the phenomenon."

I was actually reciting arguments that Ashe had made to me back when she thought I was some kind of genius simply because I owned a bookstore.

Tommy didn't know what the hell I was talking about, and so before he could embarrass himself I added, "You know, Darwin says that a species evolves. But a species ain't one thing, it's millions, maybe more. So outta all the people in the world, are we all at the same place on the evolutionary ladder? Is there just one ladder or a thousand of 'em? Some people smarter than others, some stronger. You got a genius like George Washington Carver and a beast like Adolf Hitler. How are they related? Are they at the same place?"

"That's what the Constitution and the Bill of Rights say," Tommy offered weakly.

"True," I agreed. "But that's a moral stance, not a scientific one. And the original document only referred to white, Christian, male landowners. Darwin throw a much bigger net than that one there."

Somebody overhearing our words would have thought that I was going down the wrong road. But that someone wouldn't have been listening between the lines. In his own estimation Tommy was a superior specimen. He only dealt with white people and was better educated than 99 percent of the Negro race. He would have felt that he could dismiss me unless I intimidated him physically or intellectually.

Tommy could have kicked my ass up and down the block, so I used the only muscle I had.

It worked too.

"Angel Allmont and I used to go out," Tommy told me. "We saw each other for a couple of months. But I had to let her go. She was pretty and everything, but I need a lighter-skinned girl in the business I do, and she had a wild side.

"And now that I think on it . . . her new boyfriend might have been called Useless. Something like that."

"Have you talked to her in the last week or so?" I asked.

"No. She was goin' out with your cousin and they got tangled up with a flimflam man named Hector. I think that's what she said his name was."

"Hector what?"

"I didn't ask."

"How you know he was bent?"

"Angel said that they were doing business where they were going to make ten thousand dollars in a month," Tommy said in a muted voice. "That kinda money don't evolve from honest labor."

I smiled at his inside joke.

"You know where I can find her?" I asked.

"Man's Barn."

"She moved outta there."

"Oh," Tommy said, not really caring. "I don't know, then. All I can tell ya is that the one time I met your cousin he told me that he played billiards at Jerry Twist's and that he could get me in there any time I wanted."

He looked at me.

I returned the stare.

"That all you after, Mr. Minton?"

"I guess so."

"Any time you need me to tell you more about Darwin, you just drop on by."

I wondered as I left if he believed that he had lectured me.

18

JERRY TWIST'S WAS A pool parlor on Slauson, occupying the second floor of a lime-colored two-story building in the center of the block. The bottom floor housed Ha Tsu's Good News Chinese restaurant.

Good News was unique inasmuch as it was the only Chinese restaurant I'd ever been to that had a bouncer— Harold Crier.

Harold was big and dark. He wore a black eye patch and had hands like catchers' mitts. Harold was fat, but I'd seen him chase a would-be patron who had slapped him after being refused entrance. The runner was young and sleek, but the forty-something and ponderous Harold ran that boy down after two blocks.

The story goes that Harold met Ha Tsu while trying to rob him late one Monday night. The armed robber made the mistake of getting too close to the restaurateur and before he knew it the smaller man had grabbed Harold's gun wrist and jabbed him in the eye with a fork from the counter. When Harold woke up, he was in the back room on a cot with a Chinese doctor ministering to him.

Ha Tsu made Loretta's hatred of white people seem like mild perturbation. Loretta's anger came from a specific event over a relatively short period of time. But Ha hated whites for the domination of China. He hated white people the way Sitting Bull hated them. He hated them so much that he wouldn't even turn Harold, an armed robber, over to the cops. He told Harold that he could either die there on that bamboo cot or take a job as the sentry at the front door of Good News.

"You want me to be a guard?" Harold had asked.

"You perfect," Ha told him. "You know when somebody bad comes to rob me, and when they see your eye they know what they get."

"Hey, Paris," the bouncer said in greeting. It was late afternoon, I remember, and there was hot sun on my back. The big bodyguard was sitting on a high stool, leaning against the wall next to Good News's double green doors.

"Harold. How's it goin'?"

"Cain't complain. I'm eatin' good an' stayin' outta jail. How's Fearless?"

Almost everyone who knew me did so by way of Fearless. I didn't mind.

"He's fine. Doin' a li'l stint wit' Milo Sweet."

"Yeah," Harold said. "I hear that Albert Rive been lookin' for Milo."

"Where you hear that?"

"Whisper. He come around lookin' for Al."

"What about my cousin — Useless Grant?"

"Useless your cousin, man? Damn. I don't know if that's good or bad."

"What you mean by that?" I asked.

"I guess it could come in handy bein' related to a snake. I mean, maybe the snake tell ya where all the other snakes be hidin'."

We both laughed.

"But have you seen 'im?" I asked.

"Not for two, three weeks, I haven't. No, sir. I don't work Tuesday, Wednesday, though. Maybe he come by then."

ON THE INSIDE HA TSU's looked more like a rundown fishing boat than a dining room. There were ceramic lobsters, shrimp, and other shellfish placed everywhere: on counters, on the walls, hanging in clusters from ropes over and next to each booth. There were dark-colored glass floats hanging by the dozen in fishnets, and the booths were of unfinished wood with peeling sea-green fake-leather cushions for seats.

The counter was nice. Formica and chrome. The cracked green linoleum was clean and without splinters.

"Hi, Paris," Mum, a young Chinese woman, said. She was related to Ha Tsu somehow and worked as a waitress every day of the week.

Ha was behind the counter. I liked the middle-aged Chinese partly because he was one of the few men I knew who was shorter than I. He liked me because he believed I had a sense of humor.

"Paris," he hailed. "How you doing?"

"Not bad, Ha. What's goin' on around here?"

"Color people study revolution," he said, cocking an eye at unseen spies.

"They should be studyin' their ABCs," I said.

Ha laughed and slapped my forearm.

"You right about that, bruddah," he agreed. "But you know I hear 'em talkin'. They not happy. Soon the world know."

"Maybe I better stock up on *The Communist Manifesto*," I offered.

"Put your money in gold," he advised, and I wondered about the treasure he must have buried somewhere.

"What's good today?" I asked the warlord of Watts.

"Chicken with walnuts, snow peas, and my extra-fancy white rice. Each grain inch long."

"I'll take it."

"You like it."

Ha went away to let me consider the next part of our talk.

Most people thought that I was harmless at best. I read books and stayed in most of the time. I didn't have any kind of reputation except in the sex category, and even there I was no Fearless Jones. Women would leave their date to be with Fearless.

As I said, most people didn't pay me any attention. Not so with Ha Tsu. His eyes were nearly shut all the time, but he saw everything. He heard everything too. When I came nosing around he realized that my questions and actions had purpose. He had heard the stories about people I looked for.

Don't get me wrong. On the whole I was innocuous. But now and then I did work for Milo and helped Fearless when he got into a jam. And when I did, and Ha Tsu saw me, he knew that I had something going on.

I didn't want be out in the streets looking for Useless. I didn't want to find thousands of stolen dollars or moldering bodies. But there I was.

Ha brought my afternoon repast. It was delicious. He poured us both cups of fragrant jasmine tea and sat with me, as there were few other patrons at that hour.

"You look for Al Rive?" Ha Tsu asked.

"No. Why?"

"I hear Milo want him." Ha hunched his shoulders and opened his mouth. He was missing some teeth.

"No. For my cousin," I said. "Useless Grant."

"He your cousin?"

"Uh-huh. And I have never been thankful for that fact." Again Ha laughed.

"You should come work for me, Paris," he said.

"Why's that?"

"Then I laugh all times."

"Have you seen Useless?"

"Five days."

"Really? How was he?"

"He okay, I guess," Ha said. "Talking 'bout how he gonna get rich."

"How?"

"Off of white devils." Ha smiled a smile that would frighten a child of any age.

"How's he gonna do that?"

"I don't know. But he tell me that if you got a man by his dick, even if he white he gonna go where you say. Your cousin funny too."

At the end of the counter was a doorway covered by a black-and-white-checkered curtain. Behind the curtain was a steel-bound door to some stairs that led up to Jerry Twist's pool parlor. Only certain people were allowed up into Jerry's place. If you were Van Cleave or Fearless Jones, or with somebody of that stature, you could go up any time you wanted to. But a schlub like me didn't have a chance without an invitation.

"You think I could go up that way?" I asked my host.

Ha grimaced at the fabric. His left eye enlarged and he said, "It's a magic carpet. Only open for men with power."

"Open sesame," I said.

Neither the curtain nor the restaurant owner moved.

Abracadabra, Shazam, hail hail. I said all these words, but the fabric did not flutter.

Ha shrugged and walked away from me.

I went into my pocket and came out with a dollar.

"Hey, Mum," I called to the waitress.

She came over to me with a dazed and innocent look on her face. Mum was dressed in the black-and-white uniform of half the waitresses in America. But she carried it off with more elegance and beauty than Jayne Mansfield could have imagined.

"Yes, Paris?" she asked, but I heard another question.

"You got change for a dollar?"

"For you."

When I think back on my youth, remembering moments like those, I realize that I have squandered my life.

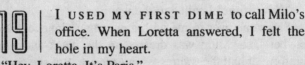 I USED MY FIRST DIME to call Milo's office. When Loretta answered, I felt the hole in my heart.

"Hey, Loretta. It's Paris."

"Hello, Paris," she said in a friendly but professional voice. I could tell that she was going to wait for me to bring up the conversation we'd started the night before — and also that there was no pressure for me to hurry.

"Lookin' for Fearless," I said.

"Milo went home to study an argument he's going to present," she said. "He's trying to be readmitted to the bar."

"Fearless say where he was going?"

"No. He just drove Milo."

"Thanks."

"Sure, Paris. Is that all?"

"I had a great time last night," I said.

She hummed her agreement and then said, "One day you'll come to understand what a wonderful man you are, Paris Minton."

•   •   •

I CALLED TWO BARS and three restaurants that Fearless frequented, with no luck. I left messages for him, but no one had any idea when he'd show up.

I could have called Mona. Maybe I should have called her. If you woke her in her bed from a deep sleep and asked her where Fearless might be, she would probably know. That man was on her mind twenty-four hours a day.

But I hesitated. One day I might really need Mona's help and if I called all the time she could begin to resent me. It's always a delicate thing dealing with your friends' girlfriends.

So instead I dialed a Ludlow number. He answered on the first ring.

"Yeh?"

"Bobby?"

"You know it is, Paris. What you want?"

Bobby Frank was known as the Two Dollar Man. He'd perform any errand for the discreet payment of two George Washington notes.

If someone wanted to get word to his mother that he was in jail and needed bail, Bobby would take the message to her door for two bills. If you wanted your mother and your cousin to know, then that was four — unless the cousin and the mother lived under the same roof.

Bobby lived in a studio apartment with a portable Zenith TV, a mini-refrigerator filled with cheap beer, a perpetual carton of Kools, and a big black telephone. He kept a ledger sheet that had three live columns: name, estimated cost, and paid. Cost was always a multiple of two, and you had to have an X in the rightmost column or Bobby wouldn't work for you again.

"I need Fearless to meet me down at Ha Tsu's ASAP," I said.

"You ain't paid me for that thing I did last month, man."

"I ain't seen ya."

"Well, you coulda come by," Bobby said.

"Yeah. You right, man. I'll tell ya what, you tell Fearless when you see 'im to give ya the four dollars. Tell him that I said to settle my bill." This accomplished two ends. It meant that Bobby would definitely get paid, and it let him know that Fearless wanted the information Bobby had. Either detail was enough to get him up and out.

"I was gonna call him," Bobby complained. He liked to complain.

"Milo's only three blocks from you, B," I said. "And anyway, Fearless ain't there."

The Two Dollar Man sighed on his end of the line.

"I hear Milo got trouble wit' Albert Rive," the Two Dollar Man said. This was often the case with Bobby. He stayed at home to get his business calls, but being at home most of the time made him lonely. On top of the two dollars, I had to pay a little interest in conversation.

"It's Al got trouble," I said. "He got Whisper and Fearless on him. He be lucky to make it to jail."

"I hear you got trouble too, Paris."

I wondered how he could have known about Three Hearts and her evil eye.

"What kinda trouble?" I asked.

"Mad Anthony says he gonna kill your cousin and he got some choice words about you too."

"Where you hear that?"

"Around. People be sayin' that Useless better keep his butt indoors."

"You know where Useless is right now?" I asked.

"I'll tell you what I told Tony's cousin."

"What's that?"

"Useless ain't gone be found he don't want it."

"You think you can find Fearless?" I asked then. "Could you find him?"

"Oh, yeah. I think I know where he's at."

He probably did. For a man who stayed inside 90 percent of the time, Bobby had more knowledge about the comings and goings of Watts personalities than a station full of cops.

WHEN I GOT BACK TO GOOD NEWS the evening clientele had begun to arrive. My plate was still at the bar, but Ha had moved to the back in order to work with his immigrant kitchen help.

There were four waitresses on duty, two more than he needed at that hour, but the trade would be brisk soon.

Mum came up to my station and smiled, not that she needed to; she would have been beautiful frowning or crying or bemoaning the dead. Her skin was olive with a hint of lemon therein, and her dark eyes were both wise and youthful — I never really knew how old she was. Unlike the common impression that most people had of Asian women, Mum was full of good humor, quite forward, and blessed with a great figure.

I was appreciating this last quality when she asked, "So how are you, Mr. Paris?"

"Quite fine, Miss Mum. Quite fine. I got money in my pocket and someplace to be in the morning. I don't have a job, which is a good thing, and nobody's trying to get me put outta my house."

She didn't have to smile to maintain her beauty, but it didn't hurt.

"How are you, honey?" I asked.

"Getting better."

"Better? Was something wrong?"

"All kinds of things," she said, pushing a shoulder forward deliciously.

"Like what?"

"I move outta my place on Grand Court over to Peters Lane. I got a nice green door with a red lantern over it."

"You like the new place better?"

"Yeah. It's closer, and you know I don't get off till ten and so I like to get home before the news."

"It's closer but is it nicer?"

"It's nicer because I don't have stupid Vincent in there anymore," she said with a sneer.

"Who's Vincent?"

"He call himself my boyfriend but he wasn't no friend to me. Don't have a job, don't do a thing. When my mothah get sick he won't even go with me to the hospital."

"How's your mom?" I asked, following my cue. "Is she okay?"

Mum smiled and put her hand on mine.

"You're sweet, Mr. Paris. She much bettah now I have free time to come see her every day."

"Sometimes gettin' rid of a boyfriend is better than gettin' one," I said.

She laughed and laughed. At Ha Tsu's Good News I was a laugh riot.

I SAT ON MY STOOL watching the devotees of Ha Tsu's cuisine come in. It was a loud establishment when it was in full swing. Some people recognized me and came my way, but after a while I pulled out a paperback copy of *The Stranger* by Albert Camus. *My mother died today, or maybe it was yesterday* . . . I liked reading about the heat of North Africa combined with the oppression of European culture.

NOW AND THEN a well-dressed man or two would show up and speak to one of the waitstaff. They'd linger around the checkered curtain until Ha would come out and admit them to the stairway to Jerry Twist's.

Mum came by every fifteen minutes or so to touch my hand and ask if I needed anything.

The Stranger, Meursault, found himself getting deeper and deeper into trouble just for living a life in the world.

"HEY, FEARLESS!" someone shouted. "What's happenin', man?"

My friend was wearing a loose white shirt with big red flowers patterned on it and dark brown pants. Fearless's hair was always close cut, and he had a slight limp from one time when he saved my life by taking two others.

He slapped hands and kissed women all the way to the counter. Fearless was popular, and unlike Van, no one felt that he was about to go crazy on them.

"Paris," he announced. "What you need?"

"I got a hankerin' to see some pool bein' played," I said.

"Well, let's go there, then, my man," he said.

I must say that no one in my life elated me like Fearless did.

Ha had appeared next to the snooker entrance before we reached the curtain.

"Boo!" Fearless said to the curtain, and it was pulled away. The door opened onto a dark passage lit by only one weak blue bulb.

As we ascended the narrow staircase I wondered about magic: those who had it, and those who did not.

20

WE ONLY HAD ONE FLIGHT of stairs to make a plan. After that we'd be in enemy territory. Fearless was used to that kind of pressure. He'd been a hair-trigger killer all through Europe for the U.S. army. They'd whisper a sentence or two into his ear, and he'd go out among Aryans, shooting and slaying and burning down.

"What's the thing, man?" he asked me on the first step.

"Useless been hangin' around Twist's for some time now," I said. "He told Ha that he been takin' money from white men, that he had 'em by the dick."

"The dick?" Fearless echoed. "Damn."

We were halfway to the second floor.

"You know what we need," I said. "Where is Useless and, failing that, what does Twist know about Useless that we don't know?"

"Beats a knife in the ribs," Fearless said.

For some reason, that caused me to grin.

The door to Jerry Twist's was red. Dark red in a dark

stairway. The faint light imbued the portal with a throbbing quality.

I let Fearless do the knocking.

He only rapped one time before the blood-colored door swung inward. Framed in the darkness of that doorway and lit by the weak light from the stairs stood K. C. Littell, one of the many mysteries of Watts.

K.C., from almost any perspective, was a white man. He had pale skin, wavy brown hair, and eyes that hadn't seemed to decide on which shade of brown they actually were. His features, however — lips and nose — were small but not quite Caucasian. A white man might have been fooled by K.C.'s appearance. Many Negroes like him had disappeared into the white world. They lived there, married to white spouses, raising white children, belonging to white PTAs. But not K.C. He was a virulent Negro. Something in his upbringing, something about his appearance made him want to bathe himself in the color he'd been denied.

"Happenin', Fearless, Paris," he sang.

"Nuthin' to it, brother," I said.

"We wanna come in a minute, K.C.," Fearless said. "That okay?"

The pale guardian pretended to think for a moment. But he knew that he didn't have the authority to bar Mr. Jones's way. No. There wasn't a president or king worth his salt who couldn't see the royalty in my friend.

K.C. nodded and stepped aside. We entered the vast room, assailed by darkness and light.

There was enough room for fifteen tables in Twist's enormous poolroom — but he only kept six. They were spaced out like islands of light on a sea of black. Each table, handmade and imported from Copenhagen, was under three hanging lamps delivering rich and buttery radiance. Every table was occupied by professional pool men from all over the country. If you were a black man and you played pool, gaining entrée to Twist's was the highest accolade you would ever receive.

The only sound coming from the room was the clacking of billiard balls. There were at least a dozen men in there playing, but I never even heard a murmur.

Somewhere in the darkness was our quarry. Jerry's desk was against one of the walls. He never had his lamp turned on and kept a penlight for the few times he had to read or sign something.

Each player paid a hundred dollars a night for the privilege of playing at Twist's. The winners left a 10 percent tip for the host if they ever wanted to play there again.

If someone needed water or whiskey or both, K.C. called down to Ha Tsu and he had one of his waitresses bring up the order.

It wasn't known what the relationship between Ha and Jerry was. No one even knew who owned the building they occupied. Were they partners or did such brilliant and unusual men just happen to come together in that place at that time?

"Mr. Jones," came Jerry's moderate alto. "Paris."

Over to our left Jerry materialized out of night.

Mr. Twist looked nothing like his name. He was short and stout with googly, watery eyes that most often seemed to be gazing somewhere above your head. His lips were like those I'd imagine on Edward G. Robinson's grandfather. All in all he looked like an uncomfortable cross between a man and a frog. He was good with a stick, better at business, and had the air of danger about him. He was one of those men — like Cleave and Fearless — who lived outside the rule of law.

Jerry was from Louisiana too. He'd grown up not seven miles from the hovel I called home. He was my senior by a decade, but I remembered him — ugly and gawking, different from the rest. I used to think that we had something in common. But years later I realized that the only experience we shared was our separateness from the people around us.

"Hey, Jerry," Fearless replied.

I nodded, noticing that I didn't deserve a *mister.*

"What you all doin' here?" he asked, peering at a spot both above and between us.

"As you know," I began. "Useless Grant's my cousin. . . ."

I told an edited version of the story. There was no reason to mention Tiny or Jessa, stolen money, or the particulars of my meeting with Mad Anthony. I didn't even tell Jerry that Useless's mother was the one who had initiated our search.

When I'd finished talking, Jerry was quiet for quite some time. Finally he sighed and glanced at Fearless.

"You in this, Mr. Jones?" he asked.

"All the way up to my elbows."

"Come on, then," he said, turning toward the depths of his establishment.

He guided us along an invisible path, between tables, to the wall opposite the entrance. There he opened a door and admitted us to his office.

I had expected dazzling light, crystal chandeliers, mirrors on every wall. But instead Jerry's office was almost as dim as the poolroom. There was a red lamp on the desk and weak blue radiance coming from the wall on my left, enough light for us to see the chairs we were meant to sit in.

Jerry placed himself in the manager's seat and lit up a cigarette without offering us one. I took out my own pack and shook it at my friend. Fearless waved away my wordless offer.

"Okay," Jerry said. "Now, what does all this falderal got to do with me?"

"I'm just worried about my cousin," I said. "And I hear you been seein' him on a regular basis."

"That's business, Paris," he said. "You know most people come in here don't speak ten words the whole night."

"But you got eyes like a eagle and a owl," I said. "You see ten times what normal men see and twice that at night."

"I ain't seen nuttin' on Ulysses Grant," he said, and I knew by his use of my cousin's proper name that he was lying.

Fearless knew it too.

"Look, Jerry," my friend said, "we not tryin' to get nobody in trouble. We not tryin' to mess up nobody's game. Paris here just need to talk to Ulysses, that's all."

Jerry took a moment. He wasn't considering the request, it was just that he was trying to show respect, that he was at least thinking about what Fearless was saying.

"I'm sorry, Mr. Jones," Jerry said. "But you know I got a reputation to maintain. I don't tell nobody's business to nobody. If I was to talk to you it might get out. Ulysses might figure out how Paris fount him. An' if he did, my whole game is out the windah."

"When he came to my house he was worried for his life," I said.

"The last time I seen 'im he was just fine," Jerry said.

"When was that?"

"Five days ago."

Jerry stared at me and Fearless, resolute in his conviction. Whether it was because he was committed to his reputation or some more intricate involvement with my cousin, I was not sure. But I did know that I had to break Mr. Twist's resolve.

"Okay," I said. "You know I don't wanna make you do somethin' go against your moral code. But I got to bring Three Hearts over here for you to tell her that."

"Three Hearts? What's Three Hearts got to do with this?" Jerry was looking me directly in the eye.

"That's Useless's mama, man. She got everything to do wit' it."

"She, she down Louisiana," he said.

"Not no mo'," Fearless said, nodding sagely.

"She in L.A.?"

"Right outside'a Watts," I said. "I can have her here in twenty-two minutes—tops."

"I cain't tell her nuthin' more than I told you," he whined. "Why she got to come here?"

"That's her boy," I said reasonably. "He's missin' an' you the last one seen 'im. You know Three Hearts gotta talk about that."

"Paris," he begged, "you know that woman. You know what they say about her."

"An' it's all true," I pronounced. "That's why I'm'a bring her to you. I don't want that evil eye on me."

Jerry gulped loud enough for us both to hear. He bit his lips and clasped his hands.

Then he said, "This shit cain't git out, man."

"You got our word," Fearless said.

I do believe a tear escaped Jerry's eye.

"Last time I seen Ulysses," Jerry said, "he was worried that a man named Hector was after him. He told me that his girl, Angel, had turned against him and he was gonna have to run."

"Why he tell you?" I asked.

"He needed money."

"And you a bank?"

A sour taste passed Jerry's big lips and he looked to the left. Then he looked back at me and said, "Ulysses been fleecin' rich white people. Blackmailin' 'em, I think."

"How?"

"I don't know. All I do know is that he been bringin' me money, lots of it, an' I been helpin' him put it into accounts that the IRS won't see. You know, foreign shit."

"How you do that?"

"That ain't got nuthin' to do with what's goin' on with Ulysses," Jerry said.

"Okay," I said. "All right. What's this guy Hector got to do with all this?"

"Hector LaTiara," Jerry said. "French-assed nigger. Think his shit don't stink. I met him one time. He got somethin' to do with Ulysses' business, but don't ask me what 'cause I don't know."

"You know where he live at?" Fearless asked.

Jerry just shook his head. His lips were hanging

loosely, as if he had just run a desperate race and was exhausted.

"I'm sorry," I said. "And I appreciate the information. Three Hearts will too."

"You keep that witch away from me," Jerry said.

"Don't worry," I promised. "I'll keep her curses all to myself."

21 ON THE WAY OUT we were distracted by a pool game. A man made an exceptionally good shot, sinking two balls and putting his shooter in prime position. Fearless put a hand on my arm and we waited until the player — a dark-skinned, elegantly dressed man — finished his run and the game. I was about to go when Fearless whispered, "Let's see what this other dude could do."

The other player was light-skinned, fat, and sweating. He wore a flouncy Bermuda shirt with big purple and green patterns printed on it. He was smoking and drinking and seemed a little pixilated. But when he leaned over to shoot, he was all business.

It was some match. If either guy got a clear shot the game was over. It was pool on a whole other plane than the one where I lived. These men were masters.

We probably watched for two hours before I made to leave. Those men were going to play until sunrise, and I had things on my mind. Fearless could have stayed but he followed me out.

•   •   •

MUM WAS GONE by the time we got downstairs. So was the bulk of Ha's crowd. I took a phone book from behind the cash register and looked up Hector LaTiara. He lived on a street called Saturn.

Harold Crier wished us good night at the door. Fearless and I wandered down the street. He had parked next to me in an empty lot there.

"What you think about what Jerry said?" I asked Fearless.

He shook his head. "You cain't evah tell wit' Jerry, man. He might be lyin'. He might be straight. I mean, I believe it about this Hector dude 'cause you knew his name anyway."

Fearless couldn't read the newspaper without help, but he knew people. He could tell what a man felt by watching him blow his nose.

"Yeah. But he called Useless Ulysses," I said. "That means he got somethin' goin' with him."

"Doin' business, like he said," Fearless reasoned.

"Naw. It's more than that."

"Maybe. But maybe it don't mattah. I mean, unless he killed Ulysses, why we wanna bother with him?"

It was true.

"You wanna go roust this Hector dude?" Fearless offered.

It was maybe midnight.

"I got my gun."

"Naw, man. We don't know who's up in the house with him, an' there's no reason to get on his bad side right off. Anyway, I'm tired. Ain't got much sleep in the last few days." Everything I was saying was true, but I had an ulterior motive.

Fearless could see the deception on my face, but he didn't challenge me.

"Okay, man," he said. "You know where I be in the mornin'. Call me when you need me."

He jumped into Milo's red Caddy and drove off in a great swoosh.

I stood in that empty dirt-floored lot wondering how I got there. I looked down the street at Good News. The lights were still on, but the restaurant was closing down.

There was no visible light from upstairs, but I knew that the men up there would be playing until six or seven. Somewhere Useless was either breathing or not breathing and Three Hearts was awake in her bed, fretting about her wayward son.

And there I was: one kind of man in another kind of world.

I DROVE AROUND FOR A WHILE because I didn't know the neighborhood very well and because the street I was looking for was only one block long. It took me five minutes just to find it on the gas station map.

When I finally got there I realized that the street was little more than an alley — I couldn't park on it without blocking the road. So I put my auto on the cross street and walked down one side of the alley and back up the other. By then it was almost one thirty in the morning. My heart was pumping with anticipation and trepidation. The streets were empty, which made them perfect for a crime. I was alone, which made me the perfect crime victim.

I saw no doorway that had what I wanted. I should have gone home, but I walked up and down the alley/lane again.

Finally, in frustration I looked up and saw a crimson glow from a third-floor apartment.

It was a lantern.

I climbed the stairs. Reaching the red light, I came upon a green door.

I knocked and the door came open almost immediately.

Mum had been lovely in her waitress getup but she was a knockout in her orange silk gown.

"I wondered if you were going to come," she said.

"Not me," I replied. "I been thinkin' about this for a long time."

Mum had nothing on under the thin material. I wanted to take her in my arms right then, but I could tell by the way she held herself that she needed a different approach.

She ushered me into a large room that was sumptuous; there was really no other word for it. The light was low but unlike Jerry Twist's — you could still see. On one side there was a large bed covered by a canopy with gossamer violet-colored silk hanging down on three sides. Next to the bed stood an eight-foot mirror in a cherrywood frame. A red hassock sat before the mirror; to its side was a small table covered with makeup containers, cream pots, brushes, and perfumes. I could imagine Mum sitting before her mirror, preparing herself for our rendezvous.

The other side of the room had a low couch and table. The couch was golden with red pillows and the table was blond, set for drinks.

Mum shut the door and came up close to me. She reached into my breast pocket and retrieved my cigarettes and matches. She put a cigarette between my lips and lit it. Then she guided me to the sofa and pressed until I sat.

While she poured me a drink in a deep bowl of a glass, she said, "I've been waiting for a man to make me laugh."

She passed me the glass. Cognac. Good cognac.

"You just moved in here?" I asked.

"I know how I like things," she said.

"I can see that."

"I want to give you pleasure, Paris," she said.

Why was in my chest, but he refused to make himself known.

Mum sat next to me and gave me a kiss. It wasn't as passionate as Loretta's had been, but it was nice. We did that for a while: kiss and then sip fine liquor from the big glasses, then kiss some more. My hands wanted to feel her orange fabric, but she kept them down.

After our third drink she lifted me by the elbows and brought me to another room. It was a bathroom with a huge freestanding, high-collared tub. It was filled with water. She tested it with a bare foot up to the ankle and then turned on the hot.

"I'm going to undress you," she told me. "Just let me do it. Don't help or touch me."

I didn't.

The water was hot and the liquor did exactly what it was supposed to. I was very excited sexually, but I would have been happy going to sleep while Mum cleaned me with a sea sponge scrubber.

I closed my eyes and let my mind wander. Somewhere between here and there a thought came to me in the form of a question: *Why would Hector LaTiara want a French dictionary?*

But even that didn't disturb me.

When I opened my eyes Mum had disrobed and was stepping into the tub with me.

"YOU'RE A NICE MAN, PARIS," Mum said. She had one arm behind my head and the other across my chest. We were in her big bed, enveloped in silk and soft, soft cotton. I was clean and completely satisfied.

"What a man wants to hear is that he's big and strong and almost scary," I replied, though I was thinking about a door that had opened in my mind.

Mum giggled.

"I'm stronger than you are," she said.

"We'll never find out now, will we?"

"Why were you at Jerry's with Fearless Jones?" she asked then, and I wondered again why she had lured me over.

"Lookin' for my cousin Useless."

"Useless Grant is your cousin?"

"Everybody says that in the same way," I said. "And I know why. Useless is a motherfucker. Have you seen him?"

"Every once in a while he talks to Ha Tsu. They like to laugh together."

"They do business together?"

"I don't know Ha's business. I'm just a waitress." She was getting nervous.

"And I'm just a bookseller," I said. "What can you do?"

"You sell books?" Mum seemed shocked.

"Yeah. Why?"

She jumped up and pulled back the red fabric at the head of the bed. There were eight bookshelves filled with hardbound Chinese texts. I perused them. Most were complete ciphers to me. But on the bottom shelf I saw the names Aristotle, Plato, Marx, Spinoza, and Hegel printed over Chinese cuneiforms.

"I like some'a these guys," I said. "But I prefer the older generation. Herodotus, Homer, and Sophocles."

"You have read them?"

"Sure."

"I used to study ancient thinkers. My father sent me to New York to study. But then the Japs came and killed my family. They destroyed everything and made my country crazy. I came here and Ha Tsu took me in."

I put my arms around her, and after a while she fell into a deep sleep. I was soon to follow, but before I nodded off I thought about the man looking for the French dictionary, the man who was after Useless.

My dreams were darker than Jerry Twist's office.

22 | *IF HECTOR LaTIARA HAD BEEN to my store, he was probably there looking for Useless*—that was the thought going through my mind when I was almost awake, lying there between floral-scented sheets. And if Hector had been to my place once, he might have been there twice, even three times. He might have been armed and he might have run into Tiny Bobchek.

But what did any of that have to do with smoked bacon?

I hated Useless, hated him in that way you can only despise a family member. All of a sudden I was worried that the Bobchek murder could be tied to me in some way. If the police could somehow identify the corpse, they might tie him to Useless and then Useless to me. The next thing I knew, somebody who knew more than I did would be confessing to the crime, incriminating me, and getting a reduced sentence as he did so.

I would have liked to pour orange juice and hot butter all over him.

"Paris," the breeze whispered.

I should have agreed with Fearless the night before. We should have gone to Hector's house. It was too late to go to the police. They wouldn't understand us taking Tiny to the strawberry field. Killer Cleave wouldn't understand me telling them about it.

"Breakfast," the gentle wind sighed.

I opened my eyes to see Mum kneeling before me, naked and proffering a silver tray holding bacon and eggs, orange juice, and coffee.

My waking dream had put a pall on the day, but I smiled for Mum and kissed her gently.

"This what you call a Chinese breakfast?" I asked the young woman.

"No. But you're not what I call a Chinese girl's boyfriend either," she replied.

We ate and talked about her family. I asked where they had come from in China and why were so many people killed.

Mum told me that her clan hailed from central China originally. She blamed the Japanese for their demise. She hated that people with a virulence that rivaled the worst white racists I had met in the South. While she spoke I thought of Loretta. I wondered if Mum would have hated my Japanese friend.

Then I wondered about the people I hated because of their skin color or whatever. It seemed rather arbitrary to me—unnecessary, or maybe not that, maybe it was necessary to hate someone, just capricious who it was that you hated.

After breakfast I put on my clothes. At the door Mum hugged me and we kissed. She peered deeply into my eyes then.

"You cannot be my boyfriend," she said very seriously.

"You're very beautiful," I replied with a smile.

"But —"

"So I'm happy for what I got here," I said. "It's like a dream in here. And now when I come to Good News I know I can talk to you about philosophy over hot and sour."

Mum's eyes widened, and maybe there was a gleam of disappointment there. She might have been thinking that I took it so well maybe I could have been a good secret lover. Or maybe she wanted me to be a little broken-hearted after that night of perfect love.

Either way, she kissed me again and, unknowingly, sent me off to war.

SEX WITH A WOMAN IS ALWAYS a two-edged sword for me. The last woman I had been with, Jessa, was the source of all kinds of trouble. I was still deep in that morass, my clothes newly perfumed with Mum's exotic scents, when I decided that it would be okay for me to go to the address on Saturn where Hector LaTiara lived.

There were many forces that brought me to his block. There was the manhood I felt from the act of love with Mum. There was the urgency I felt about the murder that had happened in my home. And there was the feeling of invisibility I had at times.

I didn't expect to confront Hector. I just wanted to get the lay of the land before Fearless and I went up against the *French-assed nigger.*

I got in my car and sat there for a while. I thought about the assumptions I had made and the mistakes that attended those assumptions.

Very often I blamed Fearless for my problems. He'd get into trouble trying to do right in a world where everything was wrong. When he felt that he needed to think his way out of a problem, he always came to me. And if I got involved, trouble came down in a deluge.

Sometimes I wouldn't answer Fearless's calls. Sometimes I would refuse him bail money.

But now here I was, in trouble deep, and I didn't question whether or not Fearless would be there the moment I needed him. I can't say that I felt guilty about my infidelity, but I did see the truth of it. If Fearless wasn't in my life, I'd already be in jail over Tiny Bobchek's murder. And if not for my friend, knowing anything about Hector LaTiara wouldn't have done me one lick of good.

IT WAS ABOUT ELEVEN when I drove down the 1600 block of Hauser, then left onto Saturn. It was a narrow street there below Pico. The dwellings were single-family houses and two- and three-unit apartment buildings. Most everybody was at work. The yards were empty. The birds were cheeping.

There was no car at the address given for Mr. LaTiara. The apartment building was red and cream stucco, tall for L.A., three floors. I sat there patiently, remembering Mum's kisses, fearing the iron bars of California justice.

At twelve fifteen Jessa stumbled out of the arched entrance to Hector's building. She was wearing a pale green dress that didn't seem done up right. She looked confused standing there on the concrete path to the first-floor entrance of the building.

Another problem I have is that I don't have enough respect for women. I'm not saying that I don't try to be civil by opening doors and keeping my eyes in check. The problem is that I don't fear women enough.

Seeing Jessa, I jumped out of my car and made it across the street before considering what her presence there might have meant. She was turning in a slow circle, looking up as if the sun had robbed her of her senses.

"Jessa, what are you doing here?" I asked, coming up to her.

At first she didn't respond. Then she looked me in the eye. After a moment, I think she recognized me. I thought she was going to tell me something, but then she screamed and socked me in the jaw.

Then next thing I knew I was flat on my back on the lawn.

I sat up, befuddled. Jessa was screaming again but she was also running. I watched her go down the street at a good clip and wondered what I should do.

I decided that going back to my car would be a mistake. If anyone saw me, they might get the license plate, and then the police would have my name and Jessa's face at least. I couldn't walk down the street—I just couldn't. And so I decided that going into the red building was my best choice.

It might not have been a good decision, but I was a little shaken by Jessa's sucker punch.

Once inside the entrance of the building, I was presented with two choices. To the left was a circular stairway that led to the apartments above, and straight ahead was the doorway to the first-floor abode.

Another easy choice. The door to the first-floor apartment was open.

I walked in gingerly. If there was someone there, I didn't want to scare them.

The foyer was a small room in its own right. Salmon pink walls and a dark wood chair with an ivory white cushion in the seat. The carpet was a yellow background supporting dozens of woven red roses. There was a telephone on the floor, marking a place where a stand should have been, I imagined. And there was a portrait of a white woman on a horse. The woman and horse were on a path in front of a white fence. In the distance was an apple orchard, beyond that a mountain range.

I remember much more about that foyer. I remember the baseboard around the floor and the yellow-and-red light fixture on the ceiling. I could spend a great deal of time on the dimensions of the room and the odd shape of it . . . but that's because of what happened in the next room, the room I should never have entered.

It was a den of some sort: half office, half study. It was dark. There was a desk behind which were closed drapes. There was a high-backed office chair, and sitting on it was Hector LaTiara, the man who had come to me looking for a French dictionary, the man Useless was so frightened of.

He was wearing a vanilla-colored jacket and a white shirt, both of which were bad choices because of his throat being slashed open. Thick, gelatinous blood had flowed, lavalike, down the fair material. An arc of blood had sprayed across the papers on his desk.

One of his eyes was wide with fright, the other half closed. His lips, even in his last moments, curled into a superior sneer, as if he were trying to convey to his murderer that he had been through worse than this.

I was mesmerized by the brutality and the blood. My

gorge rose, but I wouldn't turn away. My body shook, but I wouldn't take a step. A voice in the back of my mind was screaming, "Run! Run! Run!" But I stayed in place, gawking at the paradigm of murder.

My breathing had become very shallow. I was almost panting, with very little oxygen getting to my brain. So I put my hands on my knees and squatted down like a sprinter after a hard-run race. It worked. I took in deeper breaths, and the paralysis began to lift.

But bending over, I put myself closer to the corpse.

His left hand held a broken pencil. He'd probably snapped it when he first felt the razor on his throat. There was blood on the pencil and all over both hands. You could see that he'd grabbed for the wound without releasing what he held. Then, as he died, the hands came back down to the note he'd been writing:

Martin Friar, UEC, 2750.00

"Mr. LaTiara?" a frail voice called.

How I moved so swiftly behind the maroon drapes I cannot say. All I know is that one moment I was frozen in awe, reading the upside-down note, and the next I was behind the thick fabric. There was a tiny tear through which I could see the room beyond the dead man's chair.

"Mr. LaTiara?"

And then, long moments later, a small and ancient white woman doddered in. She had the blue hair of an old woman and a face that would have fit on the smallest of animals.

"Oh, no," she whispered, and I was convinced, absolutely, that she would fall down dead from fright.

But I was wrong. She moved closer to the desk than I had dared and stared deeply at the man. Her tiny face became steely and she turned away, walking from the room with more fortitude than she had coming in.

My enemy became that telephone in the foyer. If she stopped there to call the police, I was done for. Either she'd see me or they would come and find me.

I could sneak up on her, knock her senseless, and run—but no. She was too old and I was too close to my mother.

A minute passed and I heard nothing.

Another minute.

I moved out from behind the curtain and into the foyer. The woman was gone.

I went back into the foyer and through another door. This led to a kitchen, which had a back door that led to a yard. Then there was a fence, another yard, an alley, a street. I ran as fast as I could until I was in the driver's seat of my jalopy again. As I turned the ignition, I heard the far-off whine of sirens.

My heart was beating like bongo drums; my soul was deep in the ecstasy of escape.

23 I DROVE DIRECTLY FROM the scene of the murder to Santa Monica Beach.

Whenever I am frightened I head for water. Don't ask me why. I'm not a good swimmer and I don't know the first thing about boats. My uncle always used to say that the fish must have known it was me at the other end of that line because they never took my bait.

But despite all that, the water makes me feel secure. The Mississippi and the Gulf of Mexico were my solace in Louisiana; now that I was a Californian, the great Pacific was my protector.

I went to a bench in a park that stood maybe a hundred feet above the ocean at the end of Olympic Boulevard. There I sat and tried to make sense out of a life that, if I were a white man, should have been as boring as a cardboard box.

The last time I had anything to do with Jessa I found her lover murdered on my floor. And now I had found her again and another man had been murdered, a man who was after my cousin Useless.

It almost made sense. Almost.

I couldn't hear the waves but I could see them, cresting white and breaking rank at the sand.

Useless was being followed by Hector. Hector, for some unknown reason, had killed Tiny. Then Jessa, who knows why, had gone away with Hector. Now Hector was dead.

There were people I had never met who were involved with Useless. There was the white man Stringly and the men who were being blackmailed or extorted or whatever. There was Mad Anthony, whom I did know.

What I didn't know was if any of this mattered to me.

At almost any other time I would have gone home and left the killing of Hector LaTiara to the LAPD. They wouldn't care too much about a black man getting his throat cut. And if they decided to investigate, it would be about the criminal life he lived and not about some Negro bookseller from South L.A. But I had already tried to ignore a crime that had come to me via my cousin. Tiny's corpse was stalking me still. Hector might do so too.

After this last thought my mind went blank. I couldn't get any further into the problem. I was not the kind of man who made bold decisions about events that could harm or kill me. I moved behind drapes, sought out shadows. But there I was in the light of day between the rock (Three Hearts) and the hard place (her son).

"BAIL BONDS," Loretta Kuroko answered on the first ring.

"Loretta."

"Hi, Paris," she said happily. "Hold on."

"Hello?" Fearless said.

"Hey, man."

"You sound like the house burnt down and the dog died," he said. "What's wrong?"

"I got to see you, Fearless, and this really ain't the kinda talk you can have on the phone."

"Okay, man. Fine. Milo off wit' Whisper, so I could take some time. I don't have a car, though."

"I'm out at the beach," I said. "Santa Monica."

First-time lovers and real friends don't need much language. Fearless knew my predilection for the sea when I was frightened. He knew I would find it hard to come to him.

"You at the place you usually go?" he asked.

"No. But I can get there."

"See ya in forty-five minutes, Paris. Hold on, brother."

MY *USUAL PLACE* WAS A PATCH of sand about a hundred feet south of the Santa Monica Pier, midway between the ocean and the boardwalk. I climbed down the long stairway from the park to the beach and then trudged along the shoreline to that place.

Along the way I didn't think about anything bad or threatening. I had come to the dead end of my abilities and that had led to a blank wall. There was nothing else I could do. I was actually too afraid to consider doing anything more. The blood down Hector's chest made me blind and deaf. I wasn't built for that kind of confrontation.

I made it to my place in the sand and sat down with no blanket or bottle of beer. It was just me sitting on hot silicon under a brutal sun. The heat moved around me, that and the cacophonous music of the waves.

I didn't even have a hat; nor did I desire one. I wanted the sun to beat down on me; I wanted the waves to crash senselessly. I was an innocent man, but no one would believe it. The only solace I had was the pulse of an ocean that had been there before there was even a fish to befoul it.

A CLOUD COVERED THE SUN for a moment, and my head felt a momentary coolness.

"Hey, Paris," the cloud said.

Fearless sat down next to me on the hot bed of sand.

"Hey, man," I replied. "How'd you get here?"

"Amos taxi."

"I'll pay you for the fare."

"Your mother ain't sick, is she?" he asked.

I shook my head no.

"You ain't bleedin', broken, or dyin' as far as I can see. So don't be too sad."

I laughed and threw a play punch at him. He blocked me out of reflex, and I almost began to cry.

"Tell me what happened," Fearless said, and I unburdened myself about the dead man and the white girl and my feelings of helplessness.

"Damn," Fearless said at the end of my tale. "Somebody sneaked up on him and cut his th'oat like that? That's serious bidness there. That's a assassin doin' his job right. An' what was the white girl doin' wit' 'im?"

"Hector musta killed Tiny," I said. "That's all I can think. And then, and then . . . And then either he grabbed Jessa or she ran with him."

"Why she wanna run with the man kilt her man?" Fearless asked.

"I don't know. Maybe Tiny started takin' it out on her

when I got away. Maybe Hector came in and didn't like seein' a woman bein' beat by a man. If that's the way it came down, then she might'a run with him because he saved her. On the other hand, he might'a killed Tiny out of self-defense and then took the girl to keep her from talkin'. For that matter, Jessa might have snuck up on Hector an' cut his throat to get away.

"I ain't worried about any'a that. It's Useless's part in it that bothers me."

"I don't even see how Useless comes in," Fearless agreed.

"I see how it might happen," I said. "It's just that I don't know why."

I realized that in the presence of Fearless Jones I had the courage to think again. It was a fleeting thought.

"How so?" Fearless said.

Two young white women wearing one-piece bathing suits walked near us. One of them looked at Fearless and smiled. He smiled and waved, and the two women scurried away laughing, throwing him sideways glances.

"Hector and Useless were in business getting money from white men over some kind of blackmail or threat," I said. "Useless was cheating Hector—that goes without sayin'. . . ." Fearless chuckled and I went on. "Hector's after Useless and somehow Useless decides to use me for his shill. Either he gonna leave somethin' with me or tell Hector, or somebody Hector knows, that he did. That way he have Hector comin' after me while he gets away with his plans."

"What plans?"

"He's been movin' money through Jerry Twist. Maybe he wants to go where the money is."

"And Hector comes up on you but finds Tiny and the white girl," Fearless said.

"Yeah. And then, when I'm down in the basement with the body, he comes back and searches for whatever it is Useless said he gave me."

"And then he comes back again lookin' for the dictionary," Fearless said.

"Yeah."

"But why didn't he pull out a gun or somethin' then?"

"I don't know," I said. "Maybe enough time had passed that he knew where whatever he was looking for was."

"But then why come to you at all?"

"I don't know," I said. "I don't know."

"Well, you bettah know sumpin' soon, man. Old Three Hearts not gonna wait forever. I dropped by Nadine's house just to see how your auntie was doin', and Nadine told me that Hearts was out day and night tryin' to get a line on her son. You know that's gonna be trouble for somebody."

"Shit," I said. "Damn." And with those two epithets my paralysis was completely over. "We need to look into these white businesses Useless was fleecin'," I said. "We need to get in someplace and find out what he was up to."

"Yeah, Paris. Yeah, man. Let's do it."

"Or maybe," I said, "maybe I could sell my bookstore and take my savings and move to China. They speak English in Hong Kong. I could sell books there."

"One night with Mum don't make you a Chin'ee, man," Fearless said.

"How you know about her?"

"I saw her lookin' at you," he said. "I know that look."

24

WHENEVER FEARLESS CAME to the beach he wanted fish and chips at Briny's down in Venice. Briny was an older white gentleman who had lost his left leg below the knee and his right eye during his years at sea. The one eye he had left was gray; so was his hair and the pallor under his tanned white skin.

The first time we ate at the dive, Briny was being harassed by an angry white guy. The guy, his name was Lux, had a torso that was as big as half a keg of beer. He looked as strong as any man I ever met. Lux had decided, for some unknown reason, to make Briny the object of all his hatred.

When we got to the restaurant that first time, Briny had seated us and served us without any strange looks or hesitance. Negroes at that time appreciated fair service of that type in white establishments. But his acceptance went further than that. When he'd been whole he was a merchant marine and had spent some time down in New Orleans. We swapped stories about that city, even knew a name or two in common.

Fearless and Briny were getting pretty friendly when Lux came in.

"Hey you, Riley," the big white man shouted. "Come over here and make me some whitefish and eggs. I'm hungry and I'm horny as a toad. I got some pussy waitin' down the street. It's old pussy, so I need eggs t'get it up and fish to cut the smell."

No one could read Fearless like I could. His face darkened almost imperceptibly. His eyes shifted a thousandth of an inch. Fearless didn't abide rudeness, and there was no room in his heart for a man bad-mouthing a woman, whether she was there or not. Add that to the fact that he'd become fond of Briny in the hour we'd been in the dingy restaurant and you had a recipe for trouble.

Neither one of us liked it when Briny cowered and scuttled over to Lux saying, "Yes, sir, Mr. Lux."

But still, Fearless would have probably let it ride. Then Lux had to go and throw his plate on the floor when he didn't like his eggs. He slapped our host and unleashed a string of curses and threats that one usually only heard in prison.

Lux was in the middle of a complex description of Briny's mother when Fearless tapped the big man's shoulder.

There were seven other customers in Briny's that late afternoon. They were all witnesses to the spectacle.

Lux turned his head slowly to regard my friend. Fearless is tall, but Lux was too. The white demon had at least twenty more pounds of muscle than did my friend. And Lux was fifty pounds heavier. All of those other customers must have thought that the foolish Negro was about to get his head torn off.

"What, boy?" Lux asked.

"Let's step outside," Fearless said, gesturing at a window that showed a small backyard Briny used as a kind of dump for large appliances gone bad.

Briny rubbed his sore jaw and gaped at Fearless.

Lux nodded and gestured for Fearless to go first.

"You first," Fearless told him. "You go out first and then I'll come number two."

It was like watching a fight on a television with the volume control broken. I have never seen my friend more vicious, accurate, or sadistic in battle. After he'd knocked Lux down for the fourth time, the big man stayed on the dirt. But Fearless wouldn't have it; he beat the man on the ground until he got up and fought again. Fearless knocked out teeth and opened cuts all over the brutal bully's face. He broke a whole rack of ribs and caused deep bruising that would follow Lux all the days of his life. When Fearless was finished, he removed Lux's wallet from his pocket and took something from it (later I found out that this was Lux's driver's license). He said something to Lux and then slapped the man until he nodded. Then he pulled Lux to his feet. The big white man pleaded with Fearless not to hit him again; that was the only thing we heard through the closed window. But Fearless didn't hit him. He merely pushed him toward the door. Lux lumbered through the room with his eyes on the floor and pain in every step. When he went out the front, Fearless came in the back.

"You got a pencil?" he asked Briny.

The ex-seaman nodded and pulled a yellow number two from his pocket. Then he handed Fearless the receipt pad he used for his patrons' bills.

"This my mother's phone numbah," Fearless said, scribbling at the counter. "If that motherfucker ever even look in yo' windah again, I want you to call this numbah an' tell her to tell me about it."

And so we became semiregulars at Briny's. Lux, who had hectored Briny for two years, never returned, and we always had to force Briny to take our money.

"Fearless. Paris," Briny hailed.

He served us fried clams and talked about Louisiana. He bought our beers, but we paid for the food.

"Briny," Fearless said after the restaurateur brought us our change.

"What, my friend?"

"Paris an' me need a phone and some privacy for a hour or two."

"My office is yours," he said. He might have said the same thing even if Fearless hadn't broken Lux almost in two.

"WYNANT INVESTMENT GROUP," a young woman said, answering my call.

I was looking out onto the backyard where Fearless had demolished Lux.

"Yes," I said. "I'm looking for a Mr. Katz."

"No Katz here," she replied in a friendly tone.

"Oh," I said. "I see. Mr. Drummund, then."

"Sorry, sir. No Mr. Drummund either. If you can tell me the nature of your call, I might be able to pass you on to someone else."

"You know," I replied. "I think I must have the wrong number. You said Haversham Investments, right?"

"No. Wynant. Wynant Investments."

"I'm so sorry," I said. "Excuse me."

I made half a dozen calls like that while Fearless sat back on a walnut chair, smoking one of my Lucky Strikes and staring up into space. He wasn't listening to me or worrying about anything. I'm sure he was the same in the lull between battles during the war.

There was a V.P. named Katz at Casualty and Life Insurance Company of St. Louis. I got as far as his assistant.

"He's tied up at the moment," the man said. "May I tell him what your business is?"

"My name is LaTiara," I said. "Hector LaTiara. I've recently come into a great deal of money. Seventy thousand dollars that I've inherited from my uncle Anthony."

"Yes?"

"I don't know anything about investing and so I wondered if we could set up an appointment or something."

"I'm sure one of the junior agents at the firm would be happy to advise you, Mr. LaTiara. Mr. Katz, however, only deals with portfolios of a million dollars or more."

"You mean my money's not good enough for him?" I said. For some reason I really was insulted.

"It's good," the snooty young man replied. "It's just not enough money."

I knew the type. It had nothing to do with race, even though he must have been a white man. He was the sort that identified with his master so closely that he believed he was the arbiter of those million-dollar investors. Here he probably didn't make seventy dollars a week, but he still sneered at my paltry seventy grand.

I hung up on him.

Three calls later, at Holy Cross Episcopal, I found a

rector named Drummund—or least I got a woman who answered using his name.

"Reverend Drummund's office," she said in a well-worn but not world-weary voice.

"Hector LaTiara," I said, but there was a hesitation in my tone.

"Yes?"

She didn't know the name, hadn't heard it before—I could tell. I could have come up with a story, but I held back.

"Hello?" she said.

Still I remained silent.

"Is anyone there?"

I put the receiver down softly, this time because of caution rather than petty anger. I took a deep breath and let it out slowly.

"What's wrong?" Fearless asked me.

"I don't know what to say."

"What you mean?"

"So far," I said, "you an' me been outside the place where Useless an' them been workin'. Nobody knows us and nobody can tie us up with the crimes."

"If there is a crime."

"There's two dead men, Fearless," I said. "How much more crime do you want?"

"I mean about the money," my friend replied. "We don't even know if there ever was any money in them wrappers."

"You think Jerry Twist woulda lied about that?"

"Go on," Fearless said. "Tell me why you cain't talk to them but you can chatter all ovah me."

"Drummund don't know us," I said. "Katz neither. I

cain't just walk in on 'em, 'cause they're important men. They ain't gonna have nobody like you or me walk in their offices, not unless we tell 'em about LaTiara or Useless."

"Cain't tell 'em 'bout Ulysses," Fearless said. "Hearts wouldn't like that."

"That don't even mattah," I said. "'Cause if we call 'em an' tell 'em 'bout how we know about them bein' blackmailed or whatevah, they might just call the cops. They don't know Hector's real name, I'm sure'a that, and so when the police ask us and then find Hector dead, where will we be?"

Fearless smiled. Smiled. Here I was explaining how our whole enterprise was stalled in the water, and he just grinned as if I had told a half-funny joke.

"You'll figure it out, Paris," he told me.

"Aren't you listening to me, man?" I asked. "I'm sayin' I don't know what to do."

"That's okay," he said. "That's how everything start. First you don't know an' then you do."

25 | THE DAY WAS WENDING into evening while Fearless and I walked along the shore. We were friends, there was no doubt about that, but our relationship was also hard to define. Sometimes I was like the big brother who could read complex documents and decipher the logical knots that faced my simpleminded friend. At other times he was like the ideal father that had never abandoned me, protecting me from danger. On that particular evening he was this selfsame father who saw my troubles and only said that he believed in me and that I would see my way through in time.

Maybe all true friendships are like that: like rolling rivers rather than edifices of stone. I don't know. All I had on my mind was how I could get information from Katz and Drummund without them calling the cops on me.

"You tired, Paris?" Fearless asked, as the setting sun ignited the pollutants in the evening sky, making a fiery red sunset that had all of the ecstasy and terror of a heart attack.

"Naw, man. I couldn't sleep if I wanted to."

"That's good. 'Cause you know I think we gonna have to work hard tonight."

"Why's that?"

"Al Rive's in town."

"Really? He really came back?" I asked.

"Yeah, brother. First he put his mother in the soup an' now he wanna hurt Milo for turnin' on the heat. Whisper fount him out, but before we could get there he was gone. Tomorrow I be full-time either chasin' Al or body-guardin' Milo's butt."

"You a good friend, Fearless."

"Why not? Friendship is free."

WE DROVE FROM THE BEACH down to Nadine Grant's many-flowered home.

As we were walking through the gated fence toward the front door, Three Hearts was coming out. She was wearing all white, which was never a good sign. White was what Three Hearts wore when she was bringing God with her on her mission, whatever that mission was. It was lore in our family that Three Hearts wearing white meant that she was going to someone's funeral— and that someone didn't need to be dead yet.

"Hey, Hearts," Fearless said, holding out hands of greeting and restraint.

"Out of my way, Fearless," she commanded. "I got places to be."

"Who's drivin' you?" he asked, both friendly and stern.

"Toby Battrell," she said, waving a white-gloved hand at the street.

Standing there next to a 1940s wood-paneled station wagon was a teenage boy. His shirttails were hanging out and his plump body seemed to be made from fudge.

"That's a child right there, Hearts," Fearless said. "What's his mama gonna say when you put him out there in front'a Mad Anthony or some other crazy fool like that?"

"Toby will stay in the car."

"In the middle'a the night in places where Ulysses might be? Hearts?" Fearless entreated. "You cain't be draggin' no child around where trouble grow. You know that, baby."

"Who said that I'm goin' out lookin' for trouble?" Three Hearts said to the ground at her feet.

"Toby," Fearless called.

"Yessir?"

My friend flipped a coin across the void. The boy made a valiant effort, but he missed and had to run after the silver disk as it rolled down the asphalt.

"That's a dollar," Fearless said when the awkward ballet was through. "Go on home now. Me an' Paris will drive Mrs. Grant."

When the boy flashed a grin I decided I liked him. He jumped into his station wagon and rolled away to safety.

"Now, where you wanna go, Hearts?" Fearless asked my auntie.

I didn't speak because I would always be a child in the eyes of my family. Even with my mustache they treated me according to my size and temperament. That's why Three Hearts could use Toby on a risky venture and not realize how wrong she was.

But Fearless was born an adult. People always listened

to him; even white folks cocked an ear when they were in trouble and Fearless offered to help.

"There's a house down around Compton," she said. "I wanna go there."

"What's there?" I asked. I just couldn't keep quiet.

"Ain't none'a your business."

"Hearts," Fearless said. "We your people here. Why you wanna stonewall us?"

Three Hearts looked up into my friend's eyes with something like evil festering in hers. I did not know another man or woman who knew Three Hearts that wouldn't back down from that stare.

Fearless grinned.

"I ain't scared'a you, Hearts," he said. "You know I'm tryin' to help ya. You know you need us wit' you to help your son. So don't be pullin' no evil-eye stuff on me."

Nadine had come to the screen door. She was looking at the encounter with something like fear in her face.

Three Hearts began to tremble. Her fists were knotted in rage. I swear I felt lightning gather in the sky. It took all of my courage not to step away from Fearless.

"It's that girl," Three Hearts hissed. "I found out from a woman. I'm goin' down there to get her spell off my son."

FROM THE BACKSEAT of my car on the way to Compton, she told us the tale.

"I know you been lookin', Paris," she said. "An' I appreciate it, baby. But I couldn't just sit there in Nadine's house an' watch the flowers grow. I had to get out an' do sumpin'. And so Nadine told me about Toby. He done got put outta school fo' stealin' from the canteen, an' his mama want him to work. So I hired him for fifty cent a hour t'drive me. I buy his lunch an' pay the gas, an' he took me to every church around here.

"I must'a gone to twenty churches when I finally fount a woman who knew a woman that this Angel girl done messed wit'. I knew it was gonna be sumpin' like that. Her Christian name is Allmont. She was in this one church, Triumph of the Lord Holy Baptist, when she lured Tyree Mullins inta sin. His wife, Cleo, couldn't do nuthin' about it. It was like he had a fever. He kept tellin' Cleo that it wasn't nuthin' romantic or sex but that he was just tryin' t'help the girl. He owns some property ovah in Compton an' he put her up there. She don't pay no rent, don't buy her own food or her clothes. If she get sick he there wit' her before his own chirren. That's the woman that have beguiled my poor son."

I didn't know how much truth or rumor or fabrication by Three Hearts herself had gone into that story, but I did know that Tommy Hoag had used the name Allmont when referring to Angel. Three Hearts had brought us to the door I was looking for, the door I needed to go through in order to effect a plan that had an escape hatch if need be.

Where I was satisfied, Three Hearts was seething. I could feel her evil orb roving in the backseat, looking for just the right calamity to befall the slut-Jezebel who had led her pure and innocent son down the path of wickedness.

I would have felt good if it weren't for my auntie. Her anger would get in the way of my getting her out of California and back to the superstitious boondocks of the Creoles and Cajuns. Her anger was the promise of a great explosion that would rip open the crime her son had most definitely committed. And in the aftermath of that detonation, the police might come and drag me away for extortion, theft, and multiple murders.

But I couldn't get too lost in the dangerous atmosphere in which I found myself. We were about to get to Useless's girlfriend. And if Fearless could daunt Three Hearts just enough, I might get in there and figure a way to placate her and send her and her son far away.

COMPTON WAS A NICE LITTLE TOWN at that time. The houses were almost all one-story single-family dwellings. The yards were wide and green. The sidewalks were newly laid concrete, white and unmarred by the passage of workingmen's feet. If there were trees along the curbs they were imported, because there hadn't been enough time for them to grow.

All in all, Angel's neighborhood was like a brand-new Christmas present given by a king to his patient and penitent peasants.

Angel lived at 1203¾ Snyder. Number 1203 was a large salmon pink house with a friendly family window that had the drapes pulled. At the side of the driveway was a bank of mailboxes, four of them to coincide with the addresses up to ¾.

Number 1203¼ was an emerald green place, half the size of the front building. There was a gnarled oak on one side (obviously from a time before the area was subdivided) and ten rows of corn on the other. Behind that house was a long flat building painted white and divided into two separate addresses. The one on the right was 1203¾.

Even though Three Hearts rushed forward, Fearless got there first and knocked. Three Hearts was muttering hateful curses to herself, and darkness had fallen. There was a quarter moon to our right and crickets could be heard everywhere.

The door opened and we were flooded with yellow light.

She was much more beautiful than even her photograph had promised. The medium brown skin was closer to burnished copper. The straightened hair seemed to flow so naturally that you would have thought that she was an American Indian. The surprise in her eyes and the goddess's lips' parting were for Three Hearts. You would have thought that my auntie was Angel's long-lost sister instead of the instrument of her doom.

"I love your son, Mrs. Grant," the epitome of beauty uttered.

And to my eternally enduring surprise, Three Hearts broke down crying.

26

NOT WHIMPERING OR SOBS but deep, soul-wrenching howls came from Three Hearts's chest. She made the sounds that women made when they heard that a child or a husband had died. It was a funeral cry.

Fearless put his arms around my auntie, and she fell into the embrace. He supported her across the threshold while she bawled and shrieked.

For her part, Angel was dismayed at the elder woman's desolate abandon. She clasped her hands together and guided Fearless to a broad black couch in the center of a very modern room. In front of the couch was a console that had a TV and a record player inside the red-stained maple box. There were copies of abstract paintings on the walls that seemed to be influenced by a jazz sensibility. There was one bookcase and various chairs that went together but did not match. The wood floor was bright white pine and the walls were also white. There were a dozen lamps placed haphazardly around the large space. Some were standing posts, others table lamps. All of them were on.

I liked a brightly lit room; made me feel that nothing underhanded was going on. Of course I knew brightness and honesty weren't necessarily friends.

Three Hearts moaned and shouted for some time. There could have been bloody murder being committed in that bungalow, but no neighbor called the cops. I was glad that they didn't, but then again, it bothered me too.

Angel, who was wearing a pink dress that would have been a shirt had it been any shorter, brought ice water and knelt down in front of Three Hearts.

"Here, baby," the boundless beauty said. "Take some water. Drink it down. Let it cool you."

Then Angel put her hand to Three Hearts's forehead as if she were the older woman's mother feeling for fever.

And my auntie accepted the attention. Here I would have told you that Three Hearts would have bitten that hand if it got too close. Instead she let her head loll back and her eyes close, allowing the Jezebel to minister to her.

Fearless found a bottle of whiskey and some ice and poured us both a draft. That liquor was just what I needed.

"I'm so sorry, Mrs. Grant," Angel said just as soon as Three Hearts settled down. "I know how much pain you must be in. Ulysses got in a whole mess of trouble, and I didn't know what to do."

As I have said, Three Hearts is my blood. I have known that woman since I could speak my own name. Never in all the time before that moment had I witnessed her allow man, woman, or child to lay blame at her son's feet.

"What did he do to you, child?" Three Hearts asked Angel. "I see it stitched in your face. What did he do?"

"It wasn't him," Angel said. "He couldn't help it. He got mixed up with those men and before he knew it we were in too deep."

"He tries so hard," Three Hearts sobbed.

The women hugged over their love. It was almost as if they were competing over who could love the little rat more.

I drained my glass. Fearless refilled it. I drained it again and Fearless was right on the job.

Half the way through my third glass of bourbon I looked around me. There I was, a mortal man flanked by Venus, Mars, and Juno. I wondered if Fate was standing outside the door, if he would allow me to stand up and walk away, just walk away from all that craziness. Maybe if I asked her right, Mum would take me in. We could discuss Spinoza and Karl Marx over dumplings and white rice.

That was a beautiful thought. I allowed myself fifteen seconds to wallow in it. I'd go to college and teach English at a boarding school in Jamaica.

"Excuse me," I said when the daydream was done.

Angel and Three Hearts turned to me.

Fearless refilled my glass for the fourth time.

"What is it, Paris?" my auntie asked. She didn't like her grief being interrupted.

"I know you ladies can read each other's minds and all," I said. "You seein' invisible scars and like that. But for the menfolk here who don't have your powers, could somebody please tell me where Ulysses has gone to?"

"I don't know where he is," Angel said. She rose up from her knees as if there were no gravity at her feet.

I felt some consternation because when I looked at her

the rest of the room got fuzzy. At first I told myself that it was the whiskey, but then I looked at Fearless—the world around him was clear.

So I tried not to look directly into Angel's eyes. That way I could converse with her without falling into some kind of crazy enchantment.

"But you an' him was in business," I said, all business myself.

"No," she replied.

"What about Mr. Katz and Reverend Drummund?" I said. "Mad Anthony and Hector LaTiara?"

"You know about them?" Angel asked, seeking but not finding my eyes.

"I know about thirteen churches, banks, insurance companies, and investment firms," I said. "I know about at least seventy thousand dollars that you and Use... Ulysses had in your apartment at Man's Barn."

Angel gasped at every other syllable. She fell onto a chair that sat next the sofa. Three Hearts was glaring at me for being so cruel to her new best friend—the woman she had wanted to murder less than half an hour ago. But I didn't feel the effect of my auntie's evil eye. I realized then that alcohol was proof against her spells.

"How did it work, Angel?" I asked.

"You know my name," she replied, "but I don't know either of yours."

"Jones," my friend said first. "Fearless Jones."

"Oh," Angel crooned. "I've heard all about you. You're famous."

Fearless smiled. Even he could be flattered by an angel.

"Paris," I said. "Paris Minton."

"Oh, yes. You're Ullie's cousin. He felt really bad

about that time the police arrested you. He didn't know that they'd come to your house."

"Who was the man you left with when you ran out on Ulysses?" I asked.

"It's not like it seems, Mrs. Grant," she said. "I left, but it was because Ulysses wanted me to. He said that La-Tiara was after him and he didn't want me to get hurt."

I laughed then.

I don't get drunk all that often. And I don't believe that inebriation is any panacea to a poor man's problems. But now and then a good buzz will help you through when the ground is trembling and the mountains are coming down.

"Angel," I said slowly and deliberately, "Hector is dead, had his throat cut."

"Whaaat?" Three Hearts sang.

"I have reason to believe that Hector killed somebody else tryin' t'find my cousin. So I really wish you'd stop bein' all beautiful an' perfect for just a minute and answer some simple fuckin' questions."

"Paris," Fearless said.

"You could leave any time you want, Fearless. This girl here got us up to our necks in crocodiles, and I cain't help what comes outta my mouth."

"Excuse him, ma'am," Fearless said. "He's been under some strain. He needs to know who it is killin' who out here. He needs to know it or he won't be able to sleep in his bed."

"I, I didn't know about Hector," Angel said then. Maybe she didn't.

"What were Hector and Ulysses doin'?" I asked.

Angel looked to be full of information, but she didn't say a word.

"I got to know, girl," I said, the whiskey awash in my brain.

"I don't know you, Paris," she said. "The kind of trouble Ullie is in could put him . . . and me in jail."

"I bet Hector would take jail over what he got," I opined.

"Hector was a friend of Ullie's," she said. "Not so much a friend but an acquaintance. Hector knew a white man named Sterling. Sterling knew about men," she said tentatively.

"What kind of men?" I asked.

"Men like Katz and Reverend Drummund."

"Rich men?"

"Not rich but in charge of great wealth."

"Oh, Lord," Three Hearts moaned.

"What was the hook?" I asked.

"Me," Angel said softly but without any deep sense of shame that I could tell.

"How so?"

"I'd go to them with a purse full of money. Five thousand dollars in fifties and hundreds and the promise that I had ten times that. I'd say that I wanted to invest the money in their companies or, in the case of the church, that I wanted to use it for the greater good. When they'd wonder how I made the money, I told them about a system I used in betting in poker games. Hector would set up a fake game and I'd go there with the reverend or V.P. and show them how I'd win. The game was always fixed. After a few nights they'd be hooked and get into a big game where I'd lose ten, maybe twenty thousand dollars of their institution's money. After that Hector would blackmail them, threatening to tell their employers that they'd put the company's money on the line."

At the last words, she shed a tear and swallowed a sob. I believed that they were cheating those men but not that poor Angel was an innocent who regretted her part in the scheme. She regretted Ulysses running away with her money. She regretted some killer hungering after her soft throat. But she didn't give a damn about the men whose lives she'd ruined.

I didn't care about them either, but I wasn't the one who brought them down.

"You poor child," Three Hearts said.

"You have any idea where my cousin is?" I asked.

"There's a cabin in the Angeles National Forest. Sterling owns it. Ullie liked to go up there."

27

I HAD UNLOCKED the doors of my Studebaker for the women to climb in back. I was about to get in the driver's seat when Fearless said, "Uh, Paris?"

"Yeah?"

"You bettah let me drive, man."

"Why?"

"'Cause you drunk."

I looked at him and took in a deep breath.

"I am not."

Fearless put one finger against my chest and shoved with barely any force. I would have been on the ground if the car wasn't behind me.

How many whiskies had I downed? I couldn't remember.

I fell into the driver's seat and crawled to the other side. Fearless got in and put his hand out for the key.

While I was giving it to him, Three Hearts said, "You really should watch your liquor, Paris."

"Watch my liquor? Watch my liquor? What I should do is watch my front do'."

"Paris," Fearless warned.

"That's right. If I watched the do', then Useless wouldn't come up and hide stolen property in my toilet. You wouldn't come up gettin' me so deep in trouble that I cain't even think about nuthin' else. I'm drinkin' so I don't have to run down the street yellin' like a madman done lost his mind."

I stared at Three Hearts in the backseat. She looked away in disgust. Her disdain made me so angry that I was about to rant some more, but Fearless put his foot on the accelerator, and somehow the gravity pushing me against the seat displaced the anger too. I felt a wave of pleasant intoxication and leaned back against the door.

For a long time I stared at Angel's profile. It certainly was perfect. Daughter, wife, lover, mother—she could have been everything and anything to man, woman, or child. There was haughtiness and a waiting smile, knowledge that you could never have, and simple conversation. She was the woman who was the power behind the king and the widow that survived him.

I hated Angel Allmont, but it wasn't because of my cousin. I didn't care about Useless. He could die and never be found. Three Hearts could light a candle every night for him until the candleholder overflowed with wax and her wood shanty burned to the ground—I didn't care about them. No. I hated Angel Allmont because looking at her made me feel small.

"So what else?" I said in a voice that was too loud for the small space of the car.

"Excuse me?" Angel said. She wasn't even looking at me, but she knew what I was asking and to whom my question was addressed.

"You know," I said. "What else did Sterling know about those white men?"

For a long moment I thought that Angel was not going to look at me. But then she turned and gave me the full treatment.

"I support my mother, Mr. Minton," she said. "Her and her sister, my five-year-old son, and a man who once saved me from a rapist."

Three Hearts put a hand on Angel's shoulder.

"That ain't what I asked you," I said, wondering at the man that lay inside me.

"They were men who . . . enjoyed black women," she said at last. "They hungered for dark flesh."

"Your flesh?"

"Paris," Fearless said again.

"Yes, Mr. Minton, my flesh."

"Did you use to go with them up to this here cabin?"

"There. Hotel rooms, beach houses, rectory couches, and back-alley slums." There was distaste on her lips but not shame, not humiliation.

"So you seduced them?" I asked, as if my tongue were a scalpel and her dignity a malignant tumor that had to be excised.

"If you had been there you would see it differently," Angel said in an even voice. "Their blood was boiling from the minute they saw me. Ullie told me that this was how we could save my family. I would have done a lot worse for them."

She'd beaten me. Three Hearts was now holding the girl's hands. Fearless sat there, his posture in the stoic demeanor of respect.

I turned my back against the door. I was falling into a

stupor. Soon sleep would come and take me, just as one day Death would come knocking on my door.

"PARIS," FEARLESS SAID, and I opened my eyes.

"What?"

"Cops."

I turned and looked out the back window. The flashing blue and red lights caused a chemical reaction in my brain. I don't know the names of the particular ingredients, but three seconds after I was awakened I was also as sober as a judge.

"I'm pullin' ovah," Fearless said. "Get ready."

My sobriety turned into a microscopic lens then. Fearless saying to get ready meant that he was prepared to go to war.

"Fearless," I said as he pulled to the curb.

"What?"

"We don't need to fight here."

"We got to get to Ulysses, man. These cops in the way."

The squad car pulled up behind us. They shone a bright white light from their car into ours.

"There's no reason to hurt anybody, Fearless. We'll get out of this."

A young white man was coming up to the driver's window. He was wearing a policeman's uniform and trained to enforce a certain kind of law; he was arrogant and sure of himself, but he didn't know that if I didn't talk just right he was about to be killed.

"I got it, Fearless. I got it, man."

The tension went out of my friend.

The police hadn't made it to the door yet. Fearless was

rolling down his window in expectation. But my mind was back down the road we had just traveled. Three Hearts had thought she knew Angel from the first moment she laid eyes on her. She could see something in her the way I saw things in Fearless. Maybe, I thought, maybe Hearts knew something I did not; maybe Angel was not misnamed; maybe I was just blind to her, as many and most were to my friend.

"Step out of the car," a voice said. There was no "please" at the end of his request.

UNDER THE HIGH BEAMS of their car we stood with our hands on the roof of mine. The women were on one side, while Fearless and I faced them.

"Paris Minton?" one white cop asked my friend.

"I'm Minton," I said.

While the other cop frisked Fearless, my inquisitor patted me down with one hand.

"We're going to have to bring you down to the station," the cop was telling me.

"Gun," the cop searching Fearless said.

"Paris," Fearless said to me.

"You shut up," his cop complained.

"Don't worry, Fearless," I said. "We'll pull out of this."

"Okay," he said, as my cop snapped the first manacle of the handcuffs on me.

Three Hearts had left her gun-laden purse in the car and was holding her wallet in her hand. The police checked out the ladies' IDs and told them that they had to bring Fearless and me down to the station for questioning.

"What for?" Three Hearts asked.

"I don't know, ma'am," one of them said. "We had his license plate number and name in our hot file. We're just following orders."

THEY PRESSED FEARLESS AND ME into the backseat of their prowl car. I remember, as our captors pulled from the curb, seeing Three Hearts in the front passenger's seat and Angel behind the wheel of my junk heap. I wondered, as we drove off one way and the women headed in another, if I would see both of them alive again.

28 | SOMETIMES JAIL ISN'T such a bad thing. I mean, you're locked down and treated as a threat and a danger, but if you don't have anywhere to go and freedom contains threats that incarceration does not, then a free meal, a locked metal door, and a hard cot will do.

Fearless and I were searched and thrown into a big cell that had a maximum capacity of twelve. There were fifteen men already in there when we arrived.

Some guy, I don't even remember who, said something he thought was dangerous when we walked in.

With a smile Fearless told the man, "Come on ovah here an' let's get this ovah wit'." The man could hear the threat in Fearless's bored tone. He stayed where he was, and from then on nobody bothered us. Two men even vacated their bunks so that we would have a place to rest our weary bones.

Fearless was a paradox in my life. In that cell he was my savior. Just hearing his few words and seeing the steel in his bearing, men stepped back from him and anyone with him.

But when we were back on the streets, Fearless would drag me into danger no matter which way he went.

That's why I was happy to be locked up. The bars protected me. The lack of windows meant that nobody could spy on me. I wanted to stay there for a week, maybe two, until Useless and Angel and Three Hearts were far away and forgotten. But I knew that Fearless was too responsible for that. He used his one phone call to reach Milo. All he got was the answering service. I wasn't even going to use my call, but Fearless convinced me to phone Mona and tell her to keep on Milo.

"You need a lawyer," I said to my friend.

"Why?"

"Carrying a concealed weapon," I suggested.

"I got a license," he replied.

"Since when?"

"Since I been bodyguardin' Milo. He got it for me."

"Well," I said, "we might as well get some sleep."

"You sleep, Paris," my friend said. "I'll just sit up top an' get the lay of the land."

I WAS SO FAR INTO that mess with Three Hearts that I was even dreaming about Useless.

"What the hell you want?" I asked my iniquitous cousin. We were sitting at a picnic table in a small park near Watts.

"Listen to me, Paris," he whined. "I cain't he'p it, brother. I love her."

"So? Love her, then. That don't have nuthin' to do wit' me."

"You got to find her, man. You got to bring her back."

Useless was crying. I tried to remember him ever crying before.

"Paris."

. . . Had he ever cried before? Had he shed tears?

"Wake up, man."

I knew there was a commotion going on before I opened my eyes.

A large black man was saying something in a voice that rasped like a big handsaw on hard wood.

". . . kick your ass, peckahwood," he was saying.

There was a smallish white kid in front of him trying to stand up straight and retreat at the same time.

I immediately identified with the kid because I would have been in his position in that confrontation.

"Watch yourself, man," Fearless whispered to me. "I'm'a go ovah there."

Over there. The conflict was coming down two and a half steps from our bunk. Most of the men in the room were black. After that came three Mexicans and two other white guys. No one else in that cell was going to stand up for the white kid. No one else would have stood up for me.

"Kick his ass, Leo," somebody said.

Leo socked the kid in the face, and I was amazed that the white boy didn't go down. He leaned over like a reed in a windstorm and he began bleeding from a cut that opened over his eye. But the kid stood back up. Leo grinned. And then Fearless, the Lancelot of South L.A., stood between them. He put up his hands and shook his head, and the fight was over — just like that.

He brought the boy over to bleed on our blankets.

"I coulda taken him," the kid said. He was actually

smaller and skinnier than me, pale as a newborn luna moth. "Nigger wouldn't be so bad if he didn't have his friends with 'im."

"What's your name, son?" Fearless, not thirty-five himself, asked.

"Loren."

"Loren, call the man a bastard, a motherfucker, a pussy if you want to, but when you call him a nigger you call me one, and, brother, I am a whole other kinda pain."

"All I did was ask a man to read somethin' for me," Loren said. "I got this paper in my pocket and I don't have my glasses. It's from my auntie an' she hates me so I know somethin' bad had to happen. This dude Chapman said that he didn't wanna hear a word outta none'a the white people."

"Chapman," I said. "Was that the guy hit you?"

"Naw. Chapman got called in for questioning. That motherfucker was his friend."

"You got the paper?" I asked the kid.

He reached down into his pants and pulled a small pink envelope out of his drawers.

I took it anyway.

I can't reproduce the letter here because it was far too long: five pages of tiny chicken scratches written in the grammar of some foreign land. The first page listed the reasons that Belldie, Loren's aunt, hadn't written him before. One, which I didn't read out loud, was that the boy was illiterate. There was also a theft committed, a pregnancy he caused, an incident in church that she didn't explain, and then there was the boy's temper and his steadfast refusal to work. After that there came three pages of accolades for Loren's parents and his brother Jimmy.

It was only on the last page that Belldie, in minute detail, described the collision between his parents' pickup truck and the Sun Oil truck on the highway near their farm. Jimmy was with them and now they were all with the Lord.

The funeral had been held a week later. The letter was dated six months earlier.

Loren was at our feet dripping tears and blood on the floor.

Damn. Even when I remember that letter I realize how bad some people have it. There was that white boy made a punk by black men in an inescapable cell, holding a letter about the deaths of his folks. A letter written by blood that hated him. It might have been tough being a black man in America, but I wouldn't have traded shoes with Loren — no, sir.

Toward the end of my reading of Loren's letter the cell door came open and another prisoner was added to the overcrowded room. When Loren fell to the ground crying, someone shouted, "What?" and I thought I had an inkling of who the new inmate might be.

A big man stormed up to us. He was light colored like granite with brownish lichen growing on it. He was big and muscular.

"Who the fuck are you?" he asked Fearless as Fearless rose to the meeting.

"Fearless Jones," my friend said with no particular sense of pride.

The granite man gave a flinty smile. "I heard'a you. Yeah. I heard'a you. Mothahfuckahs always talkin' 'bout how bad you are. Huh. My name's Chapman Grey. I'm a light heavyweight. Do you think you can kick my butt like these punk-ass niggahs think you sumpin'?"

The grammar didn't quite hold together, but Chapman posed an interesting question. Could Fearless stand up against a professional?

It took me seventeen seconds to find out.

Before Fearless could reply, Chapman hit him with a stiff right jab. He followed that with a right cross that sent my friend falling against the bunk.

That was one second.

Chapman pressed his advantage, coming in on Fearless with a body barrage of six or seven blows.

That took care of seconds two and three.

Fearless pushed against the rock-hard boxer, propelling himself away. The crowd around moved out from the fray. Chapman grinned and strode forward.

By then we were up to second eight.

Chapman hit Fearless in the jaw with a right hook that would have killed me and anyone standing behind me. Fearless was thrown back but not down.

I could hear the guards outside the cell shouting.

By the time Chapman was stalking Fearless again, ten seconds had passed. He threw a straight right, but Fearless stepped to the left and hooked his right arm over Chapman's. He twisted around once, throwing the boxer off balance, and then hurled Grey into the bars of our cell. Fearless moved forward then, hitting Grey in the diaphragm, the groin, and the throat. He didn't use all of his strength, but he definitely incapacitated the boxer.

By the seventeenth second, Grey was unconscious on a cot and Fearless was walking back to his corner.

Grey's question had been answered definitively. In the ring he would have torn Fearless up. But out in the real world he had better watch out.

29

LOREN CRIED ALL THROUGH the altercation. By the time the guards came, the fight was over. Things settled down, and I sat there thinking how the life I was living would be better in the remembering than it was while it was going on.

Fearless, definitely the nicest and kindest person I knew, would fight at the drop of a hat. If he were a white guy living in the middle-class world, he would have been exactly the same, but there would never be a reason for him to fight. But we were poor and black and so either we fought or we lost ground. That's all there was to it.

Despite the smell of sweat and urine, despite the blood and tears on my cot, I still felt more secure than I had for many days. While Fearless listened to Loren talk about how much he loved his mother, I lay back and closed my eyes.

The nimbus Sleep sensed my repose and began slowly to drift in my direction.

"Minton, Paris," someone shouted, and Sleep scurried

away to the corner where she resided next to Death and Despair.

"That's me," I said, rising from my bunk.

"Come with me," a man in a suit said. He was accompanied by two large policemen. Each of them took an arm as they led me through the labyrinth of the Seventy-seventh Street precinct.

We came finally to a small door, a really small door. I remember thinking that due to some mistake in planning, this door and the room it led to had to be cut down in size. I could walk through with no difficulty at all, but I was six inches below six feet. The men holding my arms had to duck to get through, their heads nearly grazing the ceiling of the room we entered.

Two fat detectives were waiting in there. One wore a suit that was too green to be a suit and the other wore a suit of spotted gray, though I don't think the spots were intentional. They were both white men, but that goes without saying; all detectives were white men back then. They were the detectives and I was there to be detected.

"Mr. Minton?" Green Suit asked.

"Yes, sir."

"Have a seat."

I sat on a wooden stool placed on the other side of the table from the detectives. The men who had brought me there left without being asked.

The game began in earnest then. The goals of this particular sport were different on the opposite sides of the table. For the detectives to win they'd have to get me to admit to certain suppositions that they would posit. For me not to lose I'd have to avoid admission while keeping from being damaged beyond repair in the process.

"Tony Jarman," Spotty said. It was like a low ante in a high-stakes poker game.

I knew what he wanted me to say, but I squinted and cocked my head to the side. *What?*

"Don't fuck with us, Minton," Green Suit said.

"I don't know no Jarman, man. What could I tell you?"

"Mad Anthony," Spotty amended.

"Oh," I said, but my expression said, *Uh-oh, so you know about that?*

"Yeah," Green Suit said. "Oh."

I put up my hands, trying to halt the train coming at me. I went right into my explanation because in the game we were playing it was in my best interest to get it over quickly. The longer they played, the better chance they had to win.

"Let me explain," I said.

I told them about Three Hearts but not about Useless's visit. I told them that I was looking for Useless but not about his business or his confederates. I told them that Man from Man's Barn had told me that Useless knew Mad Anthony and that Anthony had kicked my butt for talking to him. I added that Fearless broke Anthony's jaw because that was just the kind of friend he was.

After all that, I smiled, thinking that my points added up to an even number.

"Why are you looking for Mr. Grant again?" Spotty asked.

"His mother thinks that the woman he's with is not right for him. She came up to see him and tell him so, but he had moved and she didn't know where he was."

"What's the girlfriend's name?" Green Suit asked.

"Debbie, I think. Don't know the last name."

"What she look like?"

I shook my head. In that game there was a point deducted for every word someone on my side spoke.

Green Suit walked around the table so that he could hit me if I tried that shit again. I let my eyes get big, very big.

"Hey, hey, man," I said. "I don't know nuthin' about her. I never met her."

Green Suit was uncertain. He believed that me and my kind were stupid but wily. That was trouble for him because he never knew when to slap my face or shake his head in disgust.

He hit me hard enough to knock me off the stool, then he shook his head. Doing both was against the rules even in our freewheeling game.

"Get back on the chair," Spotty said. He had a red face and Saint Bernard–like jowls.

"That's not what I wanna hear," Green Suit told me.

"Man, I was just lookin' for Useless. That's all."

"Where is Grant?" Green Suit asked.

"He moved to Man's Barn and then he disappeared."

"What did Useless have to do with Mad Anthony?" Spotty asked.

"He gambled a lot. Played snooker for up to a dollar a ball," I said. "I thought that Anthony might be bankrollin' him."

"And you say this Fearless broke his jaw?"

"Yeah. But that was just a fight in a café. Anthony left after that an' everything was peaceful."

Green Suit laughed at my choice of words, and I knew that Anthony was dead.

30 | HAVING RECEIVED JUST ONE slap made me a nonloser. Someday I'd tell my grandchildren about that evening in jail. By that time there'd be racism on Mars and jails for black men up there.

They took Fearless in for questioning after me. He wouldn't tell them anything either. And Fearless was the kind of man that policemen didn't batter around needlessly. They could tell right off that he'd die before saying something he didn't want to say, and despite popular belief, the police needed good reason to beat a man to death under interrogation.

Finally I got to sleep. By then I was used to the sour smell of the cell. Chapman Grey asked for a doctor. They took him away and he never returned. I didn't miss him.

I don't know what time it was when I woke up, but it felt like early morning. There was no window, so I couldn't tell for sure.

I bummed a cigarette off an old guy named Joshua

who was in there for stabbing his wife. He didn't understand why they had arrested him.

"Me an' Gladys be fightin' all the time," he told me.
"Damn, she shot me one time in 'forty-eight. The police
asked me if I was okay an' that was that."

Soon after he said this, I found myself thinking about
Jamaica again.

An hour or so later a policeman called out, "Minton
and Jones."

We were brought to a processing room where all of our
property, including Fearless's .45, was returned.

When we walked out into the waiting room, I expected
to see Milo or at least Loretta, and maybe Whisper. But
instead, Jerry Twist, the African frog, was squatting on
the bench.

"Fearless," he said, breaking convention with familiar-
ity, "Paris."

"What are you doin' here, Jerry?" I asked.

"That all the thanks I get for goin' yo' bail?"

"What are you doing here?" I asked again.

"Let's go outside," the master stickman suggested.

It was the best idea. He might have had something to
say that one wouldn't want the police to overhear. But I
was loath to go out of that jailhouse.

On the street it was maybe 6:00 or 7:00 a.m. Cars were
cruising past. Twist led us to a big blue Chrysler parked
across the street.

"Where you want me to drive ya?" he asked.

Fearless gave him an address three blocks down from
Nadine and we drove away.

"What's it like on the inside'a that jail?" Twist asked

me as we went down Central. "You know I have never been arrested in my life."

Only the best and worst of men could make that claim.

"How did you come to bail us out of jail, Mr. Twist?" I asked again.

"Answer up this time, Jerry," Fearless added.

He gave a slight shrug and said, "Ulysses called me and asked me to do it."

"Ulysses?" That was both of us.

"Yeah. He called and said that he saw his mama an' them an' they told him that you was arrested. I called cop houses till I fount you."

"Why?" I asked.

"Because Ulysses axed me to, that's why. I done told you all that I'm doin' business wit' him."

"Where is he?"

"I don't know. He called from a phone booth, said that he was with his mama an' that girl, that Angel." Jerry smiled at the thought of her. There was something obscene about a man that ugly lusting after a goddess.

He made a turn on a block three numbers lower than Nadine's.

"You could stop anywhere around here," Fearless said.

"I'll take you to the do', man," our driver offered.

"Here's fine."

"Whatevah you say." Jerry pulled to the curb, and I jumped out, followed by Fearless.

I put my head in the window before he could drive away.

"You know about that cabin Useless stay in around Angeles National Forest?" I asked.

"Sure do."

"You know where it's at?"

"Red house on Bear Pond Lane," he said without straining his memory. "Got a airplane wind vane on top. It's off Route Seventeen. The exit have a sign for fresh honeycomb underneath it. You take that exit, make a right, and go till you see Bear Pond Lane. Turn there an' go a mile or two. You'll see it."

When he drove off I actually had a chill.

"What was that all about?" I asked Fearless.

"I don't know," Fearless replied. "It was like a wild hyena had run ya down and then he lick yo' hand instead'a rippin' a steak outta yo' thigh."

"Uh-huh."

THERE WAS A LIQUOR STORE at the corner. Fearless and I went in to buy orange soda, potato chips, and devil's food cupcakes. We were starving. After eating our junk food meal at the bus stop bench we strolled on down to Nadine's.

She hadn't left for work yet. As a matter of fact, she was still dressed in her housecoat. The robe was mostly white with some pink and green sewn in. It looked more like an overgrown pot holder than anything else.

"Hi," she said to us at the door. "I wondered when you were going to bring her home."

"Who?" I asked.

"Hearts, of course."

"She ain't here?"

"She was with you."

We came in and sat around a small dining table. Nadine was the kind of woman who overdid everything. Where there should have been one chair she'd put three; where a three-foot table would fit nicely she'd place a table five feet in diameter. There were seven prints of paintings hung from the wall and little doodads all over the place.

"So you got taken off to jail an' that devil girl took off with Hearts?" Nadine asked us.

"We couldn't help gettin' arrested," I said.

"Hm."

"Does my aunt have your phone number?" I asked then.

"Of course."

"And she haven't called?"

"Wouldn't I tell you if she did?"

"Nadine," I asked. "Could you stay home from work today?"

"What?" she gasped. You would have thought I'd asked her to take off her clothes and lie out on the bed.

"My aunt may call you," I said calmly. "She might be in trouble. If you aren't here when she calls, we might miss the only chance we have to help her."

"I use my job to pay the rent," Nadine explained.

"You have sick days."

"But I'm not sick."

I'm so used to people who steal and cheat and lie that when I'm faced with someone like Nadine I'm thrown off balance. Nadine would have walked a city mile to return an extra nickel she got in change from a fifty-dollar transaction. Her idea of life was to look back over all the decades of work and play and be able to say that she never did a wrong thing or took advantage of a single soul. She'd turn on Jesus if he broke a commandment, wouldn't have a choice.

"Call them," I said. "Tell them you need a personal day — that there's a family emergency and you need to stay home to man the phone."

No lie there.

But still Nadine hesitated.

"You know I don't live no fast an' loose life like you, Paris Minton. I have responsibilities."

I could have told her that running a bookstore was a responsible position. I could have told her that trying to save Three Hearts's life was something important. But instead I said, "Please. For my auntie."

Nadine never did say yes, but we left with the tacit understanding that she would stay home. She even let us borrow her red Rambler.

THE RIDE OUT TO THE COUNTRY would have been nice if it wasn't for our mission. The old pines seemed sage and peaceful. The grasses waving in the breeze were lovely. We climbed out of the Los Angeles basin, leaving the dirty yellow miasma of smog beneath. There was fresh air and wild birds and blue sky behind billowy white clouds.

"There's the honey sign," Fearless said, pointing at the rude painting of a beehive leaning up against an exit sign.

We took the exit and the turn, drove seven miles to the Bear Pond Lane turnoff, and went two more miles to the red house with a weather vane in the shape of an airplane.

There was no driveway or lawn, just a large square of dirt in front of the house. Behind stood tall, dirty green pines.

My car was parked in front of the house. When I looked in the window I saw that the key was in the ignition.

The thing I remember most about that country cabin was the quiet. It wasn't that there was no noise but that each sound was particular, as if it were waiting its turn: Fearless's door slamming, a robin's cry, the wind through a welter of leaves and pine needles. Even though I was tense and worried, I recognized the beauty of the moment.

"Nice, huh?" Fearless said. Then he took the pistol out of his belt and made sure the safety was off.

I followed him to the front door.

He knocked.

No answer.

He knocked again. I tried the door, but it was locked.

Fearless motioned for me to follow him around the back.

There was a well-swept dirt path leading around the side of the house, marked off from the wild by a white lattice fence. Big white flowers bloomed here and there.

The back door was unlocked.

The cabin was just one big room with a thirteen-foot ceiling and rustic furniture. There was a cast iron woodstove against one wall—that was the kitchen. Other than that the left side was a living area with couches and chairs. The right side had a big bed with a thick mattress and animal furs for blankets.

Everything was neat and tidy, which told me that Useless had probably not been around very much. The only things out of place were one turned-over chair and a good deal of half-dry blood in the center of the pine floor.

Without a word we searched the house. Actually, I searched while Fearless moved around. He didn't have the kind of concentration to look for clues.

It was all a waste of time. There wasn't a personal item in the cabin. Not a name or bus ticket, not a photograph or letter. All there was was a drying pool of blood and a fallen chair.

31 I FOLLOWED FEARLESS on the ride back to Los Angeles. We dropped Nadine's car off at her house and went in to see if Three Hearts had called.

She hadn't.

Things had gotten a little more serious, and I was forced to take a chance.

Mad Anthony was probably dead, probably murdered. I wanted to stay away from Katz and Drummund, the men the murdered man had beaten. I wanted no connection with a murder, and so Mr. Friar, at United Episcopal Charities, became the object of our labors.

The office was in a three-story brick building on Olympic, about a mile west of downtown proper. There was a small park across the street that had on permanent display a cast iron statue of a woman wearing a Spanish veil. She was crying, and her hands were held out about a foot from either side of her face. There was no plaque for explanation, no reason for or account of her pain. The statue made me like the small recreation area. The mystery of the sculpture allowed casual viewers to come up with their own reasons for such powerful emotions.

At the edge of the small patch of green was a bench that gave us a good view of United Episcopal Charities.

"What's the plan, Paris?" Fearless asked me.

"You still got that chauffeur's uniform you used to wear?" I replied.

"Uh-huh."

"You wanna go and get it and put it on?"

"Sure." He stood up.

"While you at it, you could stop by that Western Union office on Manchester and pick me up a blank form there, maybe three or four."

"Sure thing, man. What you gonna do?"

"I just wanna sit for a while, Fearless. This next step gonna be a big one, an' I wanna clear my head. You know?"

My car was parked two blocks down. I walked there with Fearless and got a book out of the trunk before he drove off. Then I went back to my park bench and pretended that I was just an everyday Joe hanging out in the park.

THE TITLE OF THE PAPERBACK BOOK was *Aelita,* written by Alexei Tolstoy and published by Raduga Publishers, Moscow. I had gotten the newly printed copy from a socialist librarian who worked in Santa Monica. He'd told me that this was a translation of a Russian novel by a guy who had been through the early days of the revolution. Most of the books he had written were naturalist novels, but this was science fiction. He thought I'd find it interesting.

I did.

At that time I, and most other Americans, believed that Russia didn't allow for any kind of independent thinking, that all Russians lived in similar barrack-like rooms and were brainwashed so that they couldn't really have an imagination. But the first few pages of this book brought this belief into question. There was nothing overtly political about the story. It was more about adventure and love and men seeking their destiny among the stars.

I was amazed that any Russian could have such thoughts.

"You there," someone said in a loud, unfriendly voice.

It was a policeman hailing me from the passenger's side of his patrol car.

"Yes, Officer?" I was determined not to stand and walk toward him.

"What are you doing?" he asked.

"Reading a book," I replied. I held up the Communist-condoned fiction in case he didn't believe it.

For a moment the young white patrolman didn't know what to say. So he leaned over to conspire with his partner. They parked, disembarked, and walked over to flank me and block the sun.

"Stand up," the officer who had spoken to me before said. His only distinguishing characteristic was a red pus-filled pimple on the left side of his forehead. Other than that his brown-eyed, thin-lipped, brown-haired, frowning visage was something I had seen again and again throughout my life.

His partner was taller and deadly handsome but with nearly the same features. The contrast of like images intrigued me, but this wasn't my show.

I stood up, holding my book like a talisman.

"What are you doing here?" the handsome man asked me.

"Reading my book," I said.

"What are you doing reading here?"

"I like the literary quality of the statuary."

That bought me three seconds of silence.

"Let me see your book," the handsome speaker said.

I handed it over. He flipped through the pages, looking for contraband, no doubt. If he had read the frontispiece, he might have decided that I was a Communist; he might have arrested me for espionage. But his imagination wasn't at all intellectual. He was looking for swag, for small packets of heroin. He was looking for the kind of contraband he thought someone like me would be carrying.

"Let's see your wallet," he asked when the book search turned up nothing.

I obliged.

After fumbling through my well-ordered documents, he said, "Tell me something, Mr. Minton. Why aren't you at work?"

"I am," I said. "My book."

"Your job is reading?"

"In a way. I own a bookstore on Florence. I'm considering ordering a dozen copies of this book. But since it's a translation, I'm trying to see if it's of a quality to justify such an investment."

Three seconds more.

"Why don't you go to a park near your store?"

"I like this park," I replied.

"Turn around and lean against the bench," was his answer to my flippancy.

He searched me down to the cuffs in my pants.

When I turned around again, he was still looking for a way to invade me.

"How much longer do you plan to be here?" he asked.

"I don't know, Officer. I'm readin' a book. Haven't you ever read a book? It takes time."

If he were a soldier and I were the enemy, the look in his eyes would have told me that he intended to kill me the next chance he got.

"We'll be driving by in an hour," he told me.

"Good," I said. "I'll see you then."

I TRIED TO GET BACK into my book but I couldn't stop thinking about all the words the police and I had spilled. It was a complex meeting, what with the Communist publication, the racist miscomprehension, and my barely conscious desire to be put back in a cell.

This last detail was very important in light of the other two. I was a black man seeking incarceration because I felt comfortable in that state. If I were a braver individual, I would have become a revolutionary at that very moment. But as it is, I only remember it because of Useless and his determination to share his bad luck with family and friends.

FEARLESS RETURNED IN forty-five minutes or so. He looked very dapper in his charcoal-colored chauffeur's uniform. I took a blank Western Union form, scribbled down a note, folded it so that it appeared to be sealed, and addressed it. Fearless carried the dispatch to do its work.

•　　　•　　　•

HE CAME BACK OUT and sat there with me. I was a little worried that the cops might return, but I suppose they had found some real police work to keep them busy.

I tried to explain to Fearless about Communism and the American police state, and about me playing my part in the farce, but he didn't understand.

"That's just the way it is, man," Fearless said. "Cops wanna mess wit' you, you got to put 'em in their place."

I looked at my friend, not for the first time thinking that even though we were as close as two men could be, we didn't live in the same world—not at all.

32 | NOT LONG AFTER FEARLESS returned from his mission at United Episcopal Charities, a man came out the double glass doors. The white man had once been young, and hale, and handsome. He had probably been over six feet tall twenty-five years ago. Now he was five ten with silver hair and a gray blue suit that almost made up for the ravages of time.

The man carried a yellow slip of paper in his left hand. He transported this paper across the street, jaywalking toward me and my friend from another world.

I wasn't worried because I was buoyed with the kind of synthetic confidence that Fearless inspired.

As Martin Friar approached, Fearless stood up to make room for him on the bench. Realizing, whether right or wrong, who was in charge, Friar waved the Western Union note page at me and asked, "What is the meaning of this?"

His once-handsome features were still rugged and, in certain circles, no doubt, awe inspiring. But there was a glaze of uncertainty over his pale blue eyes.

"Sit down, Mr. Friar," I said.

He obeyed, and Fearless took a perch on the other side.

"Well?" the vice president in charge of investments asked.

"You know a young black woman named Angel?" I asked.

"Do you mean Monique? Monique Dubois?"

I took out the 3 × 5 I had got from Man. When the steely-faced white man saw it, his colorless lips trembled for a moment.

"Yes," he said. "That's Monique."

"She was your lover?" It was meant to be a question but came out as an accusation.

"We love each other," he said.

This present-tense reply threw me off a bit.

"You say you love the woman who set you up and then made you the victim of blackmailers?"

"It wasn't her fault. She was coerced into fooling me. But we, we . . ."

I don't know for sure, but I believe that in part of his mind Friar felt that he was being a fool and so was ashamed to divulge further intimacies of his heart.

"Yeah," I said. "That's true. Hector and Sterling were using her. I was just wondering what you thought."

"Where is she?" Friar asked, leaning toward me.

"That's what I'm trying to find out," I told the heart-broken executive. "She's with a friend'a mine, a guy named Maurice."

"What's he to her?" Friar asked, without waiting for even a second to pass.

This worried me. I had hoped to find someone who

was feeling hate for Angel. Hate is a good source of energy. It makes your allies blind and eager. Love is a much stickier form of fuel. It burns unevenly and often causes internal damage.

"He used to be her lover too," I said. "But no more. Now they're just friends."

The tension easing a little, Friar asked, "What can I do to help?"

He was moving too fast. I needed time to dicker with him, to figure out where he was coming from. Here he wanted to jump right in with both feet, and I still didn't have a good understanding of his part in the puzzle.

"I, I need some information before I could tell ya that," I said.

"What kind of information?"

"How did Sterling get to you?"

"I don't know any Sterling or that other name — Hector, you said?"

I told him about Hector and the little I knew about Sterling, the man in charge.

"I know the Negro is Paul Dempsey. He was the one who ran the game," Friar told us on that overexposed park bench. "But I don't know anything about a man named Sterling. I've only met black people since Monique and I have been together."

"When's the last time you saw Monique?" I asked.

"Two weeks ago," he said, choking a bit. "She called me and said that she was going away. She said that she was free of Paul Dempsey and that I didn't have to worry about her anymore."

"Was she gonna call you again?"

"No. She said that it would be better if I never saw her

again." Friar looked down at his expensive Italian shoes with bitter regret.

There was a very thin gold band on the ring finger of his left hand. The ring had probably always been that slender, but the way I read this man, I imagined that it had once been a big thick gold ring that had worn away over time like a Lifesaver confection under a dripping tap.

"How did you meet her?" I asked him.

"It was a church function. I got a note from a man I know telling me that there was a young Negro woman who had come into a modest sum and wanted some advice on how to make that work for her church."

"Really? What's this man's name?"

"Brian. Brian Motley."

"A white man?"

"Why . . . Yes, he is."

"And how did Mr. Motley come into contact with a young Negro woman?" I asked, trying hard to keep the sarcasm out of my voice.

"He said that he had a friend who had done work with the church, that they didn't really have a good system set up for their investments, but that this girl really wanted to help out."

"And then?" I asked.

"I . . . Well, I met her. She called and suggested a restaurant on Olvera Street. We, we met."

"I've only met her once myself," I said, feeling every word. "Her eyes are somethin' else."

Fearless grunted in agreement.

"I fell in love," Friar admitted. "Completely."

"Was that your first time?" I asked.

"I'm married, after all," he replied. "We have two children. I love my family."

"I'm sure you do, Mr. Friar. But I'm not asking you if Monique or Angel, or whatever her name really is, was your first lover. What I wanted to know was, was she your first black girl?"

That stopped him for a second. His outpouring of feeling coagulated there, just behind his eyes.

"I don't see what race has to do with love," he stated.

"But most people do," I said. "Most people feel that love is a question of race. I mean, how many interracial couples you see walkin' down Olympic, goin' hand in hand?"

"I'm not like that," he said. "I care for people for what's on the inside, not the outside."

"So Monique wasn't your first?"

"The question is crass, but the answer is no."

It took me a moment to disentangle that sentence. Once I had it, I asked him if his friend Brian Motley knew about his racial liberalism.

This question brought suspicion to Friar's gaze; suspicion but no immediate answer. Fearless turned to regard Friar — intrigued, I suppose, by the man's silence. *White Men Loving Black Women,* that's the title of a book someone should write one day.

A pale blue vein appeared on Friar's milk white forehead.

"This has nothing to do with Brian," Friar said. "He didn't even know anything about Monique."

"Angel," I said, correcting him. "Just like she didn't know that this Paul guy was going to blackmail you."

"I was a fool," Friar said dramatically. "But that

doesn't change how I felt, how I feel. It has nothing to do with race. Monique is a beautiful woman. She's sophisticated and well-spoken. She understands how a man thinks."

"She sure do," I said, appraising her effect on this man. "Tell me about your boy Motley. How does he fit in this?"

"I once saw Brian at the racetrack with a lovely young black woman. It was obvious that they were intimate. When he saw me he got very nervous. To assuage his fears I made a joke. . . ."

"What kinda joke?"

"I asked him if, if she had a sister."

Fearless and I both grinned.

"Maybe I was foolish, but I had been married for many years. My wife and I love each other, but a man has needs well past the time a woman is done with such things."

I liked the way he worded it.

"The women that Brian introduced me to were of another world. They would never run across my wife or her friends. They wouldn't want to marry. . . . Not until Monique, anyway."

"She wanted to marry you?"

"I wanted her. I told her we could go to the Caribbean, make a new life down there. . . ."

He reminded me of my own desire to run away to Jamaica.

". . . We could have children and love each other. I got down on my knees."

It was a wonder how getting down on begging knee was a sign of pride for the powerful white man. For people like me it was getting up to an erect posture that was difficult.

"So you say this Brian introduced you to more than one *sister* of his girlfriend?" I said.

"It wasn't like that," Friar said.

"I hope not. 'Cause it sounds like prostitution. That could be blackmail lettah numbah two."

"They were young women looking for a good time. We went to clubs and restaurants. Every now and then we'd take a weekend on the beach in Ensenada."

"How many?" I asked.

"I don't know," he lied. "Five."

Or fifteen.

"And did money ever pass hands?" I asked.

Friar moved his head to the side like cocking the hammer of a gun. But he didn't say anything. He didn't have to.

"But that wasn't the way it was wit' Monique," I said. "Oh, no. Monique came to you bringing money with her. Thousands of dollars. And when you asked her where she got it, she took you through private jazz clubs and into back room poker games. She raked in thousands of dollars and spent the rest of the night whispering in your ear."

Martin Friar's gaze had moved to his hands, which lay helplessly in his lap.

"You don't make a lot of money, do you, Mr. Friar?" I asked. "You manage the rich people's cash that flows into the church. You visit them at their big houses and drink tea from china cups older than your mother's mother's mother. But at home you sweat ovah the bills like all the rest of us. Got a gray-haired wife, and kids in college. Car payments for a car spends half the time in the shop. You got three good suits an' nobody to wear 'em for, and so when Monique came into your life, you just about changed religions.

"All it would take was ten thousand dollars. Ten thousand. You saw her make twice that in the time you'd been together. She never lost. Never."

"It was eight thousand dollars," he said through a severely constricted throat.

"Shall we go visit your friend Brian?" I suggested.

"Stay where you are," a familiar voice countermanded.

33 | THE PIMPLE ON THE COP'S fore-
head had burst since the last time we'd
met. In its place was a fleshy red sore.
Maybe his hat had broken the strained skin, or maybe
he'd been in a brawl with some poor soul who didn't want
to vacate his bench.

The cops came over to us, their hands hovering at their
billy clubs and pistols.

"Are you okay, sir?" the handsome white policeman
asked Martin Friar.

"What's your name?" was his reply.

"Officer Arlen," the cop said, his voice developing a
defensive tone as he spoke.

"Do I look like I'm in danger, Officer Arlen?"

"I'm asking the questions," Arlen said, bringing his
shoulders up the way a boxer does when he's forced
against the ropes.

"My name is Martin Friar," Angel's mark said. "I'm a
vice president of UEC there across the street. These two

gentlemen have come to consult with me. Do you have a problem with that?"

"This man here," Pimple Face said, "told us that he was reading a book."

"Was he reading a book?"

"He, he didn't say anything about meeting some vice president guy."

"Would you two like to come with me across the street?" Friar offered. "There you can ask about my position and my prerogative to have a private meeting with anyone I wish."

"We're sorry, Mr. Friar," Officer Arlen said. "This man just looked suspicious to us."

"Why?"

"He was, uh, you know . . . hanging out with nothing to do."

"Isn't this a city park, Officer?" Friar asked.

I liked what he was doing, but I was beginning to get nervous. I had never seen a policeman getting browbeaten by a civilian before. I suppose I had never thought it possible.

"Yes, sir," Arlen replied, "but —"

"But because these men are Negroes you decided that they were up to no good," Friar said, cutting him off. "This is a free country, Officer Arlen. Men like these have rights just as much as you and I. And if you take away this man's rights, you are hurting all of us. Do you understand that?"

Two minutes earlier I would have sold Martin Friar down the river for an extra carton of Lucky Strikes. But now I would be more likely to help him than I would Useless.

"Excuse us, sir," Arlen said. "We didn't understand."

The policeman didn't apologize to Fearless and me. He didn't really care, but I wasn't bothered by that. As Arlen and his bad-skinned partner climbed into their prowl car, I had to strain to keep from grinning at them.

Pimple Face glowered at me as they drove off.

"Damn," Fearless said. "Damn."

"Maybe we should go someplace private," Friar suggested.

"I got the car parked up the street," Fearless said.

MARTIN FRIAR TOOK US to a very nice one-bedroom apartment on a small street called Bucknell a few blocks from his office. It was on the third floor of a solid brick building and very well appointed. The maroon carpeting was plush and the white walls were bright backgrounds for the real oil paintings that hung from them. There were landscapes and still lifes, tasteful nudes, and even one abstract painting of nested quadrangles in differing hues of crimson.

"When we have important visitors from out of town, we often put them up here," Friar explained.

Fearless and I were sitting on a wooden-legged violet couch built for two and a half, and Friar sat across from us on a chair that completed the set. He'd poured us a very good cognac in large snifters.

I nursed my liquor, remembering that I had to keep my mind sharp in order not to be trapped by the sins of my cousin.

"This guy Motley," I said. "What's he do?"

"He works for an oil company now. Tiger Oil. For the past few years he's been a liaison between the charitable arm of his corporation and our service."

"What were you doing at the track?" I asked.

"I gamble. Not a lot. It relaxes me. I put aside a hundred dollars a month and either I go out to Gardena for poker or to the track. Once a year I blow five hundred in Las Vegas."

"And Motley knew all this?"

"We'd seen each other now and again at the track," Friar said. "I liked to go on Saturday afternoons."

"How long ago was it that you saw him with the black lady?"

"Three years . . . no, four."

"So he knew you liked to gamble and he knew you liked black women," I said.

"I don't see what you're trying to make out of it," Friar said. "I mean, do you think that Brian's been trying to set me up for years? That's ridiculous."

"Maybe Mr. Motley likes gambling a little more than you," I speculated. "Maybe he got into somebody who knew what you felt about women like Monique."

"That's pretty far-fetched, don't you think?" Friar said.

"We could check it out," I suggested.

"How?"

"Let's go talk to him."

"He'll be at work."

"Call him there. Ask to see him for lunch or after work if he can't make it."

My words were falling together for Friar a few moments after they were spoken. He stared at me for quite a while and then he nodded.

"Excuse me," he said. "I'll make a call from the bedroom."

I smiled. Fearless made a silent toast with his snifter.

"This is some racket," Fearless said when Friar closed the bedroom door. "He got his own little place to go to if he need a shower or a shave. That's nice."

"I wonder how many times he was here with Angel?" I said.

"You know I'd be up in here with some lady at least once a week," Fearless said with a rare lascivious smile. "You cain't have sumpin' like this here an' not take advantage."

We both took drinks then and appreciated the quiet and calmness of our surroundings.

"You see the way them cops bowed down to him?" Fearless asked after some time had passed.

"Yeah," I said. "White people."

"Uh-uh, Paris," Fearless said. "No, man. It ain't just that. It's the way he thinks too. Mr. Friar know he in charge. He know it. He know it so well that them cops know it too. An' he so sure about who he is that here he bring us up in here an' he ain't even scared or nuthin'."

"Why he wanna be scared of two Negro men, anyway?" I asked.

"You see that, man?" Fearless said. "You see? You think them cops stopped us 'cause they can, 'cause they don't like colored people."

"Well, didn't they?"

"Naw, man. They stopped us 'cause they scared. An' if they ain't scared, the people pay 'em is. That's the on'y reason they wanna keep you from readin' yo' book. That's the on'y reason they asked that white man were we botherin' him. They wanna keep on our ass 'cause if they don't, they worried we might start fightin' back."

Fearless did that every once in a while. He'd open his

mind to let me see his deft perceptions of the human heart. It's no wonder that women and children loved him so much. He was a natural man in a synthetic world. He had to be as tough as he was to survive the danger that truth brought.

While I was having these thoughts, Martin Friar came through the bedroom door. His eyes were once again glazed over with doubts.

"He was fired four months ago," the vice president said. "His home phone has been disconnected."

"Why was he fired?" I asked.

"They didn't say why. Only that he'd been let go and they didn't know where he'd gone."

"Did you look up his name in the phone book?"

"Yes. I called information too, just in case he'd gotten a new number recently."

"What about any friends?" I asked. "Or family."

"I don't know any of his girlfriends' numbers, and he was divorced two years ago."

"Maybe his ex-wife knows how to get in touch with him," I suggested.

"I don't know her maiden name."

"Does she have kids?"

"Three."

"Then maybe she's using their last name."

Friar went back into the bedroom, closing the door behind him.

"You plenty smart, Paris," Fearless said, pouring himself another shot of cognac. "It's like you look at everything like one'a them books you read."

"Yeah," I said. "I know enough to jump in the Pacific but I don't know how to swim."

Fearless brightened at that.

"That's where I come in," he said. "You know I can swim like a dolphin. Yes, I can."

When Friar returned, he told us that Mrs. Irene Motley was indeed listed. She'd known Friar from a happier time and so was willing to tell him where her ex-husband had moved. He had no phone, but that was okay because I had no intention of calling the man.

"Let's go over there," I said to Friar and Fearless.

"I should go alone," Friar said flatly. "Brian doesn't know you guys, and I'm the one in trouble."

"Hector LaTiara," I said, "the man you know as Paul Dempsey, is dead."

"Dead?"

"Murdered. Angel, who you know as Monique, has disappeared and so have Maurice and his mother. They blackmailed you and done worse. It is in your best interest to have somebody backin' you up when you go to see this guy."

"Brian's harmless. He wouldn't have anything to do with people like that," Friar said, dismissing my worries.

"Did he introduce you to Monique?" I asked.

"Yes."

"He's been involved with black people and gambling, and once you were in the same situation you got blackmailed. He's the connection between you and the trouble you're in."

Martin was quiet then, contemplative.

"He's been fired and he can't even afford a phone. You know there's something wrong there."

Friar maintained his silence.

"Look, man," I said. "They got you on embezzlement.

You can't go to the cops and you'd be a fool to go it alone. Let us go wit' you. That way we go in strength."

"Why should I trust you?" Friar asked. "I don't even know your name."

"Robert," I said, holding out my hand for him to shake. "Robert Butler, and this is Mr. Tiding. Frank."

"Why should I trust you, Mr. Butler?"

"Because I came to you," I said. "Because I didn't ask you for any money. Because I know the trouble you're in and you haven't told me a thing about it."

Friar's eyes were alive with thoughts and ideas but they hadn't, as yet, settled on a verdict.

"Because you're in trouble and Monique might be too. And maybe, if we're lucky, we might pull your fat out of the fire along with hers."

Finally the self-important white man nodded.

I let out a big sigh and Fearless rose to his feet.

34

BRIAN MOTLEY LIVED in a residence hotel called Leontine Court on the other side of downtown. The building was made from bricks that hadn't been cleaned since the day they were laid and edged in once-white marble. The sidewalk leading to the door was so soiled and marked that it was almost as dark as the asphalt of the street. There were eighteen stairs rising to the front door. The climb told me that this hotel had been a fancy place that had come down with the neighborhood. Years ago you could have ordered sirloin steak with red wine from room service. Now the men hanging out around the entrance carried their day-old wine in back pockets. The only steak they ate had gone through the grinder.

There was a solitary figure at the front desk sitting under a sign that read ROOMS $2. The gatekeeper was a small white man with large square-framed glasses. The thick lenses threw reflections around the dingy room.

"May I help you?" he asked Mr. Friar.

"Brian Motley, please."

"He's in four-A," the man, who was somewhere between thirty and fifty, said. "Across the courtyard and up the stairs to your left.

"And what about you?" the down-at-the-heels concierge asked Fearless.

"We wit' the white man, boss," Fearless said with a grin.

THE LEONTINE COURTYARD must have been beautiful at one time. The marble walkways ran through great planters walled in by granite bricks. But the palm trees and elephant's ears had all died away. The huge gardens were now used for cigarette butts and broken bottles. The men and women who perched out there on stone benches were young and old, beaten down and broken.

The sun glared pitilessly on the wide square, but the people still looked to be in shadow.

THE ONLY LIGHT ON the stairway leading to the fourth floor came through paneless windows open to the yard. Dirt was caked in the corners and long-legged spiders scrambled out of our path. There were big roaches too, and flies, and one pigeon that couldn't seem to find its way out of that hell.

FRIAR KNOCKED ON the crayon blue door. The man who answered wore shapeless maroon pants and a strap-shouldered undershirt. The shirt, once white, was now equal parts yellow and gray.

Brian Motley was unshaven but prebeard, five six exactly, and worn down to fit perfectly among the other residents of that slum.

His rheumy eyes registered Martin and then took us in. He made a slight shrug of resignation and said, "Killing me won't help you, Marty."

With that he backed away from the door and shambled down a very long, very narrow hall to a small room that wasn't worth the buildup.

Motley's floor hadn't been finished or sealed in many years. The wood was pale and fibrous. His wooden bench and chairs had been built for outside use. There was nothing on the walls — hardly even paint. The only good thing about that room was a small window that looked upon downtown with its high-rises and blue skies.

I had been in many rooms like this one since coming to L.A., but I had never seen a white man living in one. That was a real eye-opener for me. In America anyone could be poor and downtrodden. I would have spent more time thinking about that, but I was worried about someone deciding to cut my throat for finding out.

"What's happened to you, Brian?" Martin Friar asked his supplier of black women.

"Who're your friends?" Motley replied, sitting heavily on a wooden lawn chair.

"Robert," I said, holding out a hand. "And this is my friend Frank."

When Brian Motley grinned, you could see that he'd recently lost most of an upper front tooth.

"Bob, Frankie," he said. "Sit, sit. I found this couch three blocks from here. Can you imagine somebody throwing out something so sturdy? You know, there's people in China take somethin' home like this an' pay for their kids' education with it."

We all sat.

Martin was visibly shaken by the condition of his friend.

There was a half-empty pint of Thunderbird wine on the tree-fiber floor. Brian took a swig from it, considered offering us some, and then decided that his generosity would be wasted.

"What can I do for you, Marty?" he asked.

"What has happened to you, Brian?"

"Same thing happening to you," the wine-soaked white man said. "Only you haven't got to this stop yet."

"What are you talking about?" Friar asked. "What do you mean?"

"They got fifteen thousand out of me before they cut me loose," he said. "All I had to do was give 'em you and three others."

He giggled.

Then he took a swig of wine.

"Was that Sterling?" I asked, and for the first time Brian Motley's eyes showed something akin to fear.

"I didn't tell you that," he said.

"No, but I'll tell him you did when I find him."

"That's a lie!" Brian shrieked. He jumped up from his chair, but Fearless pushed him back down with enough muscle that he decided to stay put.

"It's a lie," he said again.

"Yes," I admitted. "And I'd be happy to omit that prevarication if you would tell us how we could get to the man."

From rage to suspicion is a long jump. Mr. Motley's head bounced like a child's rubber ball running out of steam. Then he said, "What?"

"We know about Angel, or Monique," I said. "We also know about Hector LaTiara. . . ."

That name struck home. Motley's head now made a viperlike motion: serpentine without the fangs.

"He's dead," I said. "Killed in his own apartment."

At this point Motley began breathing through his mouth. I didn't know what that meant. Was he frightened that someone might kill him too or was he excited that a dark cloud over his head had gone away?

"What do you want from me?"

"Sterling."

"Why should I help you?"

"Because if you don't, I'm still going to be looking for the man. And when I do find him, I will tell him that it was you who sent me. That is unless you really do."

The wine garbled my words in Motley's ears. He had to think about what I'd said for a moment or two.

"I need much money," he said at last.

"How much?" I asked.

"Two hundred," he said. "No. No. Three, three hundred. Three hundred dollars in fives and tens."

"Can you do that, Mr. Friar?" I asked.

"I don't have it on me, and my bank will be closed by the time we get there."

"I got it if the man take twenties," Fearless offered.

He pulled a large wad of cash from his back pocket. This didn't surprise me. Fearless often carried large amounts of cash. He never trusted banks.

"Bank ain't nuthin' but a robbery waitin' t'happen," he always said.

While Fearless peeled off the bills, I said, "Sterling."

"What do you want to know about him?" Motley asked, licking his lips for every third twenty Fearless thumbed.

"I wanna know the scam, his address, and his full name."

Fearless had finished counting.

Motley looked at the money like it was a glass of water and he'd spent seven dry days in the Gobi Desert.

"Lionel Charlemagne Sterling," he said. "He was once a member of the Santa Anita racing commission. He also belongs to the Greenwood Golf Club."

"He's the one you gave Mr. Friar's name?" I asked.

"First I met Monique," Motley admitted. "She brought me to a few card games and showed that she was always a winner. I put some money with her, and she won a few times. Then she told me about a big game. I put up six thousand dollars. . . . Only one of it was mine. She lost and Hector came to me. He made me take more, ten thousand more. Then, when I told him I couldn't take anything else without getting caught, he said he wanted other names. What else could I do?"

"You could have been a man," Martin Friar suggested.

I wondered what the righteous Mr. Friar would have done if gangsters had threatened his lifestyle and his family for the cost of a few names.

"Where does Sterling come in?" I asked Motley instead.

"Hector brought me to him when I said I couldn't steal anymore. He told me that they'd cut me loose if I played along. I gave them what they wanted, but my superiors found out about the money I took. They didn't want a scandal, but they fired me and blackballed me. I can't work. I can't live. My wife won't have me after those women. All I can do now is get on a bus and go back to Sacramento to my family."

He reached for the money, but I put my hand in the way.

"Write down the list of names you gave to Sterling and his address," I said.

"I don't know where he lives," Motley said, his voice quavering.

"I can find him," Friar said in that man-in-charge voice of his.

"Okay," I said. "Get a pencil and write down the names."

35 WE LEFT MOTLEY TO PACK his toothbrush and wine bottles. I had no doubt that he'd return to a previous life of white poverty in central California. There he'd live out his days, drinking rotgut and jumping at bumps in the night.

Friar had us drive him to a phone booth. There he called the Greenwood Golf Club and simply asked for the address and phone number of Lionel Charlemagne Sterling. The whole transaction took less than three minutes. They would never have let me in on those numbers. Then again, they wouldn't have let me play golf there either. But a man like Friar, even though he was not a member, was well-known to them.

"MR. FRIAR," I said to our new friend, "you've been a good partner so far, but right now I believe that we need to go our separate ways."

"I might be of help to you when you face Mr. Sterling."

"Naw, man," Fearless said. "These men serious about

their bidness. They got guns an' knives an' they know how to use 'em too. I can cover one man, but two be a stretch."

There was something in Fearless's delivery. When he talked, any man halfway near sane listened.

"Will you keep me informed?" Friar asked me.

"When we get your money back, you'll get it," I said. "And we might need some'a your kinda help by that time."

WE DROVE MARTIN FRIAR BACK to his office and then made our way to Spalding Drive in that part of Beverly Hills that lay south of Wilshire Boulevard. North of Wilshire and beyond was where the truly wealthy people lived. The south was for their Passepartout-like aides. These men were senior vice presidents with no chance for promotion or small-business owners who didn't have the vision, or the backing, to go large.

The house that fit the address Friar had given us was a small cottage with white plaster walls and a green thatch roof. Twenty blocks south and it would have cost less than five thousand dollars, but its location made it worth seven times that.

I rang the bell, and the door came open almost immediately. Maybe he was expecting someone. Maybe in this house he ignored the criminal circumstances of his life — I don't know. All I can say is that the tall and handsome silver-haired white man was smiling when he opened the door. The smile faltered at first and then turned into a panicked grimace. He gasped and turned to run. Given no choice, Fearless lunged after the probable Mr. Sterling, grabbing him by the collar of his white dress shirt. One tug and he was on his back. I was inside the door by then, pulling it shut behind me.

"Please don't kill me," the white man whined. "Please."

"Get his wallet," I said to Fearless.

"Take it," the terrified man said, almost throwing the wallet at me. "Take everything; just don't kill me."

I opened the billfold and pulled out his business card. It read: Lionel Charlemagne Sterling, Realtor.

"We got to talk, Lionel," I said.

"Please, please," he replied, staying down on his knees.

"Get up," I said. I couldn't stand to see a man kneeling and begging—not even a white man.

"Please."

"Get up," Fearless said in a voice he never used on me.

The sobbing extortionist rose to his feet, his head bowed and his shoulders sagging.

We were standing in an entranceway. To the right was a sunken living room. I thought he was going to lead us in there, but instead he leaned against a small waist-high table that stood against the wall. There was a telephone sitting there.

"I never meant to hurt anyone," he said. "It was just too much."

"Where's Three Hearts and Angel?" I asked him.

"In Pasadena," he said. "Thirteen twenty-nine Hugo." That was easy.

"Tell him that I would never turn him in," Sterling said. "Tell him. Call him."

"Why don't you call him?" I said, wondering who it was that frightened Sterling so.

"Can I?" he sobbed. Mucus was running from his left nostril. Tears flowed from both eyes.

"Sure," I said. "Calm down, Mr. Sterling. We're not here to hurt you."

My assurances seemed to frighten him even more. He began to tremble.

He turned to the telephone table, but instead of grabbing the receiver he pulled open the drawer. He turned quickly, but Fearless was even faster.

If I had been alone I would have died in that over-priced entranceway. But my friend, with his catlike instincts and reflexes, grabbed the gun and tore it from Sterling's grip.

Sterling fell to his knees and screamed like a woman. He grabbed me by my thigh and yelled again, not so loudly this time. His eyes were popping out and the rictus of his smile was the epitome of terror.

Not knowing what else to do, I grabbed his face and leaned forward.

"It's okay, man," I said to him. "We're not here to hurt you."

His grin began to quiver, and his eyes fixed on a place that was far away from that room. The grip on my thigh loosened, and Mr. Lionel Charlemagne Sterling began to fade.

"No," I said. "No, man. We're not here to hurt you."

The death grin was accompanied by a nod that did not comprehend my words.

He let go of my leg, but I grabbed his forearms in a hopeless attempt to keep him alive. But the blackmailer was dying, and nothing I could do would keep him from that fate.

When he'd fallen down on his back, Fearless touched his throat and put an ear against his mouth.

"Dead," my friend said. Then he looked up at me. "Damn, Paris."

"What? You think I knew somethin' like this was gonna happen?"

"You the one brought us here, man," he said.

"He killed himself," I said. "He was scared because'a what he did."

"Are we standin' ovah a dead white man in Beverly Hills?" he asked me.

"He died of a heart attack or somethin' like that. We didn't kill him."

Fearless just shook his head.

"Damn," he said again.

THERE WAS OVER forty thousand dollars laid out on a bed in one of the house's smaller bedrooms. I looked at it, counted it, placed it in a pillowcase, and put it down.

There was no other indication of Sterling's criminal activity in the house. We left him where he had fallen in the foyer. If we were lucky, a housecleaner or relative would find him and that would be it —*Death due to heart attack,* the coroner's report would read.

"Should we take the money?" I asked my friend.

"Yeah. Yeah, sure," he said. "Maybe we could find somebody he robbed an' pay 'em back."

WE WATCHED THE STREET until no one was out and no car was coming and then made our escape.

While driving toward Pasadena we had the following conversation:

"You really blame me for this?" I asked.

"I don't think you knew what was gonna happen," he said. "I don't think you wanted him to die. But it's just the way you go about things, man. You too much. You too hard."

"Hard? Me? Man, I couldn't beat up two outta three high school kids."

"Not hard fists, Paris. It's your mind. You treat people like they was books, man. You just open 'em up and start goin'. But really you should come up slow an' check it out first."

I didn't know what he was talking about. I had the feeling that he was telling me the truth, that I was at least partly the cause of Sterling's death. But what could I do about it? He was the criminal. Wasn't he?

36 IT WAS EVENING BEFORE we arrived at 1329 Hugo Place. The address sounded as if it belonged on a small house like Sterling's cottage. But this was a mansion. There was an eight-foot salmon pink adobe wall around the property and wrought-iron gates blocking pedestrian and vehicular passage.

There was a button for a buzzer to the right of the gateway.

"Okay, Fearless," I said. "What do you say? Do we knock or not?"

"They got your people in there, man," Fearless said. Then he tried the pedestrian gate—it wasn't locked.

A hundred feet from the entrance stood the house.

It was a big house, three floors in places. There were no lights on, no cars in the driveway.

My heart was pounding like John Henry's hammer, and I worried about a heart attack. Maybe I'd die like Sterling had, from fear. Even Fearless couldn't protect me from my own heart.

The moon was bright enough to light our way and expose us to invisible assassins. Every footstep we took on the gravel path was like a giant maraca announcing us to our enemies.

"There's a way round back," Fearless hissed.

I went with him from the lunar shade of a large stand of bird-of-paradise to the shadow of the house.

Behind the house stood a smaller, two-story building. There was a faint light coming from a few of its many windows.

We made our way to the front door, which was locked, and then around the sides, looking into windows as we went.

There was one window near the ground that was to the basement. There was a slightly stronger light coming from there. I peered into that portal, down into a room that was at least twenty feet below. There I beheld Three Hearts and Angel sitting across from each other at a wooden table. The room they were in was small and, I thought, probably locked.

I went to get Fearless. When he saw them he said, "I don't think there's anybody else here, Paris. Let's just break a windah an' get them."

"You got your gun?"

"Do a robin have wings?"

The window didn't look large enough, so we broke down a door at the back of the extra house.

We came in through a kitchen. The house was dark, and we left it like that, making our way, trying doors as we went.

"Paris," Fearless said after pushing open a door.

Just hearing my name caused a pain in my chest.

"What?" I cried.

"It's some steps leadin' down."

I wanted to run away. I would have run if I was alone. The thought occurred to me that we could have called the cops and given them the address on Hugo. We could have told them that there were women trapped in the basement.

There were tears on my face and the wide-eyed corpse of Lionel Sterling in my mind. I had forty thousand dollars in the trunk, but what difference did that make when my chest was about to explode?

"Come on, man," Fearless said. "Let's get this ovah wit'."

A light snapped on and I gasped, falling to one knee. I knew someone was about to open fire on us. I closed my eyes to pray.

"Paris," Fearless said.

When I opened my eyes I realized that he had turned on the basement light.

He took a step down on the pine plank staircase. Every step he took sighed like a crying woman. I came after, unable to keep my hands from shaking.

After thirty-seven cries downward we reached a concrete floor. Fearless found another light switch and flipped it. There was nothing in the ten-by-ten room except a sturdy and unpainted wooden door.

"Hearts!" Fearless yelled at the door.

"Fearless? Is that you, baby?" she cried.

Maybe I would have been relieved to hear her voice, but I was trying to hold down the fright Fearless had given me when he shouted. The darkness had brought me back to my own basement and the corpse I'd sat with down there. Fearless could have turned on a dozen lights and it still wouldn't have been enough for me.

"Hold on, Hearts," Fearless called. "We'll get you out. I just gotta jimmy this lock here."

It was a serious padlock held down by brass fittings that a jailer would have been proud of.

"I cain't pull off the lock wit' my hands, Paris," my friend told me. "I gotta go upstairs an' find sumpin' to pry it with."

I clamped my teeth shut so that I wouldn't beg him to stay. I nodded, hoping that he didn't see my fear.

Fearless patted my shoulder and made his way back up the stairs. I leaned against the door and slid down into a crouch.

"Fearless?" Three Hearts called. "Are you still there?"

"It's me, Auntie," I said, my voice a little high.

"Paris. How did you find us?"

The words jumbled in my mind as I tried to find an answer. We found a man who had been destroyed. We killed a man. We found some money. We buried a guy in a strawberry field.

I got dizzy and nauseous.

"Paris," Three Hearts cried. "Paris."

"I'm here, Auntie. Fearless is gettin' somethin' t'break the lock wit'."

"Where'd he go?"

"Up."

"In the house?"

"Yeah."

"Them men still up there?"

I expected to hear gunshots at that moment. Never in my life had I been more sure of a premonition. It came to me all of a sudden. The kidnappers were all asleep. They had slept through us breaking in but now they heard Fearless.

I stood up but went no further. Any moment the gunfire would begin. They might get the drop on Fearless, but then again he was the army assassin. But even if he killed them, the gunfire would bring the cops and we'd all be arrested and convicted for a dozen crimes.

"Paris," Three Hearts called.

"I don't know," I whispered. I'm sure she didn't hear me through that heavy door.

A woman sighed.

I jumped three feet.

It was Fearless on the top stair.

The heart attack tensed inside me, wondering if this was the moment to end my days.

Then Fearless was standing there in front of me. He had a big crowbar in his hand.

"Hold on, Paris," he told me. "Hold on, man."

He put a hand on my shoulder, and I grabbed his forearm the way Sterling had grabbed my thigh. I put my head against his shoulder and shivered.

"Paris," Three Hearts called.

"It's okay, Hearts," Fearless answered. "I got me a crowbar."

I let go and took a deep breath. The dread had gone from me, and I was ready to do what we had to.

"Gimme your gun," I said to Fearless. "I'll stand guard while you work on that lock."

IT TOOK FIVE MINUTES for Fearless to pry that door loose. It was a very good cell. Down in a basement and in the back of a walled mansion; even if the women had screamed, no one would have heard them. And there was no way they could have broken down that door.

Three Hearts and Angel hugged the both of us. They didn't cry or lose their composure. After a minute of greeting, they both said that they needed a bathroom.

Fearless led them upstairs and turned on the lights in the house.

"What if somebody in the front house sees us?" I asked while the women went about their toilet.

"Ain't nobody up there," he said.

"How you know that?"

"I just do," he replied.

I had been so traumatized that even this lame assurance didn't bother me. It was as if I had died and now nothing else could happen.

"When they come out, we got to go," I said.

"Okay, man. You know I got to call Milo anyway. I'm a day late for him as it is."

37 | "THEY WAS LAYIN'" for Ulysses when we got there," Three Hearts Grant said from the backseat. "There was four of 'em."

We were in the canyon, coming from the valley back to L.A.

Angel sat close to my auntie, holding her hand. The women were completely bonded now.

"There was blood on the floor," I said, wondering about the union between the mother and the lover of a fool.

"When they made to grab us, I shot the fat one," Three Hearts said. "But then the bald one, the one with the scar across his face, took my gun an' slapped me down. Angel tried to stop him, but he was too big and mean."

There was the knot. Angel's trying to save Three Hearts had assured their undying union.

"He died in the car," my aunt said almost casually.

"The fat one?" I asked.

"Yeah. He told 'em he was okay, but I hit sumpin' in

his belly. It's like he got sadder an' tireder until he was gone."

I turned around to see what my aunt looked like when she uttered these words. She had a sneer on her lips, as if she had just tasted something bitter. There was no remorse or discomfort, just a distasteful task that was only one-third done.

Angel didn't speak at all. She was the younger woman and therefore left the speaking to her elder.

I didn't push either woman because I was hoping that the whole thing would soon be over. Hector was dead, Sterling too. The men who had kidnapped Three Hearts and Angel were looking for Useless, so he was probably alive somewhere. All I had to do was leave the job up to Angel and Three Hearts. They could go on looking and I could go back to my life.

I figured that I could repay Friar and split the rest of the cash with Fearless. That way at least I'd have a nest egg if I needed to run. For a while then I wondered what a berth to China would cost.

IT WAS LATE WHEN the four of us got back to my bookstore-home. From the street we could see the shadow of a man hovering near my door.

"Who's up there?" I called.

"Paris?" he said, and all of the pains and bruises I'd collected in the last weeks came back to me.

"Ulysses?" Three Hearts called.

"Baby?" Angel echoed.

Fearless chuckled while the women rushed up the stairs, the soles of their shoes clattering on the hardwood.

•   •   •

IN THE KITCHEN at the back of my place, the women sat sentry in chairs on either side of Ulysses S. Grant IV's stool. He was grinning and holding hands with both women, while Fearless sat on my counter and I boiled water for tea on one of my three hot plates.

Sitting in front of Useless was a brown leather suitcase with two straps and three latches. It was old and weathered, but that just proved that it was stolen. Useless didn't own a suitcase. Never had. He was always out the door one step ahead of the law or some other man or woman seeking revenge. He didn't have time to pack, had no use for luggage. And so I was pretty sure that that traveling bag contained the reason why at least four men were dead.

"I knew you'd come here to see Paris, Ma," Useless was saying. "I knew it."

"What about all these things they sayin' 'bout you, Ulysses?" Three Hearts asked.

"What things?" Useless glanced at Angel with a sudden look of fear.

"Blackmailers, thugs, and murderers," my aunt said. "That's what."

"It wasn't my fault, Mama," he whined then.

It was the first time I had ever heard her cross with him. I wondered if it was his first time too.

"Is that what you're gonna tell the police when they arrest you?" she asked. "Is that what you're gonna tell the judge?"

"The po-lice ain't after me, Mama. They don't know about me."

"What about this girl here?" Three Hearts asked. "What about this sweet, innocent young thing that you done dragged down in the mud? I done read in her diary how much she loves you and how much you mean to her. How can a son of mine treat a woman's love like that?"

I wondered, then and now, if Angel was devious enough to lie in her own journal on the off chance that someone might read it and judge her.

"I tried to save her, Mama. Ask her. Ask her if it isn't true."

His entreaty was so compelling that I found myself looking to Angel for an answer. For her part, she was staring into her lap.

"It's true, Mrs. Grant," she said. "I was already messed up with Hector and them when they brought your son into the business. Ulysses was just supposed to drive me around and pick me up when I needed it. He helped to fix a few poker games we played. Ulysses wanted to take me away from them. He wanted me to stop."

I bet. He wanted her to stop, all right, but not before the coffers were full; I knew my cousin that well.

Three Hearts's face filled with love. She put her arms around her son and kissed his brow.

"Baby," she said. "I'm so sorry. I thought it was you did all that."

It was him, I thought. Didn't she know that he was up to his neck in extortion, blackmail, and now murder? Couldn't she see that everything had fallen apart because of him?

"Why were you runnin', Cousin?" I asked when I couldn't take the lies anymore.

"I ran because after Angel took off, I realized that I wanted her more than the money they paid me."

Angel took that cue to put her arm around her man's

shoulder. Three Hearts nodded at the gesture as if it proved the bald-faced lie he was perpetrating.

"What about the man with the scar?" I asked. "The man that kidnapped your mother and your girlfriend. Who is he?"

"I don't know," Useless said, shaking his head and looking pitiful.

"How did you know to call Twist to get us out of jail?"

A liar's desperation spread across Useless's face, and I knew that I had him.

But I was wrong.

"I got a call from a guy who wanted us to get back into business. He told me that he had my mama and if I wanted her to be all right I'd have to give him what I got in this here suitcase."

"What guy?"

"Paris," he replied, "you don't wanna get too deep in this, Cousin. These men is dangerous."

Now I was sure that he was lying.

"Who was it, Ulysses?"

"A white man named Lionel Sterling. He the one called me."

"He had your number?"

"He called Jerry Twist and told him that if he talked to me to tell me to call. He said that I'd like to hear what he had to say."

Useless might have been the best liar I'd ever met.

"Sterling's dead," I said.

"Oh, no," Three Hearts proclaimed. "Not another one dead."

"He wasn't dead when he called me," Useless said, approximating a man telling the truth.

"How did you know we were in jail?"

"Sterling told me. He had his men question Three Hearts about the men she'd been wit' —"

"That's right," my auntie said. "They asked and we told them that you had been arrested."

"Why would they ask you that?" I asked Three Hearts.

"I don't know."

My frustration was rising. Something was a lie here. Something wasn't true. And Useless knew what it was.

"When Fearless and I went to see Sterling," I said to Useless, "he was scared the minute he saw that we were black. That's what frightened him. Now, if he's afraid of black people so much, how he gonna get three black men to kidnap your mama an' girlfriend?"

"Maybe he wasn't scared," Useless speculated. "Maybe he only pretended to be afraid so you wouldn't suspect him."

I wanted to ask: That's why he had a heart attack an' died in my arms?

"People out here dyin' because'a you, Cousin," I did say.

"Leave him alone," my aunt countered. "You're the one gettin' people in trouble. You're the one see somebody and then he turns up dead."

That was the last straw for me. I said, "You come to my house, drag me out in the street where I get my butt kicked, thrown in jail, surrounded by murderers, black-mailers, pimps, and thieves . . ."

"Paris," Fearless said in a low warning tone.

". . . You shoot a man with your own gun, kill him dead, don't even cross your heart for a blessin' when you talk about it, and still you gonna sit there next to that liar you call a son and blame me for killin' the man Useless here just said ordered your kidnappin'."

"His name is Ulysses," was her reply.

"Maybe to you," I said. I realized that I was hovering over my relatives. "Maybe to you he's some Greek hero, some descendant of a poor slave woman got in the way of a war. But to me he's useless, hopeless, inadequate, futile, a waste of time."

Three Hearts stood up.

"I'm leaving," she said.

"Get out, then," I said, not myself at all. "Get the hell out."

"Come on, Ulysses," was her reply.

Useless stood. So did Angel.

"But you ain't takin' that suitcase."

Fearless hopped down from the counter.

"You don't wanna mess with the contents of this bag, man," Useless assured me.

"Why not? What you got in there?"

"It's the stuff Sterling used to blackmail them men."

"Fearless an' me know one'a them men," I said. "Martin Friar."

"Marty?" was Angel's first word in a while.

"He sends his best," I said to the young beauty. "I think he thinks he loves you."

You couldn't have read her face with a microscope.

"Leave the bag, Ulysses," Three Hearts said.

"But Mama . . ."

"Leave it. That's the devil's work in that bag. I'm sure Fearless will make sure it gets back to the men that have been wronged."

"Yeah," I said. "Fearless'll do it. Fearless, not Paris.

Not your nephew, who you dragged down in the trough with your son."

Fearless reached down for the bag. Useless took it by the handle.

"Don't cause a ruckus, Ulysses," Fearless said.

"Do you have a car, Ulysses?" Three Hearts's voice was stiff and angry.

"Yeah. Jerry Twist lent me his car."

"Then let's get out of here."

"Two questions, Useless," I said.

Hearts was about to protest my bastardization of her son's name, but he put a hand on her shoulder.

"What, Paris?"

"Who killed Mad Anthony?"

Useless never could lie very well in the presence of his mother. She forgave him everything and loved him fiercely. Her passion made him honest, or somewhat so.

"He was tryin' to kill me, Paris. I swear."

"What about Hector?"

"Come on, baby, let's go," Angel said.

"I don't know," Useless said to me. "I shot Tony in a alley off 'a Alameda. He would'a kilt me if I didn't, but I don't know about Hector."

Our eyes were locked for a long minute. I believed him . . . but that didn't make what he said the truth.

The three headed for the door. I followed them through the bookstore and out onto the porch. I don't think I'd ever been angrier. All the trouble I'd gone through, and my aunt still treated me like a throwaway waxed paper milk carton.

"You welcome for our help finding your son," I called after them. "Make sure you don't call back any time soon."

Three Hearts wheeled around and stared at me, her evil eye glowing in the night. But I didn't care, not one bit. A man can only be pushed so far and then he has to stand up and say what he feels.

"She'll cool down in the mornin', Paris," Fearless said at my back. "She'll see that you did right by her with the dawn."

"All I want is for them to leave me alone," I said. "I've had enough. You hear me?"

BACK INSIDE, Fearless picked up the suitcase that Useless had left in my kitchen.

"I'll hold on to that," I told him.

"You sure, man?"

"I wanna check it out."

"Okay, Paris," Fearless said. Then he chuckled. "You must be boilin'."

"She drive me crazy, Fearless," I said. "Here I done helped her do what she want, an' she still wanna look at Useless like he the one did it all."

"That's her baby there," Fearless said. "You cain't do nuttin' about that."

"It's not only that," I said. "Sterling was workin' for somebody, somebody he was scared of. That means the one who had Angel and Hearts kidnapped is still out there. That man's a killer an' he might be thinkin' about us. And you know Useless not tellin' us everything."

Fearless stood there while I ranted and gulped tea. He leaned back against the counter, with moths darting through the darkness behind him. It's not that he didn't care about what I was saying. It's just that there was nothing to do about it. Fearless lived a life filled with dangers. Walking down the street was a threat to him. But he just moved through it, living by a code that I doubt he'd have been able to articulate.

The phone rang about then.

It was after midnight.

"Hello?" I said, hoping that Three Hearts did not want to apologize.

"Paris," he said in a low tone.

"Hold on."

Fearless had followed me into the bookshop part of my home. I handed the phone to him. He muttered a word and then listened. After forty-five seconds or so he grunted and then hung up.

"You wanna go for a ride?" he asked me.

There was no doubt in my mind that Fearless meant to drive into trouble. Trouble was where he was coming from and it was most often his destination. But the alternative was to sit in my house alone with the fear of a killer who could take you out with a straightedge or a heart attack.

"Okay," I said, and Fearless clapped my shoulder.

I WAS SOMEWHAT SURPRISED that Fearless took us to Ha Tsu's Good News. I almost asked if he was lost when we pulled to the curb a block down from the restaurant–pool hall. Maybe, I thought, the blows of Chapman Grey had loosened a connection in Fearless's brain.

"Fearless?" I said, and then a brown shadow appeared

next to the driver's window. My shoulders rose, preparing for the shot I knew had to follow. My fingers gripped the door handle.

Then I saw that it was Whisper.

Fearless let down his window.

"Where is he?" Fearless asked.

"Right smack-dab across the street from Ha Tsu's," Whisper said. "Him and Rex Hathaway."

"Why here?" I asked.

Whisper hadn't noticed me. He glanced at Fearless, the question in his gaze.

"We on sumpin' together," Fearless said.

"Albert Rive been in town a week," Whisper said to me. "I been lookin' for him, but he got sneaky. Then somebody let 'im know that Fearless been seen at Good News."

"I thought Al was after Milo," I said.

"Yeah, but Fearless in the way. He must figure if he can take out the bodyguard, Milo be like a clam wit' no shell."

"Let's go," Fearless said.

"Hold up," Whisper said. "Why don't we have Paris here walk down the block just a minute before us? That way we see if he got somebody else there."

"We could go find out that for ourselves," Fearless said, defending me. "We don't need him."

Before Whisper could protest, I said, "No. I'll do it."

Whisper nodded. "Walk by across the street an' keep on goin'. When you come to the end'a the block, we'll make our move. Turn around quick an' shout if you see something."

•   •   •

I DON'T KNOW WHY I did it. I suppose my interpretation of Aristotle's logic had something to do with it.
It didn't make sense for Albert Rive to shoot me when he
was after Fearless. At worst he might accost me, ask me
where my friend was. And before I could answer, Fearless
would be on him.

But that wasn't the real reason. I just needed to do
something. I needed to move my legs to exercise my
heart. I was in deep trouble and if I stopped moving I
worried that the fear would overtake me and I'd be frozen
like a child in the arms of a make-believe monster.

I walked down the block, feeling cool on my left side,
the side that faced the hidden Albert and Rex. The bouncer,
Harold Crier, was gone from his post. I glanced up at
Jerry Twist's windows. They were dark, but that didn't
mean anything.

I passed under the red lantern of the restaurant, across
the street from the unseen killers, and into darkness. As
night shadows fell on me, I thought of Tiny Bobchek's
corpse. The image upset my equilibrium. My toe kicked
the concrete. At any other time I would have righted myself and kept on going, but in that sudden darkness, with
the apparition of the man I had cuckolded in my mind, I
tried too hard, lost my balance, and fell.

I looked back to see Fearless and Whisper running toward a recessed doorway. Then I saw a movement above.
It was a window coming open just as Fearless approached
the darkened entrance.

"Fearless!" I screamed. "Up above your head!"

My friend took flight without even a glance upward. A
rifle appeared at the window. Whisper came into view
and pressed himself against a wall. When the first shot

came, I expected to see the nondescript detective crumple
and fall, but instead the bullet ricocheted two feet from
where I lay. I looked up at the window, trying to understand how the assassin's shot could have been so far off.
The next shot shattered a barbershop window next to my
head, and I understood in a flash that Whisper had made
himself invisible, and I, with my loud cry, was the only
target in sight.

Instead of running, I looked for Whisper. He was gone.

A series of shots exploded inside the assassins' hiding
place across the street from Good News. I could see them
glimmer weakly through the windows.

I got myself to a standing position and staggered away,
around the corner. There I leaned against a wall, breathing as if I had just run a mile.

More gunshots.

A siren sounded somewhere.

The sirens continued. I moved down the street and into
an alley. I crouched behind a group of metal cans.

"What's happenin'?" someone hissed, and I almost
leaped up.

Behind me on a ledge big enough to hold him was a
man who'd made his bed there. He was black and dressed
in nighttime grays. There was hair all over his face and a
frightened glint in his eyes.

The sirens were getting louder.

"I don't know," I said. "I was walkin' down the street
an' all of a sudden there was shots."

Three police cars careened down the street I had run
from.

"Who was it?" the alley dweller asked.

"Loud and Dangerous," I said.

My new friend and I waited a while. There were no more shots. After a few minutes there was shouting: military-like orders were being given. At that point I got up and walked down toward the hubbub — just a neighborhood resident wondering what was going on.

There were at least a dozen people in front of Good News, gaping at the commotion across the street. Smaller groups of Watts's denizens appeared on stoops and in the street.

The police were taking five men from the building, all of them in handcuffs. Whisper and Fearless were among the prisoners. They'd be arrested, but that was all right; both men were certified to take in bail jumpers.

I saw Albert Rive, his brawny body sagging under the beating that Fearless had surely given him. The other men, except for Fearless and Whisper, also seemed a little worse for wear.

The moon hung at the end of the street. Under its constant stare a paddy wagon came, gathered my friends and their quarry, and took them someplace where Milo could go and set things straight.

"Hey, Paris," a man said from behind me. His hand on my shoulder weighed as much as a Christmas ham.

"Jerry."

"Wasn't that Fearless in there with them?"

"Was it?"

"That why you boys hangin' out around here?" he asked. "Layin' for Al Rive?"

"Did Lionel Sterling call you, Jerry?" I asked.

That slapped the smug certainty off the amphibian's face.

"Yeah," he breathed.

"He tell you to tell Useless to call him?"

"If that's what Ulysses say, then maybe so."

"You know a man named Hector LaTiara?"

"Never heard of him."

"What about —"

"I have to go in now, Paris," he said. "You got what you wanted. The next time I see ya, yo' mouth bettah be filled with Ha Tsu's noodles."

Jerry turned his back on me and walked up the stairs to Good News.

I rummaged through my pockets, looking for Mum's phone number. When I found it I felt as though I had located something precious, like a doctor's prescription for a whole life's worth of pain.

39 | SHE BROUGHT MY JASMINE TEA to the bed. The night before she had bathed me and loved me and even sung a Chinese lullaby while I drifted off to sleep in her arms. But Mum's greatest gift to me was that cup of fragrant tea. I sat up, realizing that her bed was positioned to receive the morning sun through a high window on the far wall.

Even in that overbuilt part of town you could hear birds chirping. I took a deep breath and a sip; Mum kissed me and said, "Your mustache tickle."

"I'll cut it off."

"No. I like it when a man tickle me."

It was a moment that I never wanted to end. We made love again, but the seconds were ticking at the back of my mind while she laughed at my mustache against her thighs.

She asked me if I had really read *The Odyssey*. I recited the first book, translated by Samuel Butler. I'd memorized those lines after I'd read that many Europeans in the old days had committed hundreds, even thousands of poems to memory and then recited them on many occasions.

But even Homer couldn't save me that morning.

I kissed the young waitress good-bye and walked out into the sultry morning—two parts serenity and three parts terror.

"GOOD MORNING, PARIS," Loretta Kuroko said with a humorous and playful suspicion in her eye.

I felt guilty under that gaze.

"Paris," Milo shouted. "I hear I owe you a favor, boy."

"You get Fearless outta jail, Miles?" I asked the bail bondsman.

"Come on over here an' sit with me," he said.

I turned to Loretta.

"Why are you looking at me?" she asked.

"Can I go?"

Her smile lost its insinuation, and we were friends again. She nodded graciously, and I went to Milo's spindly visitor's chair, my favorite piece of furniture in the whole wide world, and sat down hard.

"I need information, Mr. Sweet."

"Shoot."

I wasn't ready yet. I had relied on the habit Milo had of resisting sharing what he knew. He usually got coy and then cagey before getting up off of information. And so, because he hadn't, I took on his evasive role.

"Where's Fearless?" I asked.

"That's what you wanna know?"

"That's the first thing."

"He went off wit' that girlfriend Mona. She was already at the police station when I got there at two."

"Who was the third man?" I asked then. "The one with the rifle."

"Steven Borell," Milo said. "I don't know how Al Rive managed to fool him into that."

"Rive is in jail?" I asked, just to make sure.

"For a long time," Milo promised.

"You know a big ugly brother with a scar run up the center'a his face?"

"That's the information?" Milo asked.

"Yeah."

"What for?"

"Milo, I got problems. You know that. I helped Whisper and Fearless with your mess, now please just tell me who he is."

"Lonnie Mannheim," Milo said.

"Mannheim?"

"Yeah. I guess the Germans had slaves too."

"Does he have a gang?"

"Uh-huh. Sure do," Milo said. "Bobo and Gregory Handsome. Two Arkansas brothers who need to go home. All of 'em have worked for me at one time or another."

"Trackin' down bail jumpers?"

"That and other things."

"You know where I can find them?" I asked.

"Why would you want to?"

"Because Lonnie an' them know somebody don't like me," I said as clearly and candidly as I could. "Because I got to find him."

"If Lonnie only the door to the problem, then you in trouble deep, Paris."

"That's no news to me."

Milo frowned. He wasn't the kind of friend that would

put his neck on the line for me. But he did care in his way. He didn't want to think that I'd come to harm. And if the worst happened, he'd put on a good dark suit and come to my funeral. He might even send some lilies — if he could deduct them from his taxes.

"I don't know where they are," he told me. "When we did business together they were mostly legal. But nowadays I hear they break legs and worse for people don't like to hear bones snappin' and men breathin' their last."

That was Milo at his friendliest. He was trying to tell me to find another way in, to avoid men I couldn't stand up to. And I appreciated his concern, such as it was.

"Can I use your phone, Milo?"

The legal intellectual let his shoulders rise, indicating that he'd done all he could do. He gestured toward Loretta with one of his huge hands, and I rose from the orphan chair like an acolyte dismissed by a great teacher who had failed his task.

"HELLO," the nondescript voice hummed.

"Whisper."

"What's up, Paris?"

"Can I come over?"

"Always welcome," he said.

The words were friendly if the tone was not.

WHISPER'S OFFICE WAS on Avalon. The building was perfect for the elusive sleuth. It was three stories and narrow, made from dark red brick. The front door of the building didn't face the street. Instead you entered into a little recess, turned to the left, and walked up a small set of granite stairs that brought you to an old white door that was locked and far too pulpy to sustain a serious knock.

But for those in the know there was a buzzer inside of a black mailbox that the postman knew not to use. All the letters were put through a slot in the door; packages were held at the post office for pickup.

I pressed that button.

Two minutes later the detective opened the door, giving a rare, and momentary, grin.

"Paris."

He led me up a carpeted stairway to the top floor, where he had his office. Over the years I had been to Whisper's sanctum a few times. The visits were always about hard business, but still I stopped to appreciate his sense of style and decorum.

The main office was paneled with real oak, giving it that rich woody-brown feel. The carpet was maroon, edged in royal blue, and there were tall bookshelves on either side of his heavy oak desk. The shelves reached all the way to the ceiling, which was at least fourteen feet high. It was an intelligent room that invited you to sit and contemplate until the problem was solved.

I liked the chamber very much, but it was his one window that always grabbed me.

He must have had it put in specially. It was only a foot and a half in width but ran from a foot above the floor to six inches below the ceiling. It presented a view of the northern mountains and L.A.'s blue-and-amber skies. Something about the slender slice of the outdoors made your mind want to expand.

Whisper gestured to the blue cushioned chair that

looked upon the window. I sat down, feeling almost as tranquil as I had in Mum's arms.

"What's up, Paris?"

You could have spoken to the man for half a dozen years and he would have used only a couple of hundred words, excluding proper names and numbers.

"I need your help on something," I said.

His hands, raised palms upward toward his shoulders, asked me what.

"I need to speak to Bobo and Gregory Handsome," I said. "Them or Lonnie Mannheim. I don't know where they are and I need that information."

From his appearance, Whisper could have been a bus driver or a teacher's aide at a public school; he could have been a deacon at a small church or a single father raising nine kids. He looked like anything but a man who'd run into an open door to root out armed gunmen shooting wildly and intent on taking life.

"Thanks for last night," he said.

"Sure. You know I didn't do nuthin' except for trip ovah my own big feet."

"You might'a saved Fearless and you shoutin' took that rifleman's aim on you."

Even the thought of such an action put fear in me.

"What happened in there?" I asked.

"Fearless had knocked out both Al Rive and Rex Hathaway before I got inside. Then we went up the stairs. I started shootin'. It was an office buildin' so I didn't have to worry about people gettin' hurt. Steven Borell was shootin' down the stairs at me while Fearless went out a window and then back in through a side stairway. He jumped Borell and knocked him ovah. Nobody got killed an' the cops had their bail jumper, so they didn't question how we got it done."

Those were the most words I'd ever heard come out of his mouth.

"Thank you," he said again.

"You the ones did the work," I said.

"I'll find the Handsome brothers and Mannheim for you, Paris," he said. "Gimme a day, two at most, an' I'll have what you want."

"I can pay you," I said.

"No, brother. You already have."

40 FINALLY I DROVE HOME. I wasn't worried about losing business; people were used to my being closed at odd hours now and then. And it wasn't like there was any other bookshop in the neighborhood. The customers I had would come back when my problems were over — that is, if I lived that long.

I carried Useless's leather suitcase upstairs to my desk, thinking about the trouble he'd caused. I hadn't even let him in the front door and still my fat was in the fire. It was so pathetic that I had to chuckle. Useless was more deadly than an outbreak of smallpox in a tuberculosis ward.

I put the suitcase on the far side of my big desk.

Sun was streaming down from the window behind me. There was the scent of Mum's floral perfume rising from my shirt. A sheath of sweat was forming at the back of my neck, and I felt unsure about opening Useless's bag.

Instead I tried to think my way back along the path I had taken. It was what I did whenever I got lost on the road; I'd pull my car to the side and sit there remembering all the turns I had taken and directions in which I had gone. Whenever I did that, the right way would come to me.

I thought about Useless at my front door and Jessa after him. I remembered running down Central and being saved by Sir and Sasha. There was Ha Tsu, Jerry Twist, Auntie Three Hearts, and an Angel with horns. I thought about Tiny Bobchek with the hole in his temple. Hector had killed him. But who had killed Hector? Lionel Sterling? No. Jessa?

Mad Anthony had been murdered too. Useless had admitted to that killing. He claimed self-defense and I believed him. Mad Anthony was a killing machine. Shooting him from the back with a tommy gun was self-defense in my book.

I made a turn at Mad Anthony. He was the leg breaker. That made sense. I went from him to Hector. Hector was deep into all of this mess. He was after Useless because my cousin was going to take the money and run. Angel and Useless had found out about the counterplot and bolted. It was all falling together. There was reason in the mayhem. I was somewhere near home when I ran into Sterling. He wasn't afraid of some unknown assassin. His fear was of someone he knew and worked with.

A dead end. As if I thought that murder would ever be as neat as a road map.

I eyed the worn leather of Useless's suitcase, wondering idly who had owned that luggage before my cousin. It looked old enough to belong to Useless's great-grandfather: the general who had either loved or raped, as some versions of the story went, Three Hearts's husband's father's mother.

The name was given as a kind of oral history that would pass down from father to son, memorializing both the greatness and base nature of our beginnings.

Who had owned that suitcase? There was a leather tag holder strapped to the handle. I flipped it open, but the name, written in purple ink, had gotten wet and was nothing more than a blur.

I had spent half an hour trying to work out that name when I realized that I had gotten lost again.

From the bottom drawer of my desk I took a pair of thin cotton gloves that I kept for just such a purpose.

I undid the straps and flipped the latch of the suitcase. Inside, there was a large accordionlike folder made from durable brown paper. The folder had eighteen separate sections. Fifteen of these were in use. Fourteen of them contained an accounting sheet, between three and six black-and-white photographs, letters of love, and a little bag of receipts from hotels, restaurants, and upscale luxury stores that sold expensive clothing and jewelry.

The photographs were of the men in question gambling and in compromising positions with Angel. Some of the pictures were quite explicit, making me wonder if Useless was the photographer. The accounting sheet listed every transfer of funds from the mark to the blackmailers, also the probable dates on which the monies had been embezzled.

The letters were the most embarrassing. It surprised me that every man had written to Angel. My mother had told me a long time ago never to sign my name to anything unless I was compelled to by law or the possibility of profit. She hadn't used those words exactly, but that's what she meant.

Some of the letters were romantic, talking about forbid-
den love and freedom. Others were down in the gutter. I supposed that Angel had written to them first and they replied,
hoping for something that they didn't even understand.

The fifteenth section of the folder contained a file with
all the pertinent information on each mark. Full names,
addresses, phone numbers, names of wives, ex-wives, children, past lovers, and immediate supervisors. A few of the
men had confessed to crimes they had committed at different points in their lives.

I imagined them in the heat of their passion, whispering, whimpering, confessing at Angel's altar. There was
no contempt in my mind's eye. I could see getting down
on my knees for the absolution granted by her beauty. If
I were an older gentleman I might have been happy to
sacrifice the life I'd built for her. I mean, after all, what
good is a lifetime of accrued wealth when all it gets you
are body aches and boiled meat for supper?

None of the men had committed murder or any other
violent crime as far as the notes went. They seemed to be
well-chosen docile and bureaucratic sorts. Even Martin
Friar was only brave in his mind. He'd given up his orga-
nization's money to assure his place in Angel's heart and
to protect himself from exposure.

The more I read, the less I believed in the possibility
that one of the businessmen was responsible for the
deaths I'd encountered. This left me with the most probable cause: Useless.

My cousin messed up anything he got involved in. And
if you were there with him, the worst would come to you.
Useless had stolen the accordion folder from someone. I
knew this because the folder was too neat, too well

planned out for a sloppy mind like his. The man, or woman, who had designed this extortion scheme had it all worked out to a science. It was like an investment folder or a detailed business plan.

This meant that Useless was intimate with the mastermind of the operation. He was running from that someone and knew a name.

I didn't like my conclusion. I didn't want to talk to Useless again. My fear might have been irrational, but the idea of being in the same room with my cousin made my neck hairs rise.

Luckily I had other things to do first.

I took my car down the street to Central Avenue and drove four blocks to Eugenia's Stationery Store. There I purchased a box of manila envelopes, a ream of white paper, two black markers, and a roll of postage stamps.

For the next hour I put all the blackmailers' information into thirteen envelopes, then stamped and addressed each one to the men being blackmailed. I typed thirteen short notes that read,

It's over now. You will not be bothered again.
                                    A friend

I wrote PERSONAL AND CONFIDENTIAL on the front and back of each envelope, then I licked the adhesive and sealed the envelopes. After that I taped each one shut.

The only information I skipped was Brian Motley's. His life had already been destroyed.

After that I drove to a post office I knew in Westwood and deposited the envelopes in the box outside.

In my car coming home I had what I came later to
know as an anxiety attack. My tongue went dry and my
stomach roiled. A cold sweat broke out across my brow.
My hands clenched into fists around the steering wheel,
and I barely had the muscle control to pull up to the curb.
Sitting there, holding on tightly with my head against the
wheel, I began to shiver. I think the thing that got to me
was sending off those envelopes filled with so much
threat and turmoil. My chest began hurting again. I
wanted to cry but could not. So instead I took long deep
breaths with my eyes closed. After a few minutes I was
able to release the wheel. A few moments more and I relaxed into sobs.

When the episode had passed, I was able to drive but
unwilling to go home.

Maybe the killer would be there waiting for me.
Maybe. But I learned something about myself that afternoon. I learned that fear was so pervasive in my life that
it had no real sway over me.

After all, I was afraid of everything. A cold might be
pneumonia. A cut warned of lockjaw. Any man I met
might be the boyfriend of a woman who had neglected to
inform me about her situation.

"Scared if I do," I said, "and scared if I don't."

This made me laugh very hard. Anyone passing would
have thought that I'd gone insane there behind the wheel.

41 I MEANT TO GO see Fearless, but first I wanted to drive past my store. Maybe, I thought, I would have the courage to go in if I didn't see anyone waiting for me. I could change my clothes, take a short bath.

Three blocks from my house I decided that after all of this was over I was going to buy myself a gun, a small-caliber pistol, for times like these.

JESSA WAS SITTING with her back against my door and her knees pulled up to her face. She was rocking herself there. I think it was that gentle, futile swaying that made me park and approach her.

When I got to the top of the stairs, she looked up. Her crystal blue eyes flooded with tears.

"Paris," she wailed, rising and throwing her arms around me. "I'm so scared."

I had to bite my lower lip to keep from crying along with her.

"Calm down, Jessa," I said. "It's gonna be all right."

Tenderness only served to make her cry harder. I opened the door as fast as I could and pushed her across the threshold. She stood in the little reading-room entranceway, racked with sobs, leaning against the wall. I let that go on for a minute or two and then dragged her toward the kitchen-porch. When we passed the place where Fearless and I had come upon Tiny, she dug her nails into my forearms.

"That's where he died," she said through a series of hoarse sobs. "That's where my baby boy died."

"Died?" I asked. "Who died?"

"Tiny," she said, nodding and leaning on me as we went from the room.

"Is that where the blood came from?"

My incredulity put her tears temporarily at bay.

"Didn't you find him there?"

"No," I lied. "All there was was a little blood. I thought that it must'a been from him beatin' on you. Matter of fact, I was worried 'bout you until you decked me out there in front'a Hector's place."

"Hector shot him. He was dead on the floor."

"Hector must'a missed," I said. "Because there was nobody here. Just some blood, like I said. Did he shoot him in the head?"

She nodded at me hopefully.

"Must'a just grazed him," I speculated. "Must'a either bounced off or glanced off the side. The bullet hittin' him prob'ly knocked him out and then, after you left, he must'a woke up and run."

"You really didn't find him?" Jessa asked.

"No, ma'am," I said. "If I found a body, I'd have to call the cops, and you know I'd be in jail still, them wonderin' how a white man came here to die."

"You didn't see him?"

"If he'd been shot by a black man in my store, I'm sure he decided to cut his losses and run. Probably thought it was one of my crazy cousins."

"He's alive," she breathed. Then she giggled madly.

It was a straight-faced lie, but there was nothing wrong with it the way I figured. It took a great weight of guilt off Jessa's shoulders and successfully removed the only living witness to the murder.

"Let me make you some tea," I said, and she went to her favorite chair in my kitchen.

It was almost like old times.

WE'D GRADUATED FROM English Breakfast to peach schnapps when Jessa relaxed enough to tell me her tale.

"Tiny came back an' started beatin' on me when you got away. He was mad, and I couldn't blame him. But you know I was crazy for you, Paris," she said, as if our affair had been many years ago. "He wasn't hittin' me with his fists or nuthin', just open hand. He must'a been extra mad after he saw you naked. I don't think that he would have killed me. I don't think so, but then Hector came in."

"Did you know this Hector?" I asked.

"I had never seen him before. He yelled at Tiny to stop, and Tiny ran at him. He called Hector nigger, and Hector shot him in the head. I thought he was dead." Jessa's eyes got wide while she stared at the kitchen floor. I knew that she was seeing Tiny's body at her feet.

"What happened then?" I asked.

"Hector grabbed me by the hair and asked me where Useless was. He hit me and asked me and hit me again. I

just screamed and cried and said that I never heard about
any Useless. I didn't even know that he was talkin' about
a man."

"Did he believe you?"

"Later he did. A lot later. But then he kept slappin' me
and askin' me. Then he asked who Tiny was, and I told
him that he was my boyfriend and he'd found me with
you. I think he started getting scared about Tiny and the
gunshot, so he made me go with him out to his car."

"Did you try to get away?" I asked.

"No. I just went. I just went with him to the car, and he
drove me to that apartment where I saw you. I'm sorry I hit
you, Paris. I'm sorry. I was just so crazy after seeing Hector like that."

I wasn't ready to find out about Hector yet. I wanted to
get there slowly.

"What happened when he took you to his apartment?"
I asked.

She seemed relieved to be distracted from the second
murder.

"He brought me in and kept askin' what he should do
with me. He kept sayin' that he should kill me. I tried to
tell him that I wouldn't turn him in, but he didn't believe
it. Every time I said it he yelled at me to stop lyin'."

"Didn't the upstairs neighbors hear all that shouting?"
I asked.

"Mrs. Braughm lives by herself and she's mostly
deaf," Jessa said. "After a while Hector got to drinking.
He started slappin' me again. And I don't know how, but
my clothes started comin' off and we were doin' it right
there on the big sofa chair. I did everything he wanted me
to. We fucked like goats." Tremors went through her as

she spoke. I couldn't tell if it was pleasure or pain, passion or the desire to forget.

"What happened after that?" I asked her.

"It was like we were together," she said, amazed herself at the turn of events. "Things had been going bad for Hector. The man he was looking for, Useless, had stolen something from the man he worked for."

"What did he steal?"

"Money, I think. Hector never told me, but I'm pretty sure that it was money. Every time he'd talk to his boss on the phone or even just think about Useless, he'd get mad and start slappin' me. And if I did just right, we'd end up rutting on the floor."

"Did you try to run away?"

"I didn't . . . I didn't want to. I didn't know where to go and there was something that made me want to stay close to Hector. He needed me."

Sometimes in literature I'd come across the term *exquisite pain*. I never understood it before. My nature being such as it is, I have always shied away from any kind of suffering. But I could see where the ache in Jessa's life needed attention and Hector was the perfect mate for her.

"After a while he'd leave me alone in the apartment. I cooked for him and I never blamed him for killin' Tiny. I was the one who put Tiny in that position. I was the one that killed him."

"But you didn't," I reminded her. "Tiny was gone when I got here."

Jessa gave me a big smile, stood up, and came to put her arms around my neck. It was a sisterly hug, but all that talk about rutting on the floor had me thinking thoughts I knew were wrong.

"Why'd you come here?" I whispered into her dirty blond hair.

"I stayed at the YWCA for a few days after Hector was killed. I didn't know where else to go. All I had was a few dollars."

I walked her over to the stool that Useless had used.

"Tell me what happened to Hector," I said.

"Somebody killed him," she said, her eyes wide with the immensity of death. "They cut his throat while I was sleeping in the bed."

"Who did?"

"I don't know. All I know is that I thought I heard something and I called out his name. And then, when I came in, there he was."

She began crying again and I couldn't blame her. Even if she had killed him herself, it was something worth crying about. But I didn't think she'd killed him. No. Hector had housed her, punished her, and had brutal sex with her in every position in every room in that apartment. They were perfect together.

"Who was Hector's boss?"

"He never said," Jessa uttered. "He never even said that the man he talked to on the phone was his boss. But I could tell. Hector got respectful whenever he called."

"Did you ever answer the phone when his boss called?"

"Once."

"What did he say?"

"He asked who it was, and I told him that I was, I was Hector's girlfriend."

"An' what'd he say?"

"He wanted Hector, but Hector was out. Then he told me to tell Hector to meet him at the yard at five thirty."

"What did he sound like?" I asked.

Jessa didn't seem to understand the question.

"Was he a white man or a Negro?"

The white girl cocked her head to the side and bit her lower lip. "I don't know," she said. "There might have been a little southerner in there, but I couldn't tell."

It wasn't a total loss. I had found out some things.

"Tell me something, Jessa."

"What?"

"Hector came here one day asking for a French dictionary. Why he do that? Did Useless tell him that I had something of his?"

"No," Jessa said, her fingers jittering nervously. "Hector asked me about you. I told him that all you did was sell books. But he, he wanted to see you and for you to see him. He said that if you blinked he'd kill you like he had Tiny —"

"Like he thought he killed Tiny," I reminded her.

"Yeah."

"So I guess he didn't think I knew anything," I said.

"No. He said that you were nothing."

It's funny the things that make us mad. I was angry at the dead killer for thinking I wasn't worth a bullet.

"Do you hate me, Paris?" Jessa asked.

"No. Why?"

"Do you think I'm a whore?"

"No, I do not. I think you're a young woman got in way over her head, but it wasn't your fault — at least not all your fault. You might'a been messin' with Tiny, but he left you first. And there wasn't a damn thing you could'a done about Hector. Not a damn thing."

She tried to smile, which was more meaningful than if she had actually managed it.

"I'm'a give ya two hundred dollars and a ride to the downtown YWCA," I said. "In a couple or few days I'll come by and tell you what I think."

"Can't I stay with you?"

"Stayin' here just about as dangerous as stayin' with Hector."

I didn't have to say any more.

AFTER I PUT JESSA into a taxi I took the suitcase to my incinerator in the backyard. There I applied lighter fluid and set it afire. As the flames rose I tried to imagine Useless sneaking up behind a man and cutting his throat.

It wasn't a nice thought. But he just didn't have the nerve to kill a man like that.

Or did he?

42

FEARLESS'S FRONT DOOR was wide open. This detail made me hesitate. It was a warm day and an open door was the best way to cool down. But maybe the killer had knocked and Fearless had answered and got shot. Maybe Fearless was dead.

I couldn't take a step forward or back until those maybes were resolved. It's not that I expected a moment of brilliance to strike where I'd be suddenly aware of the reason behind that open door. I hoped that Fearless would appear or, failing that, he'd speak out.

But as I waited I began to wonder. If some killer had struck at Fearless he would only leave the door open if he'd left. If he was in there waiting for me, the door would be closed so that no one would suspect his presence.

That got me far enough to consider moving, but it was hearing Fearless laugh out loud that brought on the locomotion in my legs.

He was sitting on the sofa with Mona at his side. I

thought that she might have just snagged a kiss before I appeared because there was a lascivious look in her lovely grayish eyes.

"There he is," Fearless said aloud. "Paris. He done saved my life an' made me fi'e hundred dollars."

The sexual expectation was replaced by disappointment on Mona's face, disappointment but not anger. Later I would find out that Mona had a great deal of sisterly love and respect for me. She was a much more complex woman than I could have known back then, when all of her senses were besotted by the Hero.

"That's all Milo paid you to risk yo' life like that?" I asked.

"You wanna drink, Paris?" Mona offered.

I nodded, and she went into the tiny kitchen that was through the door next to Fearless's one room for living, sleeping, and paying his bills.

"That was a bonus," Fearless said. "On top'a what he paid me for bodyguardin'."

"Did you hear that window openin' up over your head?" I asked as I lowered into the broken-down stuffed chair next to his small sofa.

"Yeah," he admitted. "But I didn't know what it meant exactly. An' at the same time I heard it, you shouted. When you called my name it all fell inta place and I jumped."

I wondered for the thousandth time what it would be like to see the world from Fearless's point of view. In my world everything was particular and threatening, made up of sharp corners that would cut you if you got too close. But Fearless, I imagined, lived in a liquid world where everything blended together and moved in unison. In his world there were no absolute victors or complete victims, just movement between everything, all the time.

Mona brought me a squat glass of peach schnapps and ice. That was my favorite drink, and Fearless always kept a bottle in the cabinet in case I came by.

She sat on Fearless's lap. He whispered in her ear and she smiled.

"Okay," she said gladly and stood up. "Bye, Paris. I'm'a go an' let you men talk."

I rose and kissed her cheek. She smiled at me and patted my jaw line. As she sashayed toward her apartment, I closed the front door. Fearless had turned on the light before I was sitting again.

"I called you," he said.

"I stayed out last night. Seemed like a good idea."

"You got anything more about Ulysses?"

"I think it might'a been him who killed Hector."

I told him that Jessa had said Useless had stolen something from Hector's boss.

"He already admitted killing Tony," I added as a kind of proof.

"Naw, man," Fearless said. "Ulysses ain't gonna sneak up on no bad man an' cut his th'oat. Naw." Fearless shook his head, but he was wondering.

"That ain't all," I said. "Jessa said that Hector's boss-man called an' told him to meet him at the yard."

"Bubba's Yard?"

"I don't know. Might be."

"Thatta make sense. Sure would."

If you lived in Watts or some other poor neighborhood and you owned a fine or fancy car, you might avail yourself of the services of Bubba Lateman's Yard. Lateman

owned a largish piece of property on the borderline between Compton and Los Angeles. He'd built a high
cinder-block wall around it and topped that with barbed
wire and shards of glass embedded in concrete. He kept
dogs that would chew through bone and an alarm system
with a bell that could be heard for six city blocks. Com-
bine that with a high-powered hunting rifle in the hands
of an army-certified marksman and you had the safest
garage in the world.

It cost two dollars a day, which was steep in 1956, but
if you had a fine Cadillac and you didn't want it damaged
or stolen, you just might pay Bubba before you paid the
rent.

Bubba had a capacity of twenty-five cars, Milo's red
Caddy usually being one of them.

"So you thinkin' that they keepin' somethin' in the car
at Bubba's," Fearless said.

"I think that's where the rest'a the money is."

"Damn," Fearless said. "That's pretty smart. You know
Ulysses might think of it, but he wouldn't have the car to
make it real."

Nor, I thought, would he be able to run a blackmail
operation.

"You ready t'face that evil eye again?" Fearless asked
me.

"No," I said. "Could you do it?"

"Sure thing, man. That's the least I could do."

WE PARKED DOWN THE BLOCK from Nadine
Grant's home. I sat in the car waiting while Fearless
braced the family. Nadine would put up with them for a
while; Useless, after all, was blood to her. But it had to be

running rather hot in there. Useless was a slob and Angel was a stranger. It shouldn't have been too hard for Fearless to pry my cousin free.

The more I thought about it, the less likely it seemed that Useless would have killed Hector. The risk wouldn't have been worth it. And even if it made sense, Useless would have gone after the man with a gun. A knife is a brave man's weapon. And even though Useless wasn't as cowardly as I, he wasn't what you'd have called brave.

I sat in that car with the windows rolled up and the sun beating down. It was getting hot, but I was afraid even to open a window. Just that thin barrier of glass was better than nothing.

I got a little light-headed from the heat but I was only aware of the drowsiness, not its cause. So when Fearless opened the door and said my name, I was surprised. I think maybe I had passed out from all of the exhaustion, peach schnapps, hot sun, and fear.

"Hey, Cousin," Useless said as he climbed into the backseat.

I slid over to the passenger's side and Fearless got behind the wheel.

"Did Hector have a car he kept at Bubba Lateman's?" I asked Useless.

"Yeah. Sho did. Pink-an'-chrome Cadillac. Kep' it so neat it woulda passed a military inspection."

"Would Bubba let you pick it up?"

"Prob'ly. I went there wit' Hector a few times. You know I'd drive ovah there with him. An' then take him back home after he dropped it off."

"So you been to his place before?"

Fearless turned the key and the car started.

"Not for a month or two, but yeah."

Useless was getting wary. Maybe he knew what the next question might have been.

Fearless pulled away from the curb and we started our drive southward.

"So why you still lookin' into Hector an' them?" Useless asked, partly to prevent me from asking more questions.

"Because someone killed him," I said. "Because'a that suitcase you had and some things we found at Lionel Sterling's place."

Useless was silent.

"Where'd you get that bag, Useless?" I asked into the void of the backseat.

"Um."

"Come on, man," I said. "You ain't got time to make up no lie."

"I took it."

"Took it from where?"

"From, from Hector's place."

"When?"

"A few days ago."

"You just walked in an' took it?" I asked sarcastically. "He just let you walk all ovah him?"

"He, he was dead."

Fearless turned his head for a moment.

"You killed him?"

"No, man. No. He was dead. Somebody cut his th'oat. I saw the suitcase, grabbed it, and ran."

"Did you see who killed him?"

"Uh-uh. No. I just grabbed the suitcase 'cause I knew it was important. I grabbed it and hustled out the back."

"What about the girl?"

"She wasn't there."

"The white girl wasn't there?" I asked.

"What white girl? I thought you was askin' 'bout Angel."

"Hector's girl. Jessa."

"I didn't even know 'bout no girlfriend, man. I walked in, saw he was murdered, grabbed the suitcase, an' run."

He was lying—had to be. The man who had murdered Hector was certainly in on the blackmailing scheme. That man wouldn't have left all that evidence behind.

43

THE ONLY ENTRANCE to Bubba's Yard was an eight-foot-high wrought-iron gate. He had four snapping and slavering feral dogs that came out to greet us with their canine threats and promises.

Fearless pressed the buzzer while Useless and I stood a few feet away. The dogs were wolflike, maybe they were wolves, with dense pelts and yellow fangs. They wanted to look us in the eye, like bullies on a street corner. They wanted to kill us.

The dogs prowled the inside of the gate, lunging at it now and then. A man approached from the house that sat at the back end of the lot.

Bubba Lateman was a huge man. Six six or more and weighing three fifty at least. His head was bald and his hands too big even for a body his size. He had a smile on his face, but I knew how mean Bubba could be.

He was wearing overalls and railroad gloves. His skin was black and that day streaked with sweat.

"Fearless Jones," he said amid the yowling and barking of his dogs.

It was both a greeting and a threat. Powerful men who had never tested him always felt a little disdainful of Fearless's reputation.

"Mornin', Bubba," my friend hailed. "We come with Ulysses here to pick up Hector LaTiara's car . . . for his widow."

Fearless could lie if he had to. Usually it was to save some poor soul from an ass-whupping. I think that day he was also worried about having to kill those dogs.

"Hector didn't say nuthin' 'bout no wife," Bubba said.

"White girl," Fearless assured him. "Jessa is what they call her."

Bubba's eyes were tiny for his big, bald black head. When he blinked it was almost as if he were being coquettish, flirting with the object of his confusion.

"What you say about that, Useless?" Bubba asked.

There was a moment in which Useless faltered. I believed that he was wondering if maybe he could enlist the aid of this giant standing before him. Maybe Bubba could block us from getting Hector's Cadillac.

"They just drove me down, Bubba," he said. "Paris my cousin, an' Fearless his friend."

The dogs sensed something and began snarling in a different key.

"Get on back there!" Bubba commanded his curs. They whimpered and obeyed, skulking to some kennel on the far side of the property.

Bubba brought a big ring of keys out of the inside of his work overalls. He used a jagged-looking piece of brass to unlock the gate.

After we entered, and he locked up again, Bubba led us to the right, where the yard part of his business was. The largest of the wolf-dogs came to walk with him. She was a big gray creature, between seventy-five and eighty-five pounds. For all her weight, she looked starved and hungry for fresh flesh and revenge.

I had never been inside Bubba's Yard before. The automobiles parked in neat rows upon the hard desert soil were impressive. Cadillac cars and Italian sports jobs, there was even a Bentley and a Rolls-Royce Silver Cloud.

And Hector's Caddy, pink and chrome, as Useless had promised. It actually sparkled under the hot L.A. sun.

"They say you're bad, Fearless Jones," Bubba said.

"Some say I'm good," Fearless replied easily.

Bubba didn't like the joke. "What would you do if I told Bree here to jump up an' tear out yo' throat?"

Fearless glanced at Bree, who started growling on cue. He, Fearless, contemplated a moment and then looked back at Bubba.

"She's a beautiful animal," Fearless said. "Too skinny and knocked around more than she deserves. If she was to jump I'd have to grab her by the jaw an' snap her neck like a chicken. An' then, Bubba Lateman, I would have to teach you a lesson that you'd carry down into the coffin wit' you."

Bulfinch's Mythology came to me then. It seemed to me that this tableau belonged in those pages. Fearless was the hero, I was the hero's companion, Useless was the mischievous trickster, and Bubba was the ogre or giant. We were playing out roles in a history that went back before anyone could remember. The river Styx might have lain to our left, and this was just a step in our journey.

I couldn't help it: I laughed.

Bubba grinned then too. Bree turned her head toward him with a look of canine surprise on her vicious face.

"Take the car, man," Bubba said. "And lemme tell ya, if Bree here jumped at ya, you'd never have a chance."

I DROVE MY CAR while Fearless manned the Caddy with Useless at his side. We took Useless back to Nadine's house. Out front he was unwilling to see us go.

"Why you want Hector's car?" he asked us.

"I like pink," Fearless said. "It's my favorite color."

"Come on," he said. "What you want it for?"

"Useless," I said.

"Why you have to call me that?" he asked. He almost sounded insulted.

"What? Useless?"

"That's hurtful. I don't call you Dog Shit, now, do I?"

"You bettah not."

"Well, I might."

"And I might go to the cops an' say about Martin Friar and Brian Motley, not to mention Mad Anthony. I might tell 'em that you was in business with Lionel Sterling and Hector LaTiara. That's all I got to say, Useless. Because you know I never call you. I never drop by your house askin' for ice water. I don't need you, not at all. To me you truly are Useless. So get your ass back up in the house with your cockeyed mama and wait for us to call you again."

If I didn't know better I would have thought that Useless's feelings were actually hurt. He pouted and stared at the ground.

"Go on, Useless," I insisted.

He turned and walked away slowly.

For my part, I stood there refusing to feel guilty.

"WHAT YOU THINK, PARIS?" Fearless asked me when we were in my kitchen smoking cigarettes and drinking schnapps.

"I don't know."

There was a duffel bag on the floor between us. Above that was a table piled high with twenties, fifties, and hundred-dollar bills. I had stopped counting at sixty thousand dollars. Adding that to the money we had found at Sterling's, we had over one hundred thousand dollars. One hundred thousand. In 1956 that was enough to retire on.

"We got to give it back, Paris," Fearless said. "We got to."

"Why, man? They already stole it. We might get caught tryin' to put it back."

Fearless shook his head and started shoving the money in its bag.

"I got the addresses," I said. "Why don't you just let me send it?"

"First we need to make sure the cutthroat ain't a problem," Fearless said.

"What you gonna do with the money and Hector's car?"

"I'll just leave Hector's car on the street to get towed and then I'll borrah Mickey Dean's white Caddy, put the money in the trunk, an' bring it ovah to Bubba."

"You sure you wanna mess wit' that man again?" I asked seriously. "I think he wanna test you."

"Naw," Fearless assured me. "I mean yeah, he wonders, but Bubba's business. The minute I'm a payin' client, thatta put fightin' right out his mind."

Fearless hefted the bag of money over his shoulder and carried it out to the Caddy.

I accompanied him out to the street and watched as he drove away.

A hundred thousand dollars in free money, and my potential partner in crime was the most honest man in L.A.

44

THE PHONE BEGAN RINGING about ten minutes after Fearless had driven off with my windfall retirement fund.

I could have taken that money and moved to Paris, my namesake city, lived on the Champs-Élysée, and listened to American jazz in the bistros and nightclubs. I could have learned Latin and French and married an African princess.

The phone kept on ringing.

I was almost as leery of the phone as I was of people at my front door. Anybody could have been calling me: the police, Three Hearts, the killer pretending to be somebody else.

Why should I answer?

What I needed to do was to find an out-of-the-way motel where I could sleep and read until there was no more trouble roiling around me.

The phone stopped ringing.

I always forgot that it was Fearless's moral side that

did me in in the end. No matter how much money passed through our hands, he always wanted to do the right thing. Here we had money that nobody expected to see again. I had sent the victims the blackmailers' evidence — wasn't that good enough?

The phone started ringing again. That worried me. Somebody wanted to get through. If I didn't answer they might come by.

"Hello?"

"Paris," the voice intoned.

"Yeah," I said resignedly.

"I don't give information over the phone."

"Come on by, then," I said.

"Be there in five."

More trouble. Whisper could find his way into any problem. He was a real private eye. I couldn't shake the notion that it was him who had me walking in front of those armed men. It was him who was saved by my diversion.

But even in my self-centered despair, I knew that I had asked Mr. Natly for help. He wouldn't have been calling me if I hadn't called on him first.

Above my telephone I had a big round wall clock with a sweeping second hand.

Exactly three hundred seconds after I hung up there was a knock at the door. I just opened it. If it was some armed killer, then so be it.

Whisper smiled and stuck out a hand for me to shake.

I had met the detective a dozen times in my life. He had never before, to my recollection, offered to shake hands. His fleeting smile came and went. I offered him tea and he accepted.

We went into my kitchen and sat down like friends.

He used three sugars in his English Breakfast. That surprised me.

"That was a good thing you did the other night, Paris," Whisper said.

"I was so scared I couldn't even run," I replied.

"Scared is the detective's best friend," he said. "Scared makes you look harder and think longer. Scared keeps your hand on the wheel and your eye on the rearview mirror."

"Sounds like a heart attack waitin' to happen," I said.

"Naw, man. You get used to it. Find yourself sitting in your chair thinkin' 'bout things nobody else will get to for days. After a while you take actions before the fear moves you. Not so many people could be a detective, but you could, Paris."

"I don't think so."

"Yes, you do. If you didn't, you wouldn't be askin' after Mannheim and the Handsome boys."

He had me there.

"You find 'em?" I asked.

"Bobo," he said with a nod. "I decided to concentrate on him. I'm guessin' you wouldn't want to see 'em all together."

"Where?" I asked, cutting to the chase.

Whisper smiled again. He took out a slip of paper with a list of four places scrawled on it. These places, I knew, were the leg breaker's hangouts.

I took the list and looked it over. They were joints I wouldn't have felt comfortable going in for any reason. The names were often heard along with reports of fights, knifings, arrests, and murder.

"You want some company, Paris?" Whisper offered.

"Damn right."

"Let's go, then."

ALLEGRA'S DANCE HALL WAS no more than the frame of a barn behind an ironworks factory on Hooper. Back there you could lose your life in a second. It was early and no one was dancing. There were a couple of potheads smoking in the yard, but Bobo was nowhere in evidence.

"Should we ask about him?" I asked the professional.

"Not unless you want him to disappear on ya."

THE NEXT PLACE WAS a Texas barbecue stand on Santa Barbara. It was rumored that Bobo ate there at least four times a week. He wasn't hungry right then.

HARRY'S BARBERSHOP HAD BEEN closed temporarily by the police. There had been a murder over a poker game in the back room, so Harry took off a week or so, until the police got tired of checking their seal.

THAD'S BAR WAS LAST on our list.

The physical bar at Thad's was small, but there was a big room for clientele once they had something to drink. There were four bartenders, serving cheap beer, mostly. Whisper had kept Thad's for last because he'd been told that Bobo had an ex-girlfriend that worked there. He didn't expect that Bobo would be hanging around an ex, but he was wrong.

Ora, Bobo's girlfriend, was working serving drinks.

When Whisper asked her about Bobo, she just shrugged and gestured toward a corner with her jaw.

At the corner table sat a big man, a very big man. His shoulders sagged, and all you could see was the top of his uncombed head. The quart pitcher looked like a mug in his large hand.

Whisper and I went to his table. I tried to keep abreast of my new friend, but when we got to within six feet of Bobo, my legs just stopped moving.

Seeing our shadows in his beer, Bobo looked up. His brutal face seemed damaged somehow.

"What?" he whined.

"Bobo Handsome?" Whisper asked.

"Yeah? What you want?"

"Like to buy you a drink," Whisper said.

I liked the style. I had to remember to use it the next time I wanted to grill somebody.

"Sure," Bobo said, waving his hand at us.

Whisper ordered a fifth of whiskey and three glasses. Ora, Bobo's ex-girlfriend, frowned when she received the order, but she kept quiet.

Whisper introduced himself and so did I. We traded shots for a while and discussed baseball. I don't know a thing about baseball. I knew about the Negro Leagues, but if you asked me what they actually did on the field, I wouldn't have been able to answer.

But Whisper knew. He seemed to know a little something about everything. Bobo got drunker, and angry, but he wasn't mad at us.

"You evah have a friend that you really love?" Bobo asked me at one point.

"Uh, yeah," I said. "I guess."

"You talkin' 'bout Tremont?" Whisper asked.

It was the first time I'd heard that name, but I knew

from the context that he was the fat man that Three Hearts had killed.

"What you know 'bout Tremont?" Bobo asked, half rising from his chair.

"Nuthin'," Whisper said innocently. "I just heard that the cops fount his body. Somebody had shot him in the gut."

The violence in Bobo's demeanor melted into grief. Tears sprouted from his eyes, and his hands grasped at nothing.

Ora, who was a small dark-skinned woman, came over and put her hands on his oxlike shoulders. Her face wasn't beautiful, but the feeling she held for him was.

"Leave him alone," she told us. "Cain't you see he's hurtin'?"

"You want us to leave, Bobo?" Whisper asked.

"No, man. Go on, Ora. These here my friends."

"You don't even know these niggahs," she answered. "They buy you a drink an' turn your ass ovah."

"We don't wanna hurt you, Bobo," Whisper said, and I realized that in order to be a detective you had to be cruel while seeming to be kind.

"Go on, Ora," Bobo said. "I ain't no fool."

"Fuck you, then," Ora said to all of us.

She stormed away to be consoled by three or four other barmaids.

"I'm sorry about your friend," Whisper said.

What amazed me about Whisper was how simple and yet elegant his approach was at this point. If I were trying to get information out of Bobo I would have tried to fool him by making up a dozen lies. Whisper just told one lie and then soaked it in whiskey.

"I tell you one thing," Bobo said. "Don't evah put yo' trust in no light-skin, light-eyed, high-yellah niggah. Mothahfuckah done made Tremont's chirren orphans, an' he won't even let up on a dime. Wouldn't shed a tear ovah his own."

He said some other things, but I don't remember what. I let him go on for a while and then I told Whisper that I had to go see my uncle. I explained to Bobo that my uncle had tuberculosis and needed help around his house.

Bobo told me to make sure that he drank a lot of milk. Milk was good for TB.

I thanked him and ordered another bottle of booze. I figured if he got drunk enough he wouldn't be able to get in the way of my plans.

45

WHISPER DROPPED ME OFF at my bookstore. I hadn't told him a thing about what I'd learned.

He shook my hand and smiled at me again.

"You got all the right instincts," he told me. "You don't tell nobody nuthin' they don't need to know and you keep your cool."

I smiled, thinking that Whisper didn't know how scared I really was.

"When you want a real job, call me," Whisper said. "I could always use a partner."

I DROVE STRAIGHT FROM the sidewalk to Fearless's bungalow. When I got to the door, I heard Mona crying, "That's it. That's it. Oh yeah, baby, you got it."

At any other time I would have turned away. But I had to knock. Had to.

The protestations of love stopped. Two hard footsteps crossed the floor.

"Who is it?" Fearless asked, not nearly as angry as I would have been.

"Paris."

The door came open, and Fearless stuck his head out. "Yeah?"

"I know the whole thing. All of it."

"We got to do sumpin' right now?" he asked me.

"No. But I need a place to stay an' I ain't got no cash."

The head went away. A few words were traded in the room, and he returned holding out a key ring with two keys on it.

"Go stay at Mona's, man. She gonna be here tonight. Stay ovah there an' I get ya in the mornin'."

I took the keys and walked across two dewy lawns to Mona's place.

Her tiny house was well appointed, as I have said, but the best thing about it was her bed. It was high and soft, with ever so lightly scented sheets and blankets. There were half a dozen pillows and an azure night-light plugged into the socket to the right.

I fell instantly to sleep. And I didn't have even one bad dream.

I woke up once in the night wondering why Fearless didn't marry Mona. She was the perfect woman from where I lay. I glanced over at the sky-colored night-light and thought about blue tomorrows.

I'm sure that there was something psychological about my emotions, but I didn't want to know. It was rare that I came upon a night of bliss. I wasn't about to question it.

I WAS SOUND ASLEEP when someone came knocking on the door.

"Yes?"

"It's Mona, Paris."

I put on my pants and went to the door.

The look on her face told me that she'd had a pleasant night too.

"You know I almost got mad at you," she said.

She was wearing a white terry cloth robe and Fearless's big brown slippers.

"Sorry, babe. I just wanted a couple'a bucks to get a room someplace. But I tell ya this much—stayin' here made me feel like I was at the Waldorf in the presidential suite. That was the best night's sleep I ever had since I was a child in my mother's arms."

I only meant it as a show of gratitude, but I could see that my words touched Mona. She put her hand on my elbow, leaned forward, and gave me the softest kiss on the lips.

"Fearless waitin' on you," she whispered.

I put on my shirt but carried my socks and shoes across the lawns to my friend's place. Mona had shaken me up with that kiss. It wasn't a passionate thing, but there was something to it, something I didn't want to know about when my best friend had just spent the night with her.

Fearless was already dressed in a loose silvery shirt and gray slacks. His brown shoes looked new they were so shiny, and he had a fancy gold watch on his wrist.

"Watch?" I asked.

"Mona gimme it," he said. "I don't want her to think I don't appreciate it."

REESE ROUNDTREE OWNED a café a few blocks from Fearless's court. Fearless bought me fried eggs and bacon there. He had pancakes with pecan-flavored syrup.

"I thought Mona wasn't your girlfriend," I said at one point, thinking about that soft kiss.

"She ain't."

"Sounded like she was last night."

"We friends, Paris," Fearless said. "It was just a night together."

"So that was just like shakin' hands?"

Reese only had two tables inside his place, but it was early enough that his only customers were people on the way to work.

"No," Fearless said.

"She looked like a chicken sittin' on a ostrich egg when I seen her this mornin'," I said.

"What you sayin', Paris?"

"I'm sayin' that Mona wasn't just bein' friendly up in there."

Fearless took in every word and nuance, making them into convictions and feelings that held more truth than most men were capable of. He might never have understood what I was saying, but after hearing my words he would do the right thing, which was better than most men could ever do.

After twenty seconds of serious consideration, Fearless smiled.

"What's wrong, Paris?"

"What you mean?"

"I mean why you pesterin' me? Ain't you got a problem to solve?"

"Thomas Benton Hoag," I said.

"Who?"

I explained about Angel's old boyfriend, the high-yellow real estate man.

"He hired the Handsome brothers to grab Three Hearts and Angel."

"But he was Angel's boyfriend," Fearless said.

"Was."

Fearless squeezed the slender bone between his eyes with a thumb and forefinger. "How does he get in this?"

"Real estate," I said. "His company is a white company, and Sterling was in real estate too. Maybe Sterling knew some white dude, a potential client, who liked black girls and he came to Tommy askin' 'bout a girl who could show him a good time. That brings us to Angel. One thing leads to another, and an opportunity for blackmail emerges. After a while Tommy's in the catbird seat, targeting white men who have their hands on money but don't have no money themselves."

"So Angel was in on it from the beginning?"

"Maybe her. Maybe there was other girls. I don't know. Angel don't mattah. It's Tommy the one."

Fearless let the words wash over him. You could see him imagining not so much the details of the crime but the qualities of the man.

"So he like a pimp?" Fearless said at last.

"Yeah," I said. "Not to mention a kidnapper, a killer, and a blackmailer."

Fearless nodded and asked, "So what next?"

"There's one problem," I said.

"What's that?"

"That suitcase."

"Where is it?"

"I burned it."

"Then it ain't a problem," Fearless reasoned.

"Where it came from is the problem," I said.

"Ulysses said he took it from Hector's house."

"But we know he didn't," I said. "How's he gonna be so lucky to get there after the killer kills Hector and before the deaf neighbor calls the cops?"

"So what you think?"

"I think Angel had the bag."

"An' where'd she get it from?" Fearless asked. He was getting nervous, tapping the toes of his left foot on the wood floor.

"Either from Hector after she killed him or from Thomas after he did."

"You think she in it wit' him?"

"I know they were in it together at the beginning," I said. "At least that's what makes the most sense."

Fearless frowned and began tapping the toes of both his feet.

"Naw," he said. "That girl loves Ulysses. You know he's the apple'a her eye."

"How come you say that about Angel but you don't see it in Mona?" I asked.

"Mona don't love me, man," Fearless said with certainty. And before I could ask another question, he said, "She wants me. I'm everything she wants, but I ain't what she need. I ain't the man she gonna love, not really."

"But Angel loves Useless?"

"Down to the jam between his toes," Fearless said, accenting his words with a vigorous nod.

I took a deep breath and then another. I watched the line of workingmen and -women waiting for their coffees and pastries, then looked back at Fearless in his silver and gray.

We were at the end of the road. The journey had

started with Useless at my doorstep, plying his star-crossed fate. Now there was just one thing to do.

"We go to Schuyler Real Estate and deal with Thomas," I said.

Fearless nodded, put the last corner of hotcake into his mouth, and stood up straight.

46

FATE TRIED TO save us. She brought us to the real estate office, but Thomas Benton Hoag wasn't there.

The white man who was sitting at his desk wanted to speak to us because he was so angry.

"Do you know where Thomas is?" he demanded.

"We came here lookin' for him," I explained. "We thought he was here."

"Three days ago he stopped coming," the white man (I never got his name) said. "Just stopped coming. He has clients who have lost faith in this office. He has records that I can't read. What the hell kinda business is that?"

"Maybe he's dead," Fearless said.

That caught the white man up short.

"What?"

"If you had a friend," Fearless reasoned, "and all of a sudden he wasn't at work, didn't answer his phone, wouldn't you be worried that somethin' bad happened to him?"

"We went to his house," the white man, who was fat

and wore a blue-and-white pinstriped suit, said. "He wasn't there."

"Maybe he's in a ditch," Fearless suggested. "Have you called the police?"

"I, I hadn't thought of that."

"You just thought that he was tryin' to mess wit' you. You thought that he was gonna give up his commission to get drunk or take a vacation for a few days."

The fact that Thomas's boss didn't have an answer went way past racism. There was something wrong with the man. There he was working with someone who had committed all kinds of crimes and all he could think about was that he hadn't come in to work. He was a fool in baseball stripes, nameless in my mind but as American as the hot dog.

"WHERE TO?" Fearless asked when we were on the street again.

"Nadine's," I said on a sigh.

Fearless grinned and we were off.

On the ride I asked, "What can we do about this dude if we get him?"

"He probably run," Fearless said. "I mean, that's what a smart man'd do. All them dead men and his suitcase gone."

"But what if he ain't? What if he after Useless still?"

"Then we gots to stop him."

I remembered Cleave's hard words in the car on the way to Tiny's burial. I knew what Fearless meant and I wasn't sure that I could manage it. Killing was a hard business — not like selling books or finding money in a dead man's car.

This last thought made me chuckle, but there was little humor in the sound.

"Try not to worry about it, Paris," Fearless said. "You don't know what's gonna happen."

"But I got to be ready," I said.

"Ain't nobody evah ready, man. You could be layin' up in some hospital bed dyin', an' somewhere yo' boss fires you for not callin' in. How you gonna be ready for that?"

NADINE GRANT WAS HUSTLING OUT her front door when we got there.

"I don't have any more time to waste on you people, Paris," she said, trying to move around us at the front gate. "I have to get to work."

"Three Hearts in there?" I asked her.

"They moved," she said with a voice that somehow reminded me of a hammer at work.

"Where to?"

"Four houses down," she said. "The red place with the blue fence. It come open for rent and all of a sudden Hearts realized that she had three hundred dollars in her bag. Here she haven't even paid me for a banana and now she payin' rent for Useless and that nasty girl."

Nadine hurried off to her car, talking to herself about my aunt and how she did her wrong.

I wanted to leave then. I had a deep conviction that Nadine was right, that my family was something to avoid.

"Come on, Paris," Fearless said. "Let's get this ovah wit'."

We walked down the street and up to the front door of the dark red house. There was a jack-in-the-box and a broomstick with a horse's head in the yard. There were boxes with the name Georgia Arnold written on them on the small walled-in porch.

I knocked on the door, and after maybe a minute, Three Hearts answered.

"Hi, Paris, Fearless," she said.

I should have known by the way she said my name first that something was wrong. As it was, I wondered why she was no longer angry with me for calling her boy Useless.

She led us through a kind of utility room into a larger space. I could see Angel sitting on a straight-back chair, and Three Hearts gasped as someone dragged her to the side.

Fearless and I came in to see Thomas Benton Hoag holding a small-caliber pistol to my auntie's head. Next to him was Cousin Useless tied down in a chair.

"I'll kill her and you too," Hoag said. "Just gimme a reason."

It seemed odd to me that his dialect had changed to street. But then I guessed that he was under pressure and the way he spoke now was his true self.

"What's up, brothah?" Fearless asked.

"You don't scare me, Fearless Jones," Hoag said. "I want my mothahfuckin' money an' I want it now. I know you got Hector's car outta the yard. I know what he had in the trunk."

I glanced at Fearless. He was biding his time. I was sure that if Fearless could get to Hoag then there was nothing to fear. But there were eight long feet between my friend and that pistol. The time it would take to cross it was all the time you needed to die.

"How come you gave the suitcase to Useless?" I asked. Why not? It might buy us some time.

"He stole it from me," Angel spoke up. "I was holding it for Tommy after, after what he did to Hector."

"You don't have to answer to this mothahfucker," Hoag said, his handsome features warped by rage. "Now get up off my money or I shoot this here bastard first."

Hoag moved his pistol to Useless's temple, and Three Hearts cried, "No, Lord."

I realized then that I was not truly superstitious because if I had been I would have been confident that my aunt's evil eye would slay Hoag. But I was sure that Hoag would kill us all.

Fearless moved slightly, and Hoag brought up his pistol to point at his head. I could see that he had decided to kill Fearless. That was the smartest move. My friend was the only one in the room who posed a threat.

"Fearless took the money, Tommy," I said. "He took it and hid it. If you kill him then it's gone."

"The bitch got a gun in her purse," Angel said then. "I'll get it and keep it on him."

Hoag nodded and smiled at Fearless. My friend's nostrils dilated maybe an eighth of an inch. I knew that was his recognition of a near-death experience.

Angel took out Three Hearts's pistol and pointed it at Fearless. Hoag waited a second and then moved his gun so that it was pointing at the ceiling.

She must have been squeezing as she turned. The shot was perfect, hitting Thomas Benton Hoag in the center of his forehead. She kept on shooting, but he was already dead.

That was a moment of crystal clarity for me. I saw it all in less than a second. Angel was partners with Hoag, but then she fell in love with Useless. She was trying to get away, but Tommy ran her down. She convinced him that Useless was some kind of mastermind and told him that Fearless had the money.

It was all a ploy. She meant to kill him all along.

When the gun was empty Angel lowered it and her head.

"You got a phone in here?" I asked.

She shook her head.

"Run outside and start screamin'," I said. "And when the cops come, tell 'em he was your old boyfriend and that he wanted you back. Tell 'em that he was gonna rob you too."

Three Hearts was trying to untie Useless, but I told her to stop.

"Tell 'em the knot was too much for you," I said. "Him bein' tied will be proof that Hoag was robbin' you."

That was it. Fearless and I were out the back and over the fence to the block behind. We heard Angel screaming from that far away.

We took a bus home. I left my car. It would wait for me.

I don't know about Fearless, but I slept for twenty-four hours after that.

47

THERE WAS A HEARING to see whether or not a crime had been committed in the shooting death of Thomas Benton Hoag. Angel and Three Hearts and Useless all testified.

Thomas Benton Hoag had been Angel's boyfriend, but she had come to realize that she loved Useless. Tommy came on them at gunpoint, tied Useless up, and told Angel that if she didn't come with him he'd kill them all.

The judge liked the story, and there was no one to contradict it.

AFTER THE INQUIRY Angel asked Fearless about the money. He told her that he'd already returned it to the men that she blackmailed.

Actually he'd given it to Martin Friar along with the list I'd compiled and asked him to return it in the best ways he could. I told Fearless that we might as well keep the money as Friar, but Fearless said that we could trust the man. Maybe he was right.

Friar did say that we should keep 10 percent as a kind of finder's fee. It was some money, enough to support my lazy lifestyle for a year or so.

Useless was angry at our presumptions with his hard-earned, ill-gotten wages. But when I asked him about the money he'd invested with Jerry Twist, he shut up.

THAT WAS IT. A life worth remembering is hell to live.

A WEEK AFTER the inquisition Three Hearts, Angel, and Useless left for Louisiana. Two days after that I got a visit from Jessa. I had hoped that she'd just go away, but I should have known better.

She was wearing a nice white cotton dress and there was a red ribbon in her hair just begging to be undone. But I kept my hands to myself.

"Have you heard from Tiny?" she asked me after I made her tea.

"No, I haven't," I said. "And I hope I don't. You know I don't think that Tiny likes me too well."

Me talking about him as if he were still alive buoyed her spirits. In her heart I think she knew he was dead, but the lie helped some.

"Can I stay with you, Paris?" she asked toward the end of the visit.

"No, honey. Uh-uh. I like you, but all that mess was too much for me."

"Did they catch the man that killed Hector?" she wanted to know.

"I haven't heard anything," I said, knowing that Hector had been slaughtered by Tommy Hoag, "but you can be sure that the man who did it will pay for it one day."

"You really believe that?" she asked, boring into me with those diamond drill eyes.

I nodded with absolute certainty.

"You're a good man, Paris Minton," she said.

I preferred to believe that even if she knew the whole truth she would have held the same opinion.

I gave her five hundred of the five thousand dollars I'd made on the fiasco that Useless had brought to my door. I told her to go somewhere new and get a job in a café or an office.

"Meet a nice guy and start a family," I said.

She kissed me at the door, and I barely regretted not lying with her one more time.

When I was in the bookstore alone, after Jessa had gone off into her life, I wondered how Angel and Useless were doing and I was glad that I didn't have an answer.

ABOUT THE AUTHOR

WALTER MOSLEY is the author of the acclaimed Easy Rawlins series of mysteries, including national bestsellers *Cinnamon Kiss, Little Scarlet,* and *Bad Boy Brawly Brown;* the Fearless Jones series, including *Fearless Jones* and *Fear Itself;* the novels *Blue Light* and *RL's Dream;* and two collections of stories featuring Socrates Fortlow, *Always Outnumbered, Always Outgunned,* for which he received the Anisfield-Wolf Award, and *Walkin' the Dog.* He was born in Los Angeles and lives in New York.

IT'S HARD TO GET LOST when you're coming home from work. When you have a job, and a paycheck, the road is set right out in front of you: a paved highway with no exits except yours. There's the parking lot, the grocery store, the kids' school, the cleaners, the car wash, and then your front door.

But I hadn't had a regular job in a year, and here it was two in the afternoon and I was pulling up into my driveway wondering what I was doing there. I cut off the engine and then shuddered trying to fit inside the sudden stillness.

All the way home I had been thinking about Bonnie and what I'd lost when I sent her away. She'd saved my adopted daughter's life and I repaid her by making her leave our home.

In order to get little Feather into a Swiss clinic Bonnie had reacquainted herself with Joguye Cham, a West African prince. He made a home for Feather, and Bonnie stayed there with her—and him.

I threw open the car door but didn't get out. Part of my lethargy was exhaustion from being up for the past twenty-four hours.

I didn't have a regular job but I worked like a dog.

Martel Johnson had hired me to find his runaway sixteen-year-old daughter, Chevette. He'd gone to the police and they took down her information, but two weeks went by and they hadn't turned up a thing. I told Martel that I'd do the footwork for three hundred dollars. On any other transaction he would have tried to dicker with me; he would have given me a down payment, promising the balance when and if I did the job. But when a man loves his child he will do anything to have her safely home.

I pocketed the money, spoke to a dozen of Chevette's high school friends, and then made the rounds of various alleys in the general vicinity of Watts.

MOST OF THAT TIME I was thinking about Bonnie, about calling her and asking her to come home to me. I missed her milky breath and the spiced teas she brewed. I missed her mild Guyanese accent and our long talks about freedom. I missed everything about her and me, but I couldn't make myself stop at a pay phone.

Where I came from — Fifth Ward, Houston, Texas — another man sleeping with your woman was more than reason enough for justifiable double homicide. Every time I thought of her in his arms my vision blurred, and I had to close my eyes.

My adoptive daughter still saw Bonnie at least once a week. The boy I raised as my son, Jesus, and his common-law wife, Benita Flagg, treated Bonnie as the grandmother of their newborn daughter, Essie.

I loved them all and in turning my back on Bonnie I had lost them.

And so, at 1:30 in the morning, at the mouth of an alley off Avalon, when a buxom young thing in a miniskirt and halter top came up to my window I rolled down the glass and asked, "How much to suck my dick?"

"Fifteen dollars, daddy," she said in voice both sweet and high.

"Um," I stalled. "Up front or after?"

She sucked her tooth and stuck out a hand. I put three new five dollar bills across her palm and she hurried around to the passenger side of my late-model Ford. She had dark skin and full cheeks ready to smile for the man with the money.

When I turned toward her I detected a momentary shyness in her eyes but then she put on a brazen look and said, "Let's see what you got."

"Can I ask you somethin' first?"

"You paid for ten minutes, you can do whatever you want with it."

"Are you happy doing this, Chevette?"

The look on her face went from thirty to sixteen in one second flat. She reached for the door but I grabbed her wrist.

"I'm not tryin' to stop you, girl," I said.

"Then let me go."

"You got my money. All I'm askin' is my ten minutes."

Chevette settled down after looking at my other hand and around the front seat for signs of danger.

"Okay," she said, staring into the darkness of the floor. "But we stay right here."

I gazed into her big eyes until she turned away.

"Martel hired me to find you," I said. "He's all broken up over you bein' gone. I told him I'd ask you to come home but I wouldn't drag you there."

The woman-child glanced at me then.

"But I have to tell him where you are . . . and about Porky."

"You cain't tell Daddy 'bout him," she pleaded. "One'a them get killed sure."

Porky the Pimp had recruited Chevette three blocks away from Jordan High. He was a pock-faced fat man with a penchant for razors, diamond rings, and women.

"Martel's your father," I reasoned. "He deserves to know what happened with you."

"Porky'll cut him. He'll kill him."

"Or the other way around," I said. "Martel hired me to find you and tell him where you are. That's how I pay my mortgage, girl."

"I could pay you," she suggested, placing a hand on my thigh. "I got fi'e hunnert dollars in my purse. And— and you said you wanted some company."

"No," I said. "I mean you are a fine young thing but I'm honest and a father too."

The teenager's face went blank but I could see that her mind was racing. My appearance had been a possibility that she'd already considered. Not me exactly but some man who either knew her or wanted to save her. After twenty blow jobs a night for two weeks, she'd have to be thinking about rescue—and about the perils that came along with such an act of desperation. Porky could find her anywhere in southern California.

"Porky ain't gonna let me go," she said. "He cut up

one girl that tried to leave him. Cassandra. He cut up her face."

She put a hand to her cheek. It wasn't a pretty face.

"Oh," I said, "I'm almost sure the pig man will listen to reason."

It was my smile that gave Chevette Johnson hope.

"Where is he?" I asked.

"At the back of the barber shop."

I took the dull gray .38 from the glove compartment and the keys from the ignition.

Cupping my hand around the girl's chin I said, "You wait right here. I don't wanna have to look for you again."

She nodded into my palm and I went off down the alley.

Tall and lanky LaTerry Klegg stood in the doorway of the back porch of Masters and Broad Barber Shop. He looked like a deep brown praying mantis standing in a pool of yellow cream. Klegg had a reputation of being fast and deadly, so I came up on him quickly slamming the side of my pistol against his jaw.

He went down, and I thought of Bonnie for a moment. I wondered, as I looked into the startled face of Porky the Pimp, why she had not called me.

Porky was seated in an old barber's chair that had been moved out on the porch to make room for a newer model, no doubt.

"Who the fuck are you?" the pimp said in a frightened alto voice. He was the color of a pig too: a sickly pinkish brown.

I answered by pressing the barrel of my pistol against his left cheekbone.

"What?" he squeaked.

"Chevette Johnson," I said. "Either you let up or I lay you down right here and now."

I meant it. I was ready to kill him. I wanted to kill him. But even while I stood there on the verge of murder, it came to me that Bonnie would never call. She was too proud and hurt.

"Take her," Porky said.

My finger was constricting on the trigger.

"Take her!"

I moved my hand three inches to the right and fired. The bullet only nicked the outer lobe, but his hearing on that side would never be the same. Porky went down to the floor holding his head and crying out. I kicked him in his gut and walked back down the way I'd come.

On the way to my car I passed three women in short skirts and high heels who had come running. They gave me a wide berth, seeing the pistol in my hand.

"SO WHY'D YOU LEAVE HOME like that?" I asked Chevette at the all-night hamburger stand on Beverly.

She'd ordered a chili burger and fries. I nursed a cream soda.

"They wouldn't let me do nuthin'," she whined. "Daddy want me to wear long skirts and ponytails. He wouldn't even let me talk to a boy on the phone."

Even in a potato sack you could have seen that Chevette was a woman. It had been a long time since she had been a member of the Mickey Mouse Clubhouse.

I drove her to my office and let her sleep on my new blue sofa while I napped, dreaming of Bonnie, in my office chair.

In the morning I called Martel and told him everything—except that Chevette was listening in.

"What you mean walkin' the streets?" he asked.

"You know what I mean."

"A prostitute?"

"You still want her back?" I asked.

"Of course I want my baby back."

"No, Marty. I can bring her back but what you gonna get is a full grown woman, not no child, not no baby. She gonna need you to let her grow up. She gonna need you to be different. 'Cause it won't make a difference her bein' back home if you don't change."

"She my child, Easy," he said with deadly certainty.

"The child is gone, Marty. Woman's all that's left."

He broke down then and so did Chevette. She buried her face in a blue cushion and cried.

I told Martel I'd call him back. We talked three more times before I got all the way through to him. I told him that it wasn't worth it for me to bring her back, if he couldn't see her for what she was, and if he couldn't love her for what she was.

And all the time I was thinking about Bonnie. I was thinking that I should call her and beg for her to come home.

2

IT ONLY TOOK ME TEN MINUTES or so to climb out of the car.

Walking across the lawn I heard the little yellow dog barking. Frenchie hated me and loved Feather—we had something in common there. I was happy to hear his canine curses through the front door. It was the only welcome I deserved.

When I came into the house the seven pound dog began screaming and snapping at my shoes. I squatted down to say hello. This gesture of truce always made Frenchie run away.

When I looked up to watch him scamper into Feather's room I saw the little Vietnamese child—Easter Dawn.

"Hello, Mr. Rawlins," the petite eight year old said.

"E.D. Where'd you come from, girl?" I looked around the room for her village-killing father.

"Vietnam originally," the cogent child replied.

"Hi, Daddy," Feather said, coming from around the corner.

She was only eleven but seemed much older. She'd

grown a foot and a half in little more than a year, and she had a lean, intelligent face. Feather and Jesus spoke to each other in fluent English, French, and Spanish, which somehow made their conversations seem more sophisticated.

"Where's Juice?" I asked.

"He and Benny went to get Essie from Benny's mom." She hesitated a moment and then added, "I stayed home with E.D. today because I didn't know what else to do."

I was trying to figure it all out while standing there.

My son had agreed to stay with Feather while I was out looking for Chevette. He and Benita didn't make much money and only had a one-room studio apartment in Venice. When they babysat they could sleep in my big bed, watch TV, and cook on a real stove.

But Jesus had a life, and Feather was supposed to be in school. Easter Dawn Black had no business in my house at all.

The child wore black cotton pants and an unadorned red silk jacket cut in an Asian style. Her long black hair was tied with an orange bow and hung down the front, over her right shoulder.

"Daddy brought me," Easter said, answering the question in my eyes.

"Why?"

"He told me to tell you that I had to stay here for a while, visiting with Feather . . . "

My daughter knelt down then and hugged the smaller child from behind.

". . . he said that you would know how long I had to stay. Do you?"

"You want some coffee, Daddy?" Feather asked.

My adopted daughter had a creamy brown complexion which reflected her complicated racial heritage. Staring into her generous face I realized, for the twentieth time, that I could no longer predict the caprice or depth of her heart.

It was with the sadness of this separation that I said, "Sure, Baby. Sure."

I picked up Easter and followed Feather into the kitchen. There I sat in a dinette chair with the doll-sized child on my lap.

"You been having a good time with Feather?" I asked.

Easter nodded vehemently.

"Did she make you lunch?"

"Tuna fish, and sweet potato pie."

Looking up into my eyes, Easter relaxed and leaned against my chest. I hadn't known her and her father, Christmas Black, for long but the confidence he had in me had influenced the child's trust.

"So you and your daddy drove here?" I asked.

"Uh-huh."

"And was it just you and him in the car?"

"No," she said. "There was a lady with yellow hair."

"What was her name?"

"Miss . . . something. I don't remember."

"And was this lady up in your house in Riverside?"

"We moved away from there," Easter said, a little wistfully.

"Moved where?"

"Behind a big blue house across the street from the building with a real big tire on the roof."

"A tire as big as a house?"

"Uh-huh."

By then the coffee was percolating.

"Mr. Black dropped by this morning," Feather said. "He asked me if Easter could stay for a while, and I said okay. Was it okay, Daddy?"

Feather always called me *Daddy* when she didn't want me to get angry.

"Is my daddy okay, Mr. Rawlins?" Easter Dawn asked.

"Your father is the strongest man in the world," I told her with only the least bit of hyperbole. "Whatever he's doin', he'll be just fine. I'm sure he's gonna call me and tell me what's going on before the night is through."

Feather made hot chocolate for her and E.D. We sat around the dinette table like adults having an afternoon visit. Feather talked about what she'd learned concerning American history, and little Easter Dawn listened as if she were a student in class. When we'd visited enough to make Easter feel at home I suggested that they go in the backyard to play.

I CALLED SAUL LYNX, the man who had introduced me to Easter's father, but his answering service told me that my fellow private detective was out of town for a few weeks. I could have called his home but if he was on a case he wouldn't have known anything about Christmas.

"Alexander residence," a white man answered on the first ring of my next call.

"Peter?"

"Mr. Rawlins. How are you, sir?"

The transformation of Peter Rhone from salesman to personal manservant of EttaMae Harris would always be astonishing to me. He lost the love of his life in the Watts riots and pretty much gave up on the white race. He moved onto the side porch of EttaMae's house and did chores for her and her husband, Raymond "Mouse" Alexander.

The young Rhone had been working part-time as a mechanic for my old friend Primo in a garage in East L.A. He was learning a trade and contributing to the general pot for the upkeep of Etta's home. I thought that he was somehow paying penance for the death of Nola Payne because in some way he saw himself as the cause of her demise.

"Okay," I said. "All right. How's the garage workin' out?"

"I'm cleaning spark plugs now. Pretty soon Jorge is going to show me how to work with an automatic transmission."

"Huh," I grunted. "Raymond around there?"

"I better get Etta for you," he said, and I knew there was a problem.

"Easy?" Etta said into the phone a moment later.

"Yeah, Babe."

"I need your help."

"Yes, ma'am," I said because I loved Etta as a friend and I had once loved her as I did Bonnie. If she hadn't been mad for my best friend we'd've had a whole house full of children by that time.

"The police lookin' for Raymond," she said.

"For what?" I asked.

"Murder."

"Murder?"

"Some fool name'a Pericles Tarr went missin', an' the cops here ev'ry day askin' me what I know about it. If it wasn't for Pete I think they might'a drug me off to jail just for bein' married to Ray."

None of this was a surprise to me. Raymond lived a

life of crime. The diminutive killer was connected to a whole network of heist men who operated from coast to coast, and beyond that for all I knew. It wasn't that Mouse was beyond killing; just the opposite was true. But in recent years his blood had cooled and he rarely lost his temper. If he was to kill somebody nowadays it would have been in the dead of night, with no witnesses or clues left behind to incriminate him.

"Where is Mouse?" I asked.

"That's what I need to find out," Etta said. "He went missin' the day before this Tarr man did. Now he ain't around and the law's all ovah me."

"So you want me to find him?" I asked, regretting that I had called.

"Yes."

"What do I do then?"

"I'm worried, Easy," Etta said. "These cops is serious. They want my baby under the jailhouse."

I hadn't heard Etta call Ray *my baby* in many years.

"All right," I said. "I'll find him and I'll do what I have to to make sure he's okay."

"I know this ain't for free, Easy," Etta told me. "I'ma pay you for it."

"Uh-huh. You know anything about this Tarr?"

"Not too much. He's married and got a whole house full'a chirren."

"Where does he live?"

"On Sixty-third Street." She recited the address and I wrote it down, thinking that I had found more trouble in one day than most men come across in a decade.